NICOLE'S
WAR

Andrée Rushton

The Book Guild Ltd

First published in Great Britain in 2024 by
The Book Guild Ltd
Unit E2 Airfield Business Park,
Harrison Road, Market Harborough,
Leicestershire. LE16 7UL
Tel: 0116 2792299
www.bookguild.co.uk
Email: info@bookguild.co.uk
Twitter: @bookguild

Typeset in 12pt Minion Pro

Printed and bound by CPI Group (UK) Ltd, Croydon, CR0 4YY

ISBN 978 1915853 769

British Library Cataloguing in Publication Data.
A catalogue record for this book is available from the British Library.

MIX
Paper | Supporting
responsible forestry
FSC
www.fsc.org
FSC® C013604

In memory of my mother

CHRONOLOGY

20th September 1792: Battle of Valmy between French and Prussians

25th May–25th November 1937: Paris International Exposition

30th September 1938: Munich Agreement between Britain, France, Italy and Germany

3rd September 1939: Britain and France declare war on Germany

11th September 1939: mobilisation of Frenchmen

10th May 1940: Nazi invasion of France

May 1940: Evacuation of British troops from France via Dunkirk.

3rd June 1940: Bombing raid over Paris

14th June 1940: Nazis enter Paris

17th June 1940: Marshal Pétain speaks to the French people

18th June 1940: General de Gaulle speaks to the French people from exile

25th June 1940: Nazis enter Bordeaux

July 1940: Vichy government established under Marshal Pétain

3rd July 1940: British bomb French fleet at Mers-el-Kebir in Morocco

September 1940: rationing introduced in France

October 1940: Jews in France barred from certain occupations.

Jews in the occupied zone required to register with authorities

Foreign Jews could be held in special camps.

Naturalisation granted to Jews after 1927 removed

April 1941: Jewish bank accounts frozen

14th May 1941: First big round-up of Jews in Paris

June 1941: Jews barred from more occupations

New census, more curfews and exclusions imposed on Jews

Jews forbidden to attend classes at the Sorbonne

22nd June 1941: Soviet Union entered the war against Germany

20th August 1941: First round-up of French Jews

September 1941: *Le Juif et la France* exhibition at Palais Berlitz in Paris

December 1941: Japanese bombing of Pearl Harbor

May 1942: Jews required to wear a yellow star

July 1942: Jews forbidden use of the telephone

July 1942: Propaganda film *Le Peril Juif* shown in the occupied zone

Books by Jewish authors withdrawn from sale

Jews not to attend cinemas, theatres and public places

Access to shops restricted

16th/17th July 1942: Biggest round-up of Jews in Paris

4th September 1942: Men aged eighteen to fifty liable for

labour conscription

November 1942: Allies invade North Africa and Nazis take over unoccupied France

January 1943: Establishment of French military police force (*milice*)

February 1943: End of the Battle of Stalingrad (now Volgograd)

February 1943: Frenchmen required to work in Germany

February 1944: Resistance destroys files of French conscripts

May 1944: Large dogs in Paris requisitioned

6th June 1944: Allies land in Normandy (D Day)

14th July 1944: Demonstration at Place Maubert on Bastille Day

August 1944: Colonel Rol-Tanguy's call to Paris to rise

20th August 1944: Truce by Colonel Raoul Nordling between Nazis and Paris Resistance

23rd August 1944: Hitler orders General von Choltitz to destroy Paris

25th August 1944: Liberation of Paris

April 1945: French women vote in municipal elections

8th May 1945: End of the war in Europe

FOREWORD

The bus crawled through the wet streets of a wintry day towards the flat in a residential quarter of Paris where Nicolette had grown up. She was on her way to see her mother, after the death of her father a few weeks previously. Sometimes she wished that she lived further away than the city outskirts because she doubted that her edgy relationship with her mother would improve now. She had loved her affectionate and kindly father unreservedly, but her mother was too exacting. They had fought in her teenage years when Nicolette was seeking freedom from what had felt like suffocating control. She had left home as soon as possible, going to university in Toulouse, a city her father had liked and where she had lived for several years before returning to Paris.

On the phone a couple of days ago, her mother had declared that she could not face going through her father's possessions alone and she wanted help to sort them out. Understanding that it was a task better carried out together and trying to be sympathetic, Nicolette had agreed to help.

The bus lurched to a stop and Nicolette clambered out onto a wet pavement, putting up her umbrella against driving rain. She walked the few metres to her mother's block and opened the street door. On the other side of the small entrance hall, she rang the bell to the flat. Hearing an answering buzz, she slipped through the inner door and pressed the button for the tiny lift that fitted into the stairwell. It groaned its way slowly to the sixth floor where her mother, Nicole, slim and always neatly dressed, but now looking sad, was waiting for her. They exchanged brief greetings.

Nicolette's heart sank as she entered the flat crowded with her parents' possessions. It was going to be a long day. She was sorry for her mother and told herself that she must be generous and not resent claims on her time and affections. She had more time now that her children were beginning their adult lives, although her job as a teacher kept her busy.

'It's only his clothes and some papers,' Nicole was saying as if she could hear Nicolette thinking. She led the way to the kitchen where she made coffee while they discussed the funeral. It had been well attended and Nicole had felt overwhelmed by the occasion, as well as sad.

'I can't bear to see them, knowing that he's not here to wear them. They will have to go,' she said of the clothes as she opened a wardrobe door in the bedroom.

'Let's bag them up and take them to a charity,' Nicolette said.

She knew of one with an office nearby. Nicole agreed and they folded shirts and suits, putting everything usable into carrier bags. Nicole talked about the clothes associated with activities or events – a suit worn only on special occasions, a colourful waistcoat for parties and a cheerful collection of ties. Time passed more quickly than Nicolette had expected.

'We've worked hard. Let me take you out for lunch,' she said, hoping to avoid any offer of food in the flat. Nicole had never liked cooking and Nicolette's parents had been regular customers of the bistro in the street below.

'All right, but wait a minute,' Nicole said, struggling with a heavy bottom drawer in the wardrobe. Together, they opened it, revealing more clothes, which Nicole took out. Underneath the clothes were two old books, one with a spiral binding. Nicolette had never seen them before.

'Oh, they can stay,' Nicole said, folding a scarf.

'But what are they?'

'This one is my occupation diary,' Nicole said. She picked up the spiral-bound book and opened it.

'Do you mean the Nazi occupation, when you were in Paris?'

Nicolette knew that her mother had spent the war in Paris, but nothing more. Nicole, who willingly remembered her childhood friends, Miriam and Yvette, and her schooldays, had always refused to talk about the occupation. Nicolette had become more curious about this hidden part of her mother's life as she grew older, but her questions had always been met by a pursed lip and silence.

'Of course. What else?' Nicole said. 'Now, let's go for that lunch you want.'

'Wait a minute. What's in the other book?' Nicolette asked.

'Clippings from our newsletter and the paper your father worked for in London during the war.'

'Can I read them? Will you lend them to me?'

'You won't understand the story. You need to read between the lines,' Nicole said, placing the spiral-bound book back in the drawer.

Nicolette felt like a small child being denied a book that was too old for her. 'I can't read between the lines when you've never talked about it. You wouldn't, even though I've often asked.'

'It was too difficult,' Nicole said. 'But now that your father's gone, I've been thinking about the past and perhaps I could talk about it.'

'No time like the present,' Nicolette said, seeing an opening for the first time. 'Now for that lunch. We can drop these bags off at the charity on the way.'

They squeezed themselves and the carrier bags full of clothing into the lift and slowly descended to the ground floor. Outside, it had stopped raining.

PART ONE

ONE

MARCEL

Anne stood in the doorway of her daughter's bedroom, watching Nicole put on her lipstick in front of the mirror over her dressing table. Anne had never worn make-up and, without it, her pale face seemed like a rebuke.

'You're not going out, are you, Nicole?'

Nicole's parents had furnished the bedroom comfortably. Anne had made curtains and a matching cover for the bed on her treadle sewing machine. She had upholstered the stool that belonged to the dressing table and the small armchair in one corner. In the market near their flat, where she went shopping every week, she had found the rug that covered much of the polished wooden floor. A big wardrobe with a mirrored door occupied one end of the room and a chest of drawers stood nearby.

'Yes. It's the dance class! I told you, *Maman*. I'm starting tonight.'

'What about dinner? I'm just going to cook.'

'Oh, forget about me. I'll have something when I come back.'

Nicole Seymour was the adored youngest child and only daughter of a British family living in Paris. She had been born in France towards the end of the Great War. At eighteen, her face was framed by straight brown hair, cut in a bob. Hazel eyes and regular features were given life by an alert expression and a warm smile. With her friendly manner, a neat appearance and a qualification in shorthand and typing, she was a secretary for a company that made medicines.

Glancing at her mother, Nicole suppressed a feeling of irritation. Her parents often seemed to stand in her way these days. Her mother even liked to say that she had given her life to her family. Being alone at home during the day and with few friends in Paris, she looked more and more to her only daughter for company. No one had yet left home, but everyone except Anne was busy outside the family flat for much of the time.

They spoke English at home, sprinkled with French words. Nicole had been to school in Paris and was fluent in both languages. Her father spoke French well. He had learned it at work and by reading newspapers, but her mother struggled with the language.

'Have you fed Kim?' Anne said.

'Oh, I'm late. Can you do it for me, *Maman*?'

Nicole had been given a puppy by friends of her parents the previous year. She had persuaded her mother that the dog, even when fully grown, would be small enough to live in the family flat. She would look after him. He was a terrier, mainly white, with brown patches on his head and neck, and an affectionate nature. She had named him Kim and loved him immediately. Her father, Jeffrey, a man who never minced his words, liked to tease her by calling him a mongrel.

She snatched up her bag, said goodbye to her mother, waved at her father as she passed through the living room and shut the heavy front door of the flat behind her. Despite her mother's wishes, she had no compunction about going out. Her brothers, Ralph and Christopher, weren't at home either, but her parents would have each other's company for the evening.

Nicole had persuaded her friend, Miriam, to come to the dance class with her. Leaving the building, she crossed the road to the foot of the long flight of steps that led towards Miriam's flat. Her friends called them Nicole's Steps. She glanced back, as she always did, before climbing up. On the other side of the River Seine, the Eiffel Tower rose towards white clouds riding across a pale evening sky. Seeing its four legs planted in the ground, and the patterns made by its structure, long neck and small head, the tower always reminded her of a wooden giraffe that Christopher had once carved for her.

She also liked seeing the tower from elsewhere in Paris. It seemed so small from a distance and so massive nearby. From her office window, or from the market where she and her mother went shopping, she would catch sight of it unexpectedly. She almost felt as if the tower came with her when she went out. Her parents had told her about the dismay of a previous generation as it rose to dominate the Paris skyline towards the end of the last century. Yet she loved its soaring height; the impression it gave of lightness and delicacy, as well as strength; the way it seemed to watch over Paris and over her; and represent her city to the world.

She turned towards the flight of steps and began to climb. Her calf muscles ached and she was panting slightly as she reached the top. She crossed the Avenue du Président Wilson and made her way to the small street on the other side where Miriam lived. Above the growl of traffic, she could hear the cheeping of sparrows in the lime trees that sheltered the avenue. Now that it was summer, she breathed in deeply to catch the heady scent of their flowers. Mixed with petrol fumes, it was faint, but discernible.

Miriam was always quick to answer the door and that evening was no exception. She was a lively girl, with clusters of brown curls and a ready laugh. Her dark-rimmed glasses made her look serious, but her colourful chiffon dress was ready for fun.

The dance school was only a few minutes' walk from Miriam's flat. It occupied one floor of a mansion previously owned by a wealthy family and was now divided up for use by several businesses. A large room with bare boards and a grand piano at one end provided plenty of space. On arrival, Nicole threw herself into a waltz with a friend of one of her brothers. She moved with a natural rhythm and was pleased to see enough young men in the class for every girl to have a male partner.

'It's so much better than school where girls had to dance with each other,' she said to Miriam during an interval.

Miriam, talking to another girl, turned to Nicole without enthusiasm. On the way home, she admitted that she had not enjoyed the dancing and would not be continuing with the class.

'Give me a café with friends any time! Anyway, I've got two left feet. Haven't you noticed?'

Nicole could not help glancing at her friend's slim feet and Miriam laughed.

'Well, all right, I'll go on my own or ask Yvette,' Nicole said.

She and Miriam and Yvette had become close friends at school, sharing the experiences of their teenage years. They had talked endlessly about boys they knew or hoped to know, their parents' efforts to curtail their freedom, and their school and its teachers.

Nicole continued to attend the dance class, persuading Yvette to join her sometimes. They were never short of partners. One evening, during a break between dances, a new member of the class, a young man of about her age, came over to her.

'We haven't met before. I'm Marcel,' he said, smiling. He was dark-haired, with pale skin and pleasantly irregular features.

'I'm Nicole.' She shook the hand he held out to her and looked at him questioningly.

'Will you dance with me? You look as if you know what you're doing.'

Nicole assented. As the music started up again, Marcel took hold of her and they began to dance. He trod on her feet more than once. He had an easy laugh and seemed to find the whole experience amusing, not minding at all about his clumsiness and almost making a show of it. His apologies gave her the confidence to lead him in the dancing, while letting him appear to lead her. He was elastic in his movements and quick to learn. By the end of that evening, Nicole was able to look forwards to dancing with him again without flinching at the thought.

In the weeks that followed, Marcel sought out Nicole as his regular partner, while Yvette danced with anyone who was free and teased Nicole about having a boyfriend now. Marcel was only slightly taller than Nicole and they matched each other well on the dance floor. They practised ballroom dances and more modern dances like the Charleston until they were both proficient.

Nicole acquired two or three colourful, flouncy dresses for dancing. Marcel, who was still at school and studying for exams, always wore his school uniform of black trousers, jacket and white shirt. He refused ever to wear a tie outside school and did not otherwise think much about his appearance. As they became more skilful together, he whirled Nicole faster and faster around the dance floor and she would be panting and laughing when they finished.

She liked this young man with his ready smile and easy manner. Everything was a game and he made her laugh. His hair flew around his head as he danced and his enjoyment was infectious. He lacked the dapper, suited look that Nicole, a tailor's daughter, was used to in men. He was more like a parcel unravelling before it reached its destination. There was always a collar turning the wrong way, a shirt flap not tucked in or a loose shoelace so that, when he danced, his clothes appeared to be trying to escape him. Nicole found his untidiness attractive after her father's emphasis on a smart appearance. Most of all, she enjoyed teasing Marcel, not just about his clothing.

'Why did you decide to do dancing lessons?' she asked him one evening. The pianist had stopped at the end of a piece of music to confer with the dance teacher, allowing the class a short break.

'To meet you, of course,' he said.

Try as she might, she could not help blushing, but she was quick to reply. 'No, you didn't, because you didn't know I existed. So, why did you?'

'Because girls like dancing and I like girls. And then I saw you and you looked nice.'

'No, you thought I could dance and would help you. That's what you said.'

'You did help me, but I still thought you looked nice.'

She was glad the music was starting again, so she could concentrate on dancing. He was looking at her in a disturbing way and she did not know what to say next. To return the compliment would be too obvious and yet Marcel was much more attractive than the few young men she knew through her brothers.

That evening, Marcel suggested walking Nicole home and accompanied her down her steps to her flat. When he took her hand in the dark, as if to guide her, she felt stirred by his touch in a new way. At the foot of the steps, he kissed her lightly and said goodbye. She crossed the road as if walking on air.

The journey home took longer and longer each week as they dawdled. In Marcel's presence, Nicole felt more alive than ever before, more even than when laughing at the crazy world with Miriam and Yvette. She thought about him in his absence, revisiting their conversations, longing to see him again and, most of all, to touch him.

When Marcel's name slipped from Nicole's lips a second and then a third time at home, Anne raised her eyebrows and put down her embroidery. 'Who is this Marcel you're always talking about?'

'Oh, he's my dancing partner. He's so funny!'

'Dearest Nicole, I gathered that, but what do you know about him?'

'He's in his last year at school and he wants to go to the Sorbonne. He lives with his mother and brother. His father died a couple of years ago.'

'I want to meet him. He might be a schoolboy, but you're only eighteen and Paris is a big foreign city,' Anne said.

Nicole's father, Jeffrey, looked up from his newspaper. He was an enterprising and energetic man, tall and with a spare frame. He wore suits of his own making, while his hair and moustache were always neatly trimmed. His word was law at home and at work.

'So, you have a boyfriend now, young lady? It'll take a rare young man to be good enough for you.'

The next time that Marcel walked her home, Nicole invited him in. 'My mother is curious about my dancing partner.'

Marcel groaned and pretended to hold back. 'Oh, she wants to look me over and see if I'm good enough for you!'

He did not resist for long. When Nicole introduced him, Anne and Jeffrey greeted him warmly. The conversation began with dancing, but Jeffrey, in his accented but fluent French, soon moved on to quizzing Marcel closely on plans for his future, looking askance at his lack of a tie and causing Nicole to squirm with embarrassment. Marcel was her boyfriend, nothing more, yet Jeffrey was talking as if he had asked to marry her.

'I don't know. Maybe I'll be a writer,' Marcel said easily. 'I'm going to the Sorbonne when I leave school. I'm studying English and Nicole is helping to teach me!'

Nicole heard afterwards that becoming a writer sounded like nonsense to her father, who had worked hard to secure his own business in his adopted city.

She liked to play a game with Marcel when they were alone together. One day she would speak to him in English until he begged her to change to French. Another day she spoke only in French, until he begged her to teach him some English. She would correct his English pronunciation and grammar in between kisses.

'Nicole, my English girlfriend, teach me some English words for love,' Marcel said one evening on the way home after the dance class. They had descended the steps near Nicole's home and wandered towards the river.

'Passion, infatuation and crush!' Nicole said, amid much laughter.

When Marcel wanted more than kisses on the way home from the dancing class, there was nowhere to be private. A secluded corner in a local park allowed them to explore each other unobserved in good weather, but Nicole would not let Marcel go far. She was too conscious of the virginity that Anne had brought her up to preserve until marriage and her ideas about losing it did not include a park, even with Marcel. He never pressed her. Going to the park became their term for such exploration as Nicole permitted.

Marcel began to attend classes at the Sorbonne, where

he made a friend called Paul, who came from Dijon and was new to Paris. Marcel brought him to the dance class and introduced him to Nicole and Yvette. He was about their age, of average height and strongly built. Generous features and bright eyes made him seem approachable. He could already dance well and became a partner for Yvette. The four of them would meet after the class in a café now and then, and sometimes Miriam and other friends would join them. They would talk for hours about art and literature and increasingly about politics.

Marcel enjoyed the greater freedom of being a student, but he complained to Nicole about his mother one day when they were alone together.

'It's what am I doing and where am I going all the time. She says it's because she loves me, but she's interfering, so I don't tell her much anymore.'

'My parents aren't so different. My father won't let me go to art school yet,' Nicole said.

She wanted to be an artist. Shorthand and typing were practical skills that she had acquired on her father's insistence that they would stand her in good stead on the way to realising her dream.

'Rebel against your parents! Don't let them make you into a secretary. That's their idea. Go to art school instead,' Marcel said.

***

With the help of her elder son, Jean, Marcel's mother ran a shop that sold typewriters and printers. It was in a residential district across the Seine from where Marcel lived. Anything to do with him had a special allure and Nicole wanted to see the shop. She took the metro there to meet him one Saturday afternoon after work – her first visit to that quarter of Paris. She saw small shops and narrow streets, some of them lined with trees. There was a bustling, friendly atmosphere. A display of typewriters and sewing machines filled the window of Marcel's mother's shop.

A bell rang as she went in and Marcel, who worked there on Saturdays, spotted Nicole at once and sprang to her side. He introduced her to his mother and his brother, Jean. Mme Dupont, who had been talking to a customer, welcomed Nicole with a smile. She was a stout woman, her hair in a crisp perm. Nicole noticed a strong family resemblance to Marcel, while Jean looked quite different – no doubt taking after his father.

'Oh, you're the dancing partner!' Mme Dupont said.

'More than that. Nicole taught me to dance,' Marcel said.

'He's made good progress,' Nicole said, laughing because her comment made her feel like a teacher at a parents' evening.

Mme Dupont excused herself and returned to her customer. Jean was cordial, but other customers needed attention, so there was little time to talk to Marcel's family. Nicole amused herself by examining the contents of the shop instead.

'It's a specialist shop,' Marcel said, explaining that they sold to businesses as well as individuals.

'Of course you want to become a writer, growing up with all these machines,' Nicole said. 'But why is the shop so far away from where you live? My father's shop is near home.'

'I don't know, but if I lived near here, I would have gone to a different dance class and I wouldn't have met you,' Marcel said, with a squeeze of her hand. She laughed.

She was intrigued by the different shapes and sizes of the new and second-hand machines. Big, cumbersome, early ones were only for display, while the more streamlined, modern ones, like the typewriter she used at work, were for sale.

'Do you want to go into the business?' she said.

'No, I don't want to be tied to selling machines all my life!'

'Then you're lucky and so am I. My father expects my brothers to work with him, but not me. I've got more freedom, being a girl.'

Nicole did not mention her parents' ambition for her of marriage and family because Marcel might have thought that she had designs on him. Marriage lay in the distant future. She still wanted to be an artist, with a studio in Paris. She loved French art and dreamed of painting like Berthe Morisot or Suzanne Valadon. Sitting by the windows at home, she had drawn the Eiffel Tower, the Seine, and the rooftops and chimney pots of Paris under skies that were blue with sunshine, heavy with cloud or misty with rain at varying times and seasons. A pile of finished sketchbooks had grown in her bedroom.

***

'Have you heard about the international exhibition on the Place du Trocadéro?' Marcel said one evening in the summer of 1937 as he and Nicole left the dance class.

14

'Oh yes. My father was talking about it,' Nicole said, remembering that he had been impressed by a visit there.

Marcel wanted to see the exhibition and Nicole went with him after work one day. The Place du Trocadéro was only a few minutes' walk from where they lived. Many countries were represented, but they were impressed from the start by a big pavilion about life in Germany and spent most of their time there. While Marcel was drawn to the cars on show, Nicole lingered over a model flat with modern furniture in pale wood and knew that her mother would love the kitchen with its refrigerator and washing machine. Anne had to make do with a larder and would often complain about the summer heat spoiling food, while their clothes were boiled in a big washtub and put through a mangle. Nicole was sure that the shiny vacuum cleaner in the model flat would work much better than the carpet sweeper at home.

Talking to her parents that evening, she praised the German designs that she had seen, encouraging her mother to go and see for herself. Anne was interested, but Nicole was taken aback by her father's response.

'That's all very well, but the Germans are interested in more than modern kitchens and fast cars. Did you see Picasso's *Guernica* there?'

Nicole knew about the German and Italian bombing of the Basque town earlier that year. She admitted to her father that she and Marcel had not visited the Spanish pavilion and so had not seen Picasso's painting.

'I told you it was there. You weren't listening. Too busy thinking about the boyfriend,' Jeffrey said. 'What worries me is German rearmament and the weakness of the French military.' He looked stern as he gave figures about the armed forces of the two countries. France, by contrast with Germany, seemed unprepared.

Nicole was suddenly afraid. 'Is there going to be another war?'

'I don't know. It's possible, but is it likely so soon after the Great War?'

'It's not so soon. It's a lifetime to me,' Nicole said.

She had been born two months before the end of that war, but she had always regarded it as history. Her enthusiasm for German industry cooled as she considered her father's words. There was some justice in what he had said. She had been too caught up in Marcel to take much notice of her father twiddling wireless knobs in search of news lately or commenting from behind a newspaper about the prospect of another war. She felt abashed that she had missed such an important painting as Picasso's *Guernica* when she had been horrified by the bombing.

Nicole and Marcel visited the exhibition for a second time. Passing the German pavilion, Nicole felt uneasy. They were both shocked by Picasso's painting.

TWO

THREAT

Nicole's ambition to be an artist was not supported by her father, but he did not forbid it. The many paintings on the walls of their flat showed her parents' love of art, but they left Nicole in no doubt that all the demands of marriage and family had to come first for a woman.

Nicole was not deterred. In the summer of 1938, with Marcel's encouragement, she obtained a place at a small art school in the Rue du Dragon in Saint-Germain-des-Prés. It took women students as well as men and its reputation as bohemian appealed to her. She paid for her fees for the first year with her savings and she enjoyed her first term.

Jeffrey and Anne, with Christopher and Nicole, had a roast capon for their Christmas dinner that year. Anne then brought out the traditional Christmas pudding, which she had made weeks before and had been steaming in the kitchen.

Jeffrey had been busy in recent weeks, completing orders in time for Christmas. Ralph, now living in London with his English wife, Jessie, was absent for the first time from Christmas celebrations. He had taken charge of a new branch of the business that Jeffrey had set up in London. As the family watched flames of lighted brandy embrace the pudding, Jeffrey spoke.

'What if the Germans invade France when Britain is at war with Germany? The British here will be sitting ducks.'

'I can hardly believe it,' Anne said. 'The last war finished only twenty years ago. It seems like yesterday to me, being in Brittany with two small boys and you arriving just before the end of the war, Nicole. I can't believe it's going to happen again. We're too old now. I was in my thirties then and I'm nearly sixty now!'

'Unfortunately, I don't think Hitler is taking your age into account,' Jeffrey said. 'But you're right. It seems impossible that war could break out again so soon. France doesn't want it and hasn't recovered from the last war. There's no leader to stand against Hitler, but France has an army, so we should be all right.'

Despite her father's reassurance, Nicole felt anxious. Since seeing Picasso's *Guernica* the previous year, she had become increasingly aware of signs of war. Too many conversations now concerned France's readiness and Hitler's aggression to neighbouring countries. Being with Marcel or her family and friends, or immersing herself in her art studies could banish the anxious feeling, but only until a newspaper article, radio news or something said in conversation brought it back.

***

As a young tailor in England, Jeffrey had been offered the chance of a job in Paris in 1912 with an English firm. He travelled there from London for an interview. The bustling city with several completed lines of metro, the imposing new church of Sacré-Coeur in Montmartre and a busy nightlife impressed him. Paris had recovered well from a major flood two years before. Business prospects for a tailor in a city that was a world-leader in fashion were good. On being offered the job, he returned home to persuade Anne that a new life awaited them and their baby, Ralph, across the English Channel.

Jeffrey and Anne stayed in Paris when war began in 1914 and another son, Christopher, arrived the following year. As the war progressed, the fear that Paris would be invaded grew. The bombing of the city by Zeppelins and planes gave way to shelling by howitzers. Jeffrey stayed in Paris for his job, but, in 1918, Anne moved to Brittany to safeguard their two boys and to have a third baby. Nicole was born there in the summer.

On the death of his employer after the Great War, Jeffrey took over the tailoring business near the Place d'Iéna in an affluent district of Paris. The business prospered in the early 1920s and the good quality of his work as a bespoke tailor attracted influential clients, including royalty. The King of Spain was mentioned proudly at home, as was the Duke of Luxembourg. Jeffrey made clothes for Anne, as well as for himself and the two boys. His well-dressed family was a good advertisement for the business.

Growing prosperity enabled them to rent a large flat in fashionable Neuilly. A maid dealt with cleaning and laundry, while Anne looked after the children and did the shopping and cooking. A thriving British community existed in Paris and Jeffrey was a founder member of the Standard Club, where the family spent their Sundays playing tennis and cricket with other British families. Every summer saw their departure on holiday to southwest France, to Biarritz, Bayonne or some other resort on the Atlantic coast. This prosperity did not last. After the crash of 1929, the tailoring business struggled, causing the family to move from the flat in Neuilly to the smaller one across the Seine from the Eiffel Tower.

***

Nicole had grown up knowing that she would have to decide on her nationality at the age of twenty-one. French law did not allow for dual citizenship and so, as the child of British parents living in the country of her birth, she had to choose to be French or British. She talked to Marcel about it.

'Choose French nationality, Nicole,' he said, as they strolled arm in arm around the Bois de Boulogne one Saturday afternoon, stopping frequently to embrace. 'After all, you were born here. It's your country!'

'Yes, but it won't please my parents. I'll be the only French person in a British family.'

'Well, stand up for what you want. It's your life, after all. And don't forget that you're a rebel.'

Marcel kissed her, ignoring passers-by. 'I want you to be French, Nicole. Even though you look English, with your brown eyes and hair and the way you dress.'

'I hope you're not saying that I don't know how to dress.'

'That would be a terrible thing to say in a city where women are so *chic*!'

***

Paris was preparing for war. Sandbags began to appear around statues and treasured buildings. Valuable stained glass was being moved. On her visits to galleries, Nicole watched art going into hiding.

The summer of 1939 saw another holiday by the sea. The family drove south in their blue Willys-Knight, with big headlamps, wheels with spokes and a running board. On the way to Biarritz, they stayed in Bordeaux, at a *pension* that advertised a welcome to families with dogs.

They returned to Paris just as Neville Chamberlain's efforts at appeasement were seen to have failed. Hopes had been high for his agreement with Hitler in Munich the year before, but Jeffrey's worst fears and those of the British community in Paris were realised when Britain and France declared war against Germany on 3rd September. Jeffrey read the newspaper report of Chamberlain's announcement of war to the British people and quoted it to the family. All young Frenchmen between the ages of eighteen and thirty-five were mobilised.

'Have you heard the news, Nicole? I've been called up. We all have,' Marcel said as he met Nicole that evening. 'I have to report to the army on the eighth day after war was declared. That means September 11th.'

They were clattering down the steps of her building,

where Marcel had picked her up as he often did. Nicole stopped and turned to look at him. 'That's the day before my twenty-first birthday! Oh, surely you're coming to my party?'

'I'd love to, but it's impossible. I won't be here.'

'Oh, Marcel, what a shame! But I don't see you as a soldier. You're not at all military. You'll have to tuck your shirt in, cut your hair and do up your shoelaces!'

Marcel looked glum for a moment, but he spoke briskly, 'Well, let's hope for a quick French victory to see off the Germans and then we can all go home.'

Nicole could see that he was not looking forward to joining the army. They continued to their favourite café, where they were meeting Paul, Miriam and Yvette, and they all sat outside talking about the war and what it might mean for them. It was beginning to dominate their lives. Paul was a journalist by then, working for the daily, *La Presse Parisienne*. He had been called up as well and was unhappy about leaving his job, but Nicole could imagine him as a soldier. It was not simply about his orderly appearance. He was purposeful and well-organised. Beside him, Marcel seemed boyish – yet Marcel was exciting. Nicole had eyes only for him.

All the young men Nicole knew began to disappear – Marcel and Paul, students at the art school and two of Jeffrey's employees. Paris was becoming a city of women, children and older men. Their last meeting before Marcel had to report for duty took place on a September evening when they strolled near his flat. Leaves were not falling yet, but a crispness in the air hinted of autumn.

'I'll come back as soon as I get leave. I don't want to be away for long and I'm going to miss you terribly,' Marcel said, after they had talked about his new life in the army.

'I miss you now, from one day to the next, so it'll be worse when you're away for weeks, perhaps even longer,' Nicole replied.

He turned towards her and took her in his arms. 'Will you come back home with me now? My mother's out with friends and Jean has already left for the army, so we'll be alone.'

Nicole knew what he was asking and that going to war meant that she might never see him again. She could not say no to him. She felt her mother's strictures weaken and she agreed.

Marcel lived in a small street off the Avenue du Président Wilson, near Miriam and Yvette, although Nicole's Steps made them all seem further away from her. She knew his flat well from previous visits, but she had never been in his bedroom before. With eyes only for Marcel, she barely saw the furniture, the posters of film stars pinned to the walls and his overflowing bookcase. She did notice that Marcel produced a condom and was relieved that she would not have to fear becoming pregnant.

They made love with all the intensity of young people who had to part soon, not minding the discomfort of his narrow single bed as they explored each other for the first time in real privacy. When they were dressing afterwards and Marcel asked her to marry him, Nicole agreed fervently. He did not have an engagement ring to offer and they did not talk about when they would marry. It would not be possible until he returned from the war and no one knew when that might be.

At home that evening, she told her parents about Marcel's proposal. Anne was pleased and full of congratulations.

Jeffrey pursed his lips and folded the newspaper he had been reading, slapping it down onto the coffee table beside his chair.

'That young man should have some savings behind him first, not be proposing to my daughter on his way to war.'

For the first time in her life, Nicole had done something important that she would never tell her mother about. One day, when she and Marcel married, her mother would think of her as a virgin bride. Yet she did not feel ashamed or as if she had lost anything. In the days and weeks that followed, she felt that she had gained in maturity and had joined the adult world. Her eyes brightened and she was aware of a new confidence.

***

The Seymour family went ahead with the small party to celebrate Nicole's twenty-first birthday. Marcel had gone by then and so had Paul, but Miriam, Yvette, other friends from school and some from Nicole's art school came along. Christopher had not been conscripted like Marcel, because he was British, so he could attend. Ralph was in England with his family.

After a buffet supper, which ended with a cake made by Anne, Nicole and Christopher rolled back the carpet and put records on the gramophone. The young people danced to the music of Jean Sablon and Django Reinhardt. In the absence of enough male partners, the girls danced together and even Miriam, self-proclaimed wallflower, was persuaded to take to the floor. With the thump of feet on the floorboards in mind, Anne had made sure to warn the tenants underneath about noise. Thoughts of war faded for an evening.

Ralph, in England, joined the RAF. Christopher did the same from France and prepared to leave home for England. Nicole wished increasingly that the war would go away. Marcel could return and Christopher could stay at home. How stupid it was to go to war, a completely unwanted intrusion into everyone's life. Why didn't the Germans keep to their own country and leave everyone else to theirs?

'I've never thought of you as military,' she said to Christopher one day at home, repeating almost exactly her words to Marcel.

'No, I'm not, but it's a heaven-sent chance to escape tailoring. Father wouldn't dare to stop me helping to save Britain from invasion, especially as he's joined up, too.'

Blackouts and the wail of air-raid sirens accustomed people to the change from peacetime to war. Metro stations were made into shelters and so were the cellars of the block of flats where the Seymour family lived. An air of unreality attended all the preparations. No one believed that Germany would be able to invade France. The army would prevent it with the help of the Maginot Line, the series of forts that the French had constructed along the border with Germany after the Great War. Yet Nicole and her family and friends nearby noticed closed shutters in their quarter of Paris. People were leaving.

***

'Of course you'll choose British nationality,' Jeffrey said, when Nicole flourished an official letter inviting her to choose now that she was twenty-one. Her parents had retained their British nationality and both Ralph and Christopher had chosen to be British. Her future with Marcel agreed by then, Nicole was firm.

'But, Papa, I don't feel British. I was born in France and I've grown up in Paris, and I'm going to marry a Frenchman and live here.'

'Be sensible, Nicole! We're a British family and we'll need to leave France if Germany invades, because Britain is at war with Germany. You must come with us,' Jeffrey said.

'Oh, yes, of course I'm coming with you. I can't stay here on my own! I'll go to England as a French citizen and after the war Marcel and I will be married and live here. He agrees with me.'

Jeffrey sniffed. 'That boy! Don't allow yourself to be influenced by him.'

'Of course you feel British, Papa, because you were born there and grew up there, but I've never lived in England. It can't be my country in the way that it's yours,' Nicole said, ignoring her father's rudeness about Marcel.

She felt tremulous. She had never contradicted her father before and she had not forgotten his crushing of Christopher a few years previously. Her brother's love of woodcarving was displayed at home by his carvings of animals. Nicole's favourite remained the giraffe that he had made for her and that reminded her of the Eiffel Tower. One day at home, after Christopher had left his English school and the family was finishing lunch, he had announced his wish to be a cabinetmaker.

Jeffrey had waved a dismissive hand. 'I know you like woodcarving, my boy – I'm always tripping over the evidence – but that's just a hobby. You're coming into the business, so that you can help Ralph carry on after me. I'm not going to be here forever, you know.'

'I love wood, but I have no feeling for cloth. It's lifeless,' Christopher had said, his hand caressing the carved back of Nicole's mahogany chair, next to his.

Jeffrey had given a snort of laughter. 'Of course it's lifeless! It's cloth. It's not meant to move around of its own accord. The body inside moves and demonstrates the beauty of cloth. Wood doesn't do anything but sit there. Besides, the family business is cloth, not wood. What kind of fool are you, boy? You're being apprenticed to me. That's the whole point of this expensive education that you've had. You know the business is struggling and I need you. I don't want to hear any more foolishness.'

Ralph had not needed to speak, although his ringing voice and cheery manner brought life and energy to any gathering. He had been made in his father's mould and had taken up tailoring as if born to it. Ralph was as dapper as his father and a good advertisement for the business. Jeffrey had never made any secret of his pride in his elder son and a certain irritation with his younger son.

That had been the end of the argument. For several years, with a set face, Christopher had worked in the family business, at first as an apprentice tailor, until the day came when he joined the RAF and escaped into the war.

Anne also wanted her daughter to choose British nationality, but Nicole was not deterred by her parents' opposition. She was looking forward to her life with Marcel and she applied for French nationality. It was granted, as she had known it would be, because she had been born in France. She was secretly proud that she had become the rebel that Marcel had encouraged her to be, while also fearful of her father's reaction.

She need not have worried. Whether because he understood how much it mattered to his daughter, or he acknowledged his part in her French identity, or was preoccupied by the war, Jeffrey said little when Nicole showed him her certificate of French citizenship. It was a *fait accompli*.

Nicole had an address for Marcel and wrote to him with her news.

21st October 1939

Dearest Marcel

I've chosen my nationality and the government has agreed that I am French! My parents aren't too upset.

Day to day, I carry on as normal, but I long to see you. I can't imagine when that will be. If we are invaded, I shall go to England with my parents. Can I visit you in your barracks if you can't come to Paris?

All my love, Nicole xxx

Marcel's reply arrived only a few days later. Nicole had written to him in French, but his reply was in English. His letter was short as he could not talk about where he was or what he was doing.

27 Oct '39

My dearest Nicole

I've read your letter at least a hundred times. You are a French citizen! You will not regret it.

I miss you, but you cannot come here because passes are

given only to wives to visit. I hope to come to Paris on leave before too long, so be patient, my Nicole, and remember how much I love you.

Your Marcel

Little seemed to happen after the declaration of war. The government distributed gas masks and people carried them around for fear of a gas attack. Anti-aircraft balloons flew overhead. Shopkeepers with German-sounding names displayed signs indicating their French identity. Streetlamps were dimmed, while windows had to be curtained before lights could be switched on indoors. The Louvre was closed and more paintings were moved to safety. A few more people in the wealthier districts left Paris.

Parisians continued to put their faith in the Maginot Line. The British in Paris decided to await events as there was no immediate crisis and the Seymour family hung on. People were anxious and Nicole, without Marcel, felt her life shrinking. When rationing of the main items of food was introduced in February 1940, Anne complained about having to register with shops and collect coloured ration stamps from the town hall, as well as about the rationing itself, but like everyone she became used to it.

In March 1940, after six months' service, Marcel secured a few days leave, which he spent as much as possible with Nicole. They made love on his narrow bed at home, knowing his mother to be busy in her shop and grateful for his brother Jean's absence in the army. On his last night, they met in his room and, later, he saw her home. They kissed passionately at the foot of the steps across from

Nicole's flat. She did not care if her mother could see them from the living-room window. Every moment with Marcel was precious now.

THREE

INVASION

In May 1940, listening to the news of the Nazi invasion of Belgium, Luxembourg, the Netherlands and France, Nicole's thoughts turned immediately to Marcel's safety. At night before falling asleep, she relived their times together and her first thoughts in the morning were of him. She no longer received any letters from him.

Like everyone else, she followed the Nazis' progress through the country. Even after the invasion, people of her parents' generation still believed that their city would be safe and reminded themselves of the last war when the Germans had drawn back from entering Paris. Frightened of what was happening, Nicole wanted to believe they were right.

One evening in mid-May, Jeffrey came home from the shop, where he had spent the day pivoting between the wireless and his customers. He huddled over the wireless at home. 'Listen!' he said, irritably, at one point.

Anne and Nicole looked up from talking about a carving that Christopher had done before leaving to join the RAF. It was a small figure of a wood sculptor at work on a miniature of himself. Christopher had presented it to his parents as he left Paris. Nicole knew that Anne liked it, but that Jeffrey saw it as a challenge to his parental authority. If Christopher had to carry on fiddling with wood, why couldn't he carve a piece showing a tailor at work with scissors or a measuring tape, something to display in the shop and draw in customers?

A newscaster's voice filled the room as Jeffrey turned up the volume. The Nazis were approaching the city of Laon in Picardie, and Belgian evacuees and others were flooding into Paris. Turning off the wireless as the news ended, Jeffrey repeated what he had been saying for weeks.

'It's not looking good. We won't be safe here if they take Paris. They'll see us as citizens of a worse enemy than France. After all, we're British; we're at war with Germany and we're not losing.'

Faces were serious as the family talked about what to do. They had been expecting war for some time, but things were different now. They no longer talked about what they would do if the Nazis invaded, but what they must do now the invasion had happened and was increasingly likely to engulf Paris. It was alarming.

'We must get to England.' Anne's voice sounded strained.

'Ralph will have room for us and if he's been posted away from home by the RAF, Jessie will take us in. That's what they've always promised,' Jeffrey said.

Nicole looked from one to the other of her parents, conscious for the first time that they were not as calm, capable and in charge of events as they had always seemed to be. She did not blame them. This was worse than the Depression and not just a matter of tightening belts. Paris was no longer the secure and comfortable place of her childhood. The furniture in the flat might look as solid as ever, but her world trembled around her and she felt the panicky urge to run that she could see in her mother. For the first time in her life, she felt protective towards her parents – they who had always protected her.

'But the Nazis are in control in the north. How can we get past them?' she said, a frown creasing her forehead and her fear sharpening. She was familiar with her parents' stories about the Great War, but nothing like this had ever happened to her before.

'We can't go anywhere near them, but they're not in control everywhere, not yet. I'll go to England with the RAF, probably from Nantes – where I'll sell the car before I go,' Jeffrey said.

'Are you leaving us to their mercy?' Anne said with a grimace.

'Certainly not, as you well know! I've been thinking about this. The best thing for you two is a boat from Bordeaux,' Jeffrey said.

The family normally travelled to England by the Golden Arrow, taking a train from the Gare du Nord in Paris to Calais, transferring to a ferry to Dover and continuing by train to London. It was a day's journey, but it would not be possible now. The obvious French Channel ports, like Calais, Boulogne, Dieppe and Le Havre, from which they might have escaped, were either already occupied or else vulnerable to Nazi invasion.

'We've never gone that way before. How will we get there? People are already leaving Paris and the trains must be packed,' Anne said.

'I've got an idea, but I need to speak to Rick first. I'm hoping he'll take you to Bordeaux,' Jeffrey said, referring to a friend at the Standard Club.

'What about the flat? Our lovely home?' Anne took a sharp breath and looked around, as if trying to furnish her memory.

'Everyone who can is leaving Paris. I know because I've been talking to clients,' Jeffrey said.

'They'll come here, won't they?' Anne's mouth was pursed in distaste.

'We can't protect the flat from them if they invade Paris, but we'll be safe in England. We'll hold onto the flat and we'll come back here afterwards,' Jeffrey said.

'Oh, so you don't think the war will last. Well, at least I don't have to go in a plane. You've worked it all out,' Anne said.

Nicole could see the relief in her mother's face, both because Jeffrey was taking charge of events and because she disliked the idea of flying.

'I'll have to sort out something for the business. I don't want to shut up shop altogether, unless I have to,' Jeffrey said.

Nicole was torn. She was upset at the thought of leaving her home. She would miss her friends, the art school and the places she loved, but her greatest concern was for Marcel. He could have been taken prisoner or he might be part of the retreating French army. She hoped desperately that he would soon appear in Paris.

'I must know where Marcel is and what is happening to him,' she said. 'It's weeks since he's written to me.'

'Write and tell him where you're going. You may have French citizenship, but you must help your mother,' Jeffrey said.

Nicole nodded. Her parents needed her now in a way that they had never done before. When choosing her nationality, she had thought only of herself and her future, but this was different.

***

Nicole met Miriam and Yvette one evening in May, in a café on the Place d'Iéna that they knew well. The three girls had remained close since leaving school and straightaway plunged into what was most on their minds.

'My grandparents are in Rennes,' Yvette said. 'My mother thinks we should go there, but will it be far enough away?'

'It's impossible to tell. What about you, Miriam?' Nicole asked.

The two other girls turned towards their friend. Miriam was Jewish. Her parents had come to France from Poland as a young couple. Miriam and her brother, Louis, born in France, had French names. Louis liked his name, but Miriam did not want to be called Françoise and preferred her Polish middle name.

'We have relatives in Poland and the United States, but no one in France,' Miriam said. 'My parents aren't thinking of going anywhere, despite what's happening to Jews.'

She did not need to explain further. Living in the obvious path of Nazi invasion, they had all been following the news much more closely in the last year or two and were aware of the persecution of Jews in Germany and Austria.

Miriam swirled her drink, looking serious. 'We can't go to Poland now it's been invaded and the United States is so far away. My father says to lie low, that we'll be all right. It's funny, but I've never felt as Jewish as I do now.'

'It could be dangerous for you here, Miriam, if the Nazis come,' Nicole said.

'And it will be scary, waiting for the enemy,' Miriam said. 'What about you, Nicole?'

'We're going to my brother's house in London,' Nicole said. 'My father is travelling with the RAF. My mother and I will probably go to England from Bordeaux.'

'I wish I had somewhere to go, but I can't leave my parents. I'm not sure that my father's right about lying low and I feel like leaving, because we're just letting them overrun us.' Miriam's forehead was creased with worry and the three friends exchanged glances.

'The war might not last long. Maybe only a few weeks or... I don't know, a few months,' Yvette said.

'Or a few years. No, you don't know, Yvette. Think of the last one. I read somewhere that in August 1914, they said it would all be over by Christmas,' Miriam said.

A silence arose as the three friends grappled with the idea of their city being occupied by a foreign power. It was an almost impossible thought. A song by Josephine Baker on the café wireless filled the gap in their conversation.

'Do you know what happened in the canteen at the Sorbonne today? Some clumsy girl dropped a whole tray of food all over me. I was nearly drowned in soup. I had to spend twenty minutes in the toilets scrubbing myself down!' Miriam said as the song died away.

Nicole and Yvette laughed at the comical expression on Miriam's face and the war was forgotten for the moment.

'Did you realise that it's May 19th today, the date we agreed to meet?' Miriam asked.

'Well, of course. We are meeting!' Nicole said, looking blank. Then, she understood. Six years previously, visiting the Luxembourg Gardens at the age of fifteen, they had agreed to meet on the same bench, on that date, in ten years' time. Nicole and Yvette might have forgotten all about it, but Miriam reminded them every year.

'Yes, but it's only 1940, not 1944!' Yvette said.

'Four years to go! What a long time we shall have been friends by then,' Nicole said.

'Don't be late! Be there on the dot of noon in 1944, on our bench,' Miriam reminded them as they got up to leave the café.

They laughed because they would meet many times before then. Yet, descending the steps to her home that evening, after leaving her friends, Nicole began to have doubts. Normally one of them would call round or pick up the phone to the others, but was there time for that now? The war might separate them soon, perhaps for years. It was another unsettling thought among all those that had troubled her in recent weeks.

Later that evening, Jeffrey attempted a long-distance call to London. After a frustrating wait, he was put through to Jessie. He spoke loudly, repeating himself several times.

'The line was bad, but it's all right. She's expecting us

soon. I couldn't give her a date, but I promised to try and keep in touch,' he said as he put the phone down.

'It's such a relief to know we have somewhere to go,' Anne said.

Nicole sat down at the desk in the sitting room of the flat. She wrote to Marcel, adding Ralph's address in London under her name.

20th May 1940

Dearest Marcel

They are getting closer to Paris every day and we don't have much time. My father is leaving France with the RAF. My mother and I hope to go to Bordeaux and take the boat for England. We'll stay at my brother's house in London. I'll write again as soon as I know more. I wish I knew where you are. Please write soon.

Thinking of you always – keep safe.

All my love, Nicole

There was no reply. Day after day, Nicole asked her mother on her return from work if a letter had come for her.

'He's far too busy fighting off the Nazi advance to have time to write love letters,' Jeffrey said, seeing Nicole's disappointment.

The Seymour family were not sure when they would need to leave Paris. They listened to the wireless and read newspapers, desperate for news that grew more worrying as the days passed. The Nazis were clearly on the way. People were suggesting that it would be better to let them in quietly rather than suffer all the destruction and bloodshed of opposition.

Nicole warned the art school that she would be leaving soon and had no idea when she might return. She was pleased to be told that any application she made in future would be looked upon favourably. She slept badly at night, dreaming of the tramp of marching feet coming to her door and waking in a sweat in the early hours of the morning, relieved to hear only the normal night-time sounds of the city.

Paris had changed with the threat of invasion. The city was quieter, witness to the beauty of a warm springtime, with trees newly in leaf on the streets and in the parks and flowers emerging in the sunshine. People who remained were staying at home more. With the arrival of refugees driven from home by the Nazi invasion in the north, unease grew, despite the government saying that Paris would be safe.

The Seymour family followed the progress of the invasion with mounting anxiety. The Nazis were close and Parisians in the wealthier districts were continuing to leave the city. Even though the Germans had not invaded Paris during the Great War, not much more than twenty years previously, Parisians still feared aerial attack.

Jeffrey secured open tickets for Anne and Nicole on a passenger boat going from Bordeaux to Southampton. He arranged a lift for Anne and Nicole to Bordeaux with Rick, who would be driving there with his wife, Georgie, then leaving for England by boat. Nicole obtained a French passport.

On a Sunday at the beginning of June, Nicole and her parents went to the Standard Club as usual. It was a breezy, late spring day. The club was in Meudon, a suburb of Paris.

To a casual onlooker, everything would have seemed peaceful, but the conversation was all of war and the plans of the British in Paris to escape. Thousands of British and French troops were being evacuated from Dunkirk and nothing stood in the way of the Nazi advance.

Nicole played tennis before having lunch with her parents. Afterwards, they wandered towards the rose garden, which the British owners of the club had planted. The rose bushes were in flower, with more buds about to open. Nicole stopped by a bush of bright red blooms, breathing in the faint scent. She used her fingernails to cut off a small rose, barely more than a bud.

'Nicole! What *are* you doing?' Anne's voice was sharp with disapproval as she left her own inspection of a rose bush to stand beside her daughter.

Nicole slipped the rose into her handbag. 'Nobody will miss it. We're leaving soon and I want something to remind me of Paris.'

At home that evening, she secured the rose with sticky tape in the autograph book that she had begun when it became likely that they would leave. Underneath the rose she wrote: *Souvenir from the Standard Club, Sunday 2nd June 1940, before the Nazis entered Paris.* She placed the autograph book beneath a heavy dictionary to press the rose flat and willed herself not to forget it when they left for England. It contained the signatures and best wishes of everyone who mattered to her.

After work the next day, Nicole was at home, standing at a window that looked out onto the flight of steps up to the Avenue du Président Wilson. She was planning to go and see Miriam when her attention was caught.

'*Maman*, look at these planes! What on earth are they doing over there?'

Anne came to join her, screwing up her eyes to see better. 'How odd. We don't usually see planes here.' She raised her voice. 'Jeffrey, come and look at this!'

Jeffrey joined them, shouting as he looked out of the window. 'They're bombing! They're German planes bombing Paris! Get down to the shelter quickly!'

They could hear air-raid sirens now. They ran downstairs to the basement shelter where several residents were in a state of shock. Others joined them. Although not directly overhead, the sound was terrifying. When silence fell at last and they heard the all-clear siren, everyone crawled upstairs. From the wireless, they learned that the target of the raid – involving almost a thousand bombs – had been the nearby car factories of Renault and Citroën, and Paris airports. Many people had been killed. One bomb had fallen nearby and another near the Bois de Boulogne.

Anne slept badly and was pale and exhausted the next morning. After breakfast, she wandered distractedly around the flat, trying to decide what to take with her to London.

'Jeffrey, you must find out from Rick when he's leaving. I can't stay here any longer. Supposing they bomb us tonight?'

'They're not here yet. Let's wait a bit. After the raid last night, surely the government will do something to stop them. Anyway, I need to arrange for someone to look after the business,' Jeffrey said.

'You should have done that by now. I'm starting to

pack,' Anne said, but she calmed down at Jeffrey's words and allowed him to leave for work.

Every morning, Jeffrey switched on the wireless, which sat on the sideboard in the living room. The family listened in silence over breakfast. One morning, the Nazis were only seventy-five kilometres away from Paris. Given the size and strength of the enemy forces and their own lack of preparation, the French government appeared to think that lives would be better preserved if they accepted the invasion. The Nazis were heading south to Paris and it was becoming clear that they would meet no opposition.

Jeffrey was alarmed. 'The wretched government is abandoning us. I'm off to the embassy now to see what they're advising the British here to do. They'll have a plan.'

The British Embassy occupied an imposing 18th century building, the Hôtel de Charost, which Jeffrey knew from attending receptions for British businessmen in Paris. It gave the impression of elegance and strength.

'Good. Nicole, darling, stay at home today, at least until we know more,' Anne said.

Nicole was due to attend classes that morning, but, seeing her mother's fear, she agreed to stay at home. Making a phone call to explain her absence, she wondered when she would see her college and her friends there again.

Anne and Nicole remained in the flat, reassured by Jeffrey's confidence, but knowing that they must leave soon. They spent their time whittling down what they wanted to take and packing cases. Jeffrey could not take much luggage on the plane and Rick and Georgie's car would have scant room, so they would take only one case each.

Nicole packed her summer clothes and a cardigan. She squeezed in a spare pair of flat heeled shoes. Her summer coat and sensible town shoes would do for the journey. She did not want to wear her winter coat in June and there was no room for it in the case, so it stayed behind with most of her winter clothes.

'I expect Kim will have to go into quarantine when we get to England,' Anne said at one point.

'Oh, yes, of course, in case of rabies. Poor Kim. There's nothing wrong with him. How long will it be for?' Nicole asked.

'I'm not sure. It could be weeks or months,' Anne replied.

Jeffrey returned a couple of hours later, his face drawn. He sank into a chair in the sitting room. 'I went to the shop and straight on to the embassy, but there was no help from anyone and no advice. All I was told, by some gormless official, was that British people in Paris must look after themselves. And they're all clearing up and getting out, saving their skins with no thought for us.'

Anne gave a sharp intake of breath. 'We must go now.'

'There's something else. Paris is being declared an open city, so it won't be defended. We would be completely at the mercy of the Nazis. It really is time to go. And while I was out, I could hear an unusual sound above the traffic, a kind of thunder. People were saying it's the noise of the invasion. They've nearly reached Paris. I can't hear it now because the windows are closed, but go outside—'

'I believe you,' Anne said, not moving.

'I see you've packed, so I'll drive you to Rick. I rang him from the shop this morning and he's ready to set off this afternoon. We can't risk staying here any longer,' Jeffrey said. 'I went to the bank on my way back, so I can give you cash for the journey. And I've arranged for an employee, Patrick McGrath, to look after the business in my absence. I gave him last-minute instructions this morning. It's fortunate that he's an Irish citizen. They are unlikely to see him as an enemy, with the Irish Free State keeping out of the war.'

Nicole and Anne exchanged glances. Nicole was becoming used to the anxiety on her mother's normally calm face. She waited for Anne to say something reassuring, but both her parents were silent. After months of uncertainty, the moment of flight that they had all been dreading had arrived.

PART TWO

PART TWO

ONE

FLIGHT

After a scratch lunch, Nicole sat at the desk in the living room and scribbled hasty notes to Marcel, Miriam, Yvette and the art school. With her father urging her to hurry, there was no time to go to the nearest letterbox at the top of Nicole's Steps. Instead, she found stamps and then knocked on the door of their concierge, M. Lebrun, whom she had known for years. He was an elderly man with a grumpy manner, but he would occasionally do favours. He opened the door, raising his eyebrows at the letters Nicole was flourishing at him.

'M. Lebrun, we're going to England and I haven't got time... will you please post these for me? I've stamped them.'

'Well, it's all right for you with somewhere to go, but I've got nowhere, so I'm staying put, whether they come or not. I'll post them if you're in such a hurry,' he said, with a disapproving sniff.

Nicole thrust the four envelopes and a tip into his hands, thanked him and ran back to her flat. All the letters said that she was leaving today for England and those to friends gave the address of Jessie's house in London. She did not expect any replies soon, as the postal service to England had been disrupted by the invasion. Nor did she know when she might return to Paris.

At the last minute, glancing around her bedroom, she remembered the autograph book. Grabbing it from underneath the dictionary that was pressing the rose she had taken as a memento of Paris, she squeezed it into her case with the wooden giraffe that Christopher had made for her. The invaders were not having either of those precious possessions, nor her current sketchbook, her favourite box of watercolours, her pens and her bottle of ink. She sat on her case to close it, clicked the fastenings shut and carried it to the front door.

'We'll need supplies for the journey. We could be on the road for days if there's a lot of traffic leaving Paris,' Anne said, filling two string bags with food from the kitchen.

Kim was running around, anticipating a walk because of all the commotion. In the middle of carrying cases down to the car, Jeffrey stopped and stared at the dog as if he had never seen him before.

'You can't take him,' he said. 'There won't be room in the car for a dog. Find someone to look after him!'

Nicole, behind her father with her case, put it down. 'How can I, Papa? We're just about to go.'

'Then leave him on the street or give him to Lebrun.'

Nicole's face tightened. 'I won't leave him on the street. And you know M. Lebrun doesn't like dogs. No one else will take him now. They're all packing to leave, like us, but I won't abandon him to starve.'

Jeffrey shrugged. 'Rick will decide. You won't be able to argue with him, my girl.'

Once out of doors, they could hear the disconcerting thunder of the invasion that Jeffrey had mentioned. Without delay, they climbed into the Willys-Knight and set off. Rick and Georgie lived near the Standard Club in Meudon and Jeffrey drove straight there, noting heavy traffic going south. On arrival, he helped with the luggage, scowled at Kim and rang the doorbell.

Rick opened the door. He was a heavy man who enjoyed French food and wine and was a keen cricket player. His wife, Georgie, slim and elegant, slipped past him now to greet Nicole and her parents.

'Here they are. Over to you,' Jeffrey said. With a brief farewell, he was gone. He was going straight to Nantes, where he would sell the car before flying to London with the RAF. The three of them would meet again at Jessie's house in a few days' time.

Rick and Georgie were ready to leave, their luggage stowed in the boot of their car. Adding the extra cases, Rick slammed the boot shut and slipped into the driving seat, with Georgie next to him. Nicole sat in the back with Anne and Kim and the bags of food. Nothing was said about Kim and the loaded car set off.

It was obvious from the crowded roads that Parisians were already pouring out of their city by any means they could. Most people were heading south, away from the Nazi advance, and the car soon joined a heavy stream of traffic. Nicole looked out of the window as they crawled along.

People were not only driving, but cycling and walking, or pushing prams and carts laden with possessions. Cars were not only full, but mattresses and other goods were strapped to roofs. She was perturbed by the sight of French soldiers, as it meant that any defence had been abandoned.

'You won't see Marcel among soldiers going south of Paris,' Anne said, observing Nicole's scrutiny as they passed a group of soldiers.

'I can't help looking for him,' Nicole said.

As the convoy of vehicles left the city and reached the open countryside, the pace of traffic increased. They took the road to Chartres. It was late in the evening before they arrived, hoping to spend the night. They began to hunt for rooms and, after much searching, found a guest house on the south side of the town that was prepared to take them. It was expensive and Georgie was certain that the owners had put the price up on seeing the approaching crowds.

They left as soon as possible the next morning. People they spoke to along the way were all intending to cross the River Loire at Tours, thinking that they would be safer on the other side. South of Chartres, they heard planes in the distance.

'Is that the French air force?' Nicole said.

'No. they're German planes. Reconnoitring, I suppose,' Rick said. He spoke calmly, but Nicole could see his worried face in the car mirror.

The planes approached, zooming low over the line of traffic, and they caught sight of swastikas on the wings. Then, they heard shots and explosions. The line of traffic was wavering under attack. People walking alongside the vehicles were screaming and running into surrounding fields to escape from the guns and bombs.

'They're attacking us!' Georgie's voice was panic-stricken.

Planes were swooping low overhead, shooting at the crowds. Everyone in the car was frightened, but there was nowhere to hide. Nicole was terrified of a bullet through the roof of the car. She shrank down in her seat, clutching at Kim next to her, but she could not stop looking out of the window. Outside, people were falling to the ground. A man collapsed beside the car, blood spurting from his head. Through the open windows came the sound of screams.

'Shouldn't we stop and see what we can do to help?' Georgie said, glancing from side to side.

'No, we can't. We'd be even more of a target and hold up people behind us,' Rick said.

A little further on, when the car ahead of them stopped, they were forced to do the same. For a while there was chaos, but the traffic began to move again. Nicole, thinking her last moment had come, glanced at her mother. Anne looked frozen, her expression blank. Kim was whimpering, frightened by the noise, and Nicole tried to comfort him. From her seat behind Georgie, she was aware of Rick's hands gripping the steering wheel when the planes were overhead and relaxing when they retreated.

Yet the planes were not gone for good. They returned and shot the fleeing queue of traffic a second time before roaring away. Again, the line of traffic halted. Nicole saw a little girl crying. She appeared to be lost and there was blood on her clothes and legs. Letting go of Kim, Nicole jumped out of the car, escaping Anne's clutching hand and ignoring her plea not to go.

'Where's your mummy?'

Nicole put an arm round the little girl. She was about five years old and did not seem to be hurt, despite the blood. She stopped crying and pointed behind her, then started crying again.

'Nicole. We're moving – come back!' Anne called from the car.

'Tell Rick to pull over!' Nicole said. 'Don't worry,' she told the child. 'We'll find your family.'

She looked in the direction the child had pointed for anyone who might claim her. People were milling about, beginning to return from the fields now it appeared the planes had gone. She began to ask those closest to her if they knew the child as she watched Rick steer to the side of the road and stop beside a car with a punctured tyre. The driver came over to Rick.

'The tyre was shot. Can you help me change the wheel?' he said, when Rick wound his window down.

Rick got out and they changed the wheel together. Anne gave the driver's wife some of the food she had brought from the flat, including a bottle of milk, tasting it first to see that it was still fresh. With a baby to care for and few supplies of their own, the young mother, little more than a girl, was thankful.

Watching all this, holding the little girl's hand and trying to comfort her, Nicole carried on asking people if they knew the child. No one did and Rick was starting to say that they had to move on. Nicole was beginning to feel desperate. How could she abandon the child and yet how could they take her with them? To her enormous relief, an older girl came out of the crowd towards them.

'Amélie!' the little girl said with delight.

'She was lost and no one seemed to know her,' Nicole said to the older girl. 'Are you all right? There's blood on her and I thought perhaps someone had been shot.'

'She's my sister. No, I don't know where the blood came from, but she's not hurt,' the older girl said after a quick examination. The child had let go of Nicole's hand and was clinging onto her sister. 'She ran off when they started shooting. Thank you so much, *mam'selle*, for helping.'

'Well, good luck,' Nicole said, breathing a sigh of relief.

The two girls melted into the crowd and Nicole returned to the car, trying not to notice bodies by the side of the road with people clustered round them. Rick drove on, the four passengers limp with relief at their survival and scanning the sky every so often, fearful of the planes' return.

They stopped in a village overnight when Rick needed a break from driving. There was nowhere to stay, as the only hotel was already full and a spell of knocking on doors was fruitless. They sat where they were in the car, eating what little food they had and dozing uncomfortably until daylight arrived.

Nicole missed Marcel. It was a feeling made worse by not knowing where he was or whether he was all right. She was certain only that the war that had flung them apart so easily would make it difficult for them to meet again. He seemed so far away now that neither of them knew where the other was. She tried to bring him closer by remembering what they had said and done together, but she found her memories fragmentary and hard to pin down.

After an uncomfortable night, Rick was keen to drive on as soon as it was light. Although the road was heavy with traffic of all kinds, there were no more attacks from the air and the journey continued slowly. They learned from people they spoke to when they next stopped that the French government had left Paris for Tours little more than twenty-four hours after their own departure.

'Paris has been abandoned. I'm so glad we left. I couldn't have stayed there, waiting,' Anne said.

'Yes, it's good to be on the move. I feel I'm doing something,' Georgie said.

It was hard to find food, even though they had money, because so many other people were travelling. Petrol was scarce and they had to queue for it with a tin can that fortunately Rick kept in the boot. On most nights, they were reduced to sleeping in the car.

Georgie proved herself to be a capable companion. Her supply of cosmetics, which she offered to Anne and Nicole on every occasion, was cheering. Nicole and Anne had brought few with them and Georgie's hand cream and *eau de cologne* helped them to feel less grubby and more presentable now that they were unable to wash properly. They all became accustomed to disappearing behind a tree or bush when necessary. Nicole made sure that she took Kim for a walk twice a day and begged scraps of food for him from cafés.

One evening, they heard from a barman that the Nazis were near Paris, which had been declared an open city. Two days later, they were again sitting in a café when they heard news on the wireless. The Nazis had entered Paris late on the previous day, Friday 14th June, moving along the Champs-Élysées with tanks, armoured cars and anti-tank units, as Parisians watched from cafés. Machine-gun posts had been set up and wireless stations seized. That same day, the French government had moved from Tours to Bordeaux.

Stopping at a café on another day, they heard a broadcast by Marshal Pétain, the hero of the Battle of Verdun in the Great War, now a politician. He talked about the need for hostilities to end. Neither they nor the other customers understood what he meant, yet capitulation to the Nazis seemed the most likely outcome.

Later, they heard reports of a speech made by a General de Gaulle. He had spoken on the radio to the French people from exile in London, pleading with them to continue the struggle against the invader. Nicole had never heard of him before, but it was uplifting to know that he was not giving in to the Nazis as she suspected Marshal Pétain of doing.

Their crawling pace meant it took them over a week to reach Bordeaux. Arriving at last, they found a city full of refugees. Many people had arrived ahead of them. Rick parked the car and they went in search of somewhere to spend the night.

'Where is the *pension* we stayed at before? They liked dogs,' Nicole said.

'It was near the cathedral, I think, but where?' Anne said as they stood in an unfamiliar square without a map.

'Never mind. We'll find somewhere,' Georgie said.

Yet they became disheartened as hotel after hotel was full. In the end, they found a large family room, which would sleep four, in a hotel on a small street near the railway station.

'What do you think? We don't mind sharing, especially after all those nights in the car! I'm so desperate to stretch out in a bed that I'll fall asleep straightaway,' Georgie said to the others, after a brief consultation with Rick.

'It'll be fine. I'm too tired to try anywhere else and dogs are allowed,' Anne said.

They were all exhausted and slept solidly. After a late breakfast, the four of them went to the dockside offices of the shipping company in Bordeaux. They had open tickets, but they needed to book a timed departure. The journey there by car on congested streets showed them that the city was in turmoil, crowded and hot. A café where they stopped, more for news than a drink, had run out of coffee and they drank tea instead, securing water for Kim. People were talking to strangers and the four travellers picked up a feeling of anxiety, almost of panic. There was a rumour that the Nazis had laid mines in the estuary of the River Garonne to destroy any boat leaving the docks.

'I don't like the sound of that. Should we drive on and try to get into Spain?' Anne said, shaking her head.

'No. Too hazardous. Even if the border guards let us in, we could be imprisoned under Franco,' Rick said. 'We're going to have to take our chances here.'

They reached the office of the shipping company, where it was evident that the threat of mines in the estuary was not putting off fleeing travellers. It was crowded in the ticket office and Nicole waited outside with Kim while Anne queued with Rick and Georgie for tickets for a particular boat.

'Well, that's lucky. We've all got places tomorrow afternoon. Now, take this in case we're separated for any reason,' Anne said, smiling with relief as she emerged half an hour later and handed Nicole her ticket.

The next job was to sell the car. It was late in the day before they found a garage willing to buy it. Rick fumed about the price he was forced to accept by a car salesman, who was taking full advantage of his obvious desperation.

That evening, Anne tried to telephone Jessie from the hotel to tell her when to expect them, but it was impossible to get through.

'We'll telephone her when we get to England. Isn't it marvellous to think that tomorrow we'll be away from all this nightmare, sailing to England and safety?' she said, as she put the phone down.

Her smile was strained. Nicole crushed her own misgivings about the boat not being able to leave or being blown up in the estuary and gave her mother a hug.

'Yes, roll on tomorrow!' she said.

'Let me give you some money in case we get separated. You never know.' Anne handed some cash to Nicole.

'Thank you, *Maman*. I didn't have time to go to the bank because we left in such a rush in the end,' Nicole said, slipping the money into her purse.

The following afternoon, they arrived by taxi at the docks on the River Garonne. The quayside was thronged with people. Threading their way through the crowds, they arrived at their boat to find passengers already boarding. Anne, a little ahead of Nicole, was on the gangway, her case in one hand and her ticket in the other, when an official barred Nicole's way, pointing at Kim.

'Where's his certificate?'

'Here's my ticket,' Nicole said, flourishing it.

'No dogs allowed without a health certificate,' the official said, taking Nicole's ticket and handing it back to her.

'We haven't got anything for the dog. No one in the shipping office said anything about that,' Anne said.

Rick and Georgie joined in the pleading to allow Kim on board, but the official was adamant. It was against company rules to take animals aboard without a certificate of good health signed by a qualified vet. Hadn't they read the small print? He had a closed face and no sympathy whatsoever with their plight.

'What shall we do?' Nicole said.

'We'll have to leave him behind,' Anne said.

'Can't we find someone to look after him?'

'If you can, of course, but the boat's leaving in half an hour.'

'All right. You go up and I'll come and find you.'

People behind were becoming restive and Rick, Georgie and Anne continued up the gangway. With her case in one hand and Kim's lead in the other, Nicole slipped through the crowd. All these people were passengers and there was no point in asking anything of them. In the space behind the crowd, she saw shops and offices. One was selling tickets for different boat journeys. She stepped inside with Kim to find a middle-aged woman in charge.

'Please can you give a home to my dog? They won't let me take him on board.'

The woman's face, about to smile, grew stern. '*Non!*' She almost spat out the word. 'What would my cat say, silly girl!'

Nicole wasted no time on persuasion. Next door was a shop selling fishing tackle. Two men turned towards her as she entered and repeated her request.

'I'd like to help you. He looks like a nice little dog, but I can't. My mother wouldn't stand for it,' the younger one said.

'Sorry, my dear. We don't know what's going to happen with this war and we can't take on an extra mouth to feed,' the older man said.

Disheartened, Nicole withdrew. No one wanted him. A dog, unlike a car, was of no use at such a time, even in a dog-loving country. How thoughtless she had been in not finding out the rules for taking a dog on board. She was almost in tears as she turned back towards the boat. The crowd had thinned out and the gangway was empty. She tried to persuade the official who had refused to let Kim board to change his mind. It was no good. A rule was a rule and she could see the pleasure with which he repeated it. She looked at the gangway. Could she bolt past the man and onto the boat? She started forwards, with Kim, but then the gangway began to rise.

'Stop! Wait for me!'

'Too late, you've missed it,' the official said implacably.

'No, no! I've got a ticket. My mother is on that boat. I must get on it!'

The gangway was rising steadily and sailors on deck were preparing to take it on board. Grinning, the official repeated what he had said. This time, Nicole believed him. Scanning the deck, she could make out her mother, high above her. Anne was looking at the quayside, clearly searching for her, but did not see her at first. Then, she waved. As the boat began to move, Nicole waved back.

'I'll… catch… the… next… one!'

Her voice was a scream into the wind. It might have picked up her words and carried them to Anne, but Nicole did not know for certain if her mother had heard her. She watched the boat edge its way into the middle of the Garonne, moving towards the sea. Soon, she could not distinguish anyone on board. She gazed helplessly, screwing up her eyes to see better, as the boat slowly shrank in size. She could not stop looking until it disappeared from her sight because she was remembering the rumour she had heard. Her only consolation was that there did not appear to be any mines in the river.

TWO

BORDEAUX

Nicole looked down at Kim, sitting quietly at her side. She was glad not to have abandoned him, but she had missed the boat – her one chance to escape the Nazi invasion – all for the sake of a dog. She was alone in a country becoming occupied by an enemy whom she now knew would stop at nothing. Her mother might have been halfway up the estuary, but Nicole could almost hear a reprimand and, behind it, the astonishment of her father at her stupidity.

She had never been so alone in her life. Her parents, always there, even to the point of intrusion, were both gone. In the next day or so, her family would be in England, while she remained in France, not even at home in Paris, but in Bordeaux – a city where she knew no one. Her mouth opened for a scream, but she snapped it shut and told herself to grow up. She must not panic; instead, she must seek help.

She returned to the ticket office where the sour woman had refused to take Kim. It was closed. She stood outside irresolutely, putting down her case and looking around. Now that the boat had left and with many fewer people about, the quayside seemed empty and unwelcoming. It no longer stood for the escape from France that she and her parents had planned. It was late in the afternoon and would soon be evening, putting her more at the mercy of any stray person who might take advantage of her. A snuffle from Kim reminded her that he would soon be expecting his dinner and she was completely without food.

From the empty docks, it was clear that no other boats were leaving that day, so she must stay the night in Bordeaux. The hotel of the previous night was too expensive. She and Anne had been unable to find the *pension* where they had once stayed on holiday, but she searched her memory again now. It had been in a street near the cathedral; Anne had chosen it for the sign outside welcoming dogs. Her parents had liked Bordeaux, although it gave the impression of being past its heyday – its once elegant buildings blackened and crumbling. On that holiday, Nicole remembered the family had enjoyed evening meals on a restaurant terrace, sitting until late in warm air among other holidaymakers.

She picked up her case. How fortunate that she had not left it with her mother and that she had some cash, now secure in her handbag. She would find the *pension* and spend the night there. In the morning, she would go to a vet and get a health certificate for Kim and exchange her ticket for one on the next boat. She would arrive in England only a day later than her mother, exactly as her last words, shouted from the quayside into the wind, had promised.

Nicole felt calmer with a plan. First, she had to find the cathedral. Unwilling to spend money, she ignored buses and trams and began what turned out to be a long walk. People she asked on the way assured her she was going in the right direction. After about half an hour, she recognised a tower and soon arrived in the big cathedral square. A buzz of conversation arose from surrounding cafés.

She stood by the west front of the cathedral, a grimy building, its many carvings obscured by the dirt of centuries. Normally, she would have looked at it with interest, but this was no time for architecture. Streets led from the square in different directions and she chose one at random. It narrowed quickly. Soon, she had to step over litter scattered on the pavement. Hard faces stared, making her feel uneasy. She turned around and retraced her steps, her suitcase heavier now.

She walked around the cathedral, trying again to remember the name of the *pension*. It had begun with the letter "A". L'Aquitaine came to mind, but that did not feel right. Beginning to feel dispirited, she chose another street to explore. Before long, it began to curve in a way that seemed familiar and then she saw a name – L'Argentan, with a picture of a dog. That was the name she had forgotten. At last she had found it. She pushed open the door and went in.

'Oh, I don't remember you, but I never forget a dog, *mam'selle*,' the man at the reception desk said, making a fuss of Kim. His plump, genial appearance was familiar. A dog resembling Kim came up to inspect him.

'Do you have a bed for the night? I missed the boat and I need to exchange my ticket, but the ticket office is shut...' Nicole said, breathlessly.

He put up a hand to interrupt her. 'No, I'm sorry, we're full, with all the people escaping Hitler.'

Nicole's face fell and she began to turn away. Either because of her stricken look, or the appealing eyes of Kim, the man, who was clearly in charge, relented.

'Well, there is our son's bedroom. He's in the army and we don't know where, but I doubt he's coming back tonight. It's only a small room, but there'll be space for you and the dog.'

He named a price that she could afford. Nicole, exhausted as much from the strain of the day as from her walk from the docks, accepted with relief. The man gave Kim a drink and even found him some scraps of meat from the kitchen. He handed Nicole a key and told her where to find the room. It was small, but clean and comfortable and the bed was made up.

Outside once more, Nicole bought bread, cheese and fruit for her supper and ate sitting in a tiny park nearby, thankful for the warm summer air of the southern city. It would be so much harder to be stranded on a cold evening in northern France. Kim was slumped at her feet, tired from the walk. She looked around. The trees in the park were in full leaf, but beyond them she could see handsome buildings. People cutting through the park, some of them laughing and talking, others hasty and silent, appeared to be leading ordinary lives. The war had not yet reached them, but they must have known it was on the way.

Alone in the darkness of a strange room that night, she considered spending precious francs on a telephone call or a telegram to Jessie, so that Anne would have news on her arrival in London. She would try to contact her mother in the morning, after she had exchanged her ticket and could give the news of her arrival.

She longed for Marcel. She could see his face and almost smell and touch him. Yet he was so far away from her now that she, too, had left home. Would they meet again before the war was over – a war that might last for years? Would they ever be married? She allowed Kim the rare luxury of spending the night at her feet.

The next morning, refreshed after a good night's sleep and breakfast, with Kim fed once again, she paid her bill. At least the couple running the pension were not trying to take advantage of her plight. Nicole was glad of the camaraderie that she had noticed among dog owners.

'Do you know of a vet? It's for the health certificate so I can take him on the boat,' she said to them as she came downstairs with her case.

'Yes,' the man said. 'There is one near the docks.'

He gave her the name and told her where to go. Nicole decided to secure her ticket first. That was the most urgent task. She was hoping for a boat that would leave in the early afternoon, like the one she had missed. Saying goodbye, she fastened Kim's lead and left the *pension*.

In the morning sunshine, Nicole, her case in one hand, walked back with Kim to the ticket office at the docks. She had survived a night alone in Bordeaux and her hopes rose as she walked along. She would take the afternoon boat and reach England by the evening of the next day.

Arriving at the ticket office, she was relieved to see that the woman who had been so curt with her about Kim was not there. A younger woman was on duty behind the counter. Nicole put down her case as the woman turned towards her.

'I missed the boat to England yesterday and I'd like to take today's boat,' she said, producing her ticket from her handbag.

'I'm sorry, but all the tickets are taken for today's boat,' the young woman said.

'I'll go tomorrow, then,' Nicole said.

'No. This is the last boat for England. It's because of the war.'

Nicole could hardly believe what she was hearing. 'Is there no way I can go today?'

'That would only be possible if someone gives up a ticket, but we already have quite a list of people hoping for returns.'

The young woman's tone of voice had become a shade crisper. She turned to speak to another customer as Nicole wondered whether she should wait in the hope of a seat on the last boat. It sounded unlikely that she would be successful, so she left the ticket office. She did not even think to ask for a refund, so worried was she about her predicament. Since missing the boat on the previous day, all her thoughts had centred on reaching England. In some consternation, she admitted that she did not know what to do now. The feeling of panic hovered. Her parents would be worried about her and Bordeaux might be invaded shortly. The Nazis were moving fast and might not stop until they had taken over the whole of France.

She wandered around, helping Kim at one point to drink from a horse trough. Her mind was racing. Would there be boats from anywhere else on the west coast, like La Rochelle to the north, or Biarritz to the south? Lisbon was so far away, on the other side of Spain. Santander was nearer, but even if she could get there, she was by no means sure of securing a place on a boat and she was afraid of going to Spain under Franco's fascist government. Rick had dismissed that as an unwise move when her mother had suggested it. She began to feel desperate, but, war or no war, she was not abandoning her dog on the street. She might take him to a dog's home or give him away, but she would never leave him to starve. She did not need to do anything like that now, even find the vet, because they weren't going anywhere.

She longed so much for the company of someone she knew well that she began to think an incredible thought. She would go back to Paris. Marcel might be on his way back there. He would be walking, like the defeated soldiers she had seen, back to Paris and home. He might even be there by now. In the ordinary light of a day when she felt bereft, she missed him as badly as she had done in the nights since leaving Paris. She did not believe in fate, but could she find Marcel and stay with him for the remainder of the war, with Kim having brought them together?

Returning to Paris would be dangerous, even foolhardy, now it had been invaded. Yet the Nazis could be on their way to Bordeaux. At least she had chosen French citizenship instead of giving in to her father's demands to become British and she had a French identity card. To any enquiring official, she would credit her unmistakably English surname of Seymour to a distant ancestor.

The best plan was to try and get a train to Paris. She might not have enough money, but it was worth finding out. Asking the way, Nicole walked to the railway station with Kim. It was a long walk across the city, her second that day.

She arrived to see people pouring off trains from the north, but no trains seemed to be leaving the station. Joining a queue, she waited to ask advice from the ticket office.

'There are no trains to Paris today and don't ask me when there will be,' a harassed man said, shrugging his shoulders at Nicole's question when her turn came.

She sat on a bench in the station, with people milling around her. Should she try to beg a lift from someone? She had never done anything like that before and knew that her mother would disapprove. Would it even be possible? During the drive down, almost no traffic had been going north. Everyone was escaping to the south, away from the invader. Yet, if she were to stay in Bordeaux, her money would soon be gone.

In the station, she began to feel less alone. Most people there were in a similar predicament. She overheard conversations about whether people should stay here or leave and go further south. She began to talk to a woman with three small children who came to sit next to her.

'My husband is in the north with the army, but I took the children and left Chartres because they said the Nazis were coming and my neighbours were all leaving,' the mother said in answer to a question from Nicole. She looked tired and Nicole felt sorry for her.

'It can't be easy travelling with three children,' she said, aware of having only one small dog to look after.

'No, it isn't. And I've got four children, but I've lost my eldest. He's twelve. We all got on the train, but he disappeared on the journey. I thought he'd turn up when we got to Bordeaux, but there's no sign of him.' Looking in the crowd around her, the woman appeared distraught.

'Twelve is a sensible age. Perhaps he'll find his way back to Chartres,' Nicole said.

'Oh, I hope so. I can't see how else I'll find him, so we must go back. What about you, dear? Where are you from?'

Nicole explained and the woman nodded. When she stood up with her children to enquire about a train back to Chartres, Nicole wished the family well and left the station. Outside, she looked around. She was beginning to know her way and already Bordeaux seemed less strange. She would stay here for a while. That was more appealing than trying to beg a lift back to Paris. There might be a train in a few days when all the chaos had calmed down. In the meantime, she would ask to stay on at the *pension*. At least she had some money. She trudged back with Kim and her suitcase. It was hot and the sun was high in the sky. The couple, whose name she now knew was Peyriac, were not surprised to see her.

'I thought you might be stuck today, so I told the maid to leave your bed for the moment,' Mme Peyriac said. 'You can stay on here now, but you'll have to go when our son turns up.'

'Oh, thank you, of course I will. I haven't got much money, so could I work for you instead of paying?' Nicole said.

'We're short of help because we're so full, so you could do bedrooms and clear tables in return for your keep. But don't let the dog into the dining room because some people don't like them near food.'

Nicole's relief at these words showed in her smile as she assured her new employer that she would work hard, keep Kim under control and leave immediately if their son came home. She settled back into the room that she could now think of as hers. She discovered the next morning that her chores at the *pension* only occupied her until after lunch every day and her meals were included. The *pension* dog accepted Kim and both were fed with kitchen scraps. Nicole spent her free time reading newspapers, listening to the wireless and talking to people about what was happening. She tried telephoning England from a call box nearby, but the operator could not put her through. The invasion had ended any telephone link between France and England, for the present at least. Telegrams had also ceased.

'My parents will have to live on hope,' she said to Kim as they left the call box. She talked to him now that there was no one else.

Nicole wrote a letter to her mother. Buying a stamp from a newsagent, she asked about the postal service to England, but no one knew what was happening. She felt better for posting the letter and could only hope that her effort would not be wasted.

She did her best to follow the news. An armistice had divided the country into zones. Paris was in the occupied zone, as was Bordeaux and the north and west coastal areas. Central and most of southern France remained in the hands of the French government as the unoccupied zone, with Marshal Pétain in charge.

When a new government, based in the spa town of Vichy and complying with the armistice, took over in early July, Nicole felt the sense of crisis lessen. She wanted to leave Bordeaux. The Peyriacs' son could appear any day and dispossess her of her room and her funds were diminishing.

***

As everyone expected, the Nazis reached Bordeaux. They arrived with tanks, cars and motorcycles, as well as marching men. Flags with swastikas waved in the summer breeze and bands played. Their presence provoked unease, resentment and fear among people, feelings that Nicole shared. Stones thrown by children fell unnoticed to the ground.

Nicole hated the big red flags with black swastikas, which were soon displayed everywhere. She shrank from the Nazi soldiers with their marching and the way they strolled around the city like new owners or tourists when off duty. Life had changed so suddenly and so much because of the invasion. Immediate changes included all the clocks in the occupied zone going forward an hour to German time and the introduction of a curfew between 10pm and 5am. Without knowing Bordeaux well, Nicole felt strongly that the invasion diminished the city.

Once, when she was taking Kim for a walk, a Nazi soldier appeared suddenly in front of her on a crowded main street. He was young and looked lost, but she was not going to help him find his way. She dodged around him before he could speak and walked on quickly, tugging at Kim's lead. The grey-green uniform and badges and signs of rank were more than distasteful. On one man so close to her, they aroused a stronger sense of defeat than seeing soldiers in the distance or banners hanging everywhere.

The *pension* remained full and there was plenty of work for Nicole, with no sign of the Peyriacs' son. By late June, newspaper articles showed that people who had fled were going home. Nicole had no home to go to, but she found that news reassuring. The Peyriacs were too busy to talk much, but one lunchtime in early July she revealed her British origin to a pension guest.

'The British are murderers, bombing our fleet!' the man said, loudly. Others joined in and soon the whole room was condemning the British for bombing the French fleet at Mers-el-Kébir in Morocco.

'They're as bad as the Nazis.'

'They've always been the enemy.'

'Hundreds of innocent men bombed to oblivion and the fleet destroyed.'

'But they were afraid the fleet would be used against them by the Nazis. And Churchill gave a warning of twenty-four hours,' Nicole said, having heard about the bombing.

It was no good. Her attempt at defence of the British only inflamed the hotel guests and she retreated to the kitchen in dismay, fearful that in future she would have to disguise her British origin in a way that had never been necessary before.

THREE

RETURN

Nicole felt safe at the pension, but she did not forget that she might have to leave at a moment's notice. The work was easy and she began to enjoy her new independence, even while missing her parents and wishing that they knew she was safe. Avoiding the subject of the bombing of the French fleet, she found *pension* guests to talk to or even strangers in cafés, as well as the Peyriacs. The invasion had lowered the normal barriers between strangers and people on the move were talking freely about what to do.

'How long are you thinking of staying, Nicole?' M. Peyriac asked one morning as she was clearing the breakfast tables.

'I want to go back to Paris. They might have taken over our flat, but I have friends I can stay with.'

Like everyone around her, she was falling into the habit of referring to the occupiers not by a name but simply as "they". Refusing to name them was a form of resistance. She did not think of moving to the unoccupied zone, despite the appeal of freedom. She would need a permit and, with no contacts outside Paris, she would be unlikely to obtain one. Besides, she did not want to start life completely afresh in a new place. The more she thought about it, returning to Paris was her only option. Marcel might have returned. Miriam would have stayed, even if Yvette had left. She might also be able to return to the art school. There were trains now, but she could barely afford the fare and did not want to turn up penniless in Paris.

A solution came when one of the pension guests, a man some years her senior, began talking to Nicole as she served at meals. He found out her name and that she wanted to return to Paris.

'I'm driving to Tours in a few days' time, when I've finished my work here,' he said, adding that his name was Benoit. 'I'd like some company on the journey. Do you fancy a lift?'

Nicole stalled. She was not sure she liked Benoit. His manner was too familiar. On the other hand, a lift would help as her cash was diminishing.

'Well, that's kind, but I have a small dog,' she said.

'I know. I've seen you with your dog, the lucky mutt. I might pick up other people on the road, but a pretty girl like you is assured of a seat. And there'll be room for your dog – he's not too big.'

Reassured by Benoit's acceptance of Kim and the possibility of other passengers as well, Nicole accepted the offer. Benoit named a date and the remaining days at the *pension* slipped by. On the morning that they were to leave, he appeared with a large can of petrol. How had he obtained it when petrol was already in short supply? He seemed to be one of those people who found what they wanted.

They left Bordeaux on a sunny August morning. Nicole said an affectionate goodbye to the Peyriacs and thanked them for taking her in. She put her case in the boot and went to sit in the back of the car, but Benoit motioned to her to sit in front. Kim settled at her feet.

North of the city, the road was far less crowded than it had been coming the other way and they made good progress. Nicole felt relieved when Benoit picked up an old man and a small boy. They were also returning home, to a village south of the city of Angoulême and were grateful for their lift.

After dropping off the other passengers, Benoit drove on in silence for a while. They were coming into the city and Nicole was looking out of the window at quiet streets. She was startled when Benoit took his right hand off the steering wheel and laid it on her thigh. She removed it promptly.

'Don't you want a cuddle?' he said, taking his eyes off the road to look at her.

'No, I don't.' She kept her eyes on the road.

'Don't be stiff. Just a cuddle at the hotel where I stay, to thank me for the lift.'

'Thank you for the lift and stop the car now.'

Nicole was glad that they were not on a remote road where anything unwanted could happen. Benoit began to bluster, still expecting her to pay for her lift with sexual favours. She shouted at him. This worked and he stopped the car, turning an aggrieved face towards her.

'All right, if you don't want to play, you can scarper.'

Nicole climbed out of the car with Kim and grabbed her suitcase from the boot. Only when she had her case did she slam the passenger door. The car drove off immediately and Nicole and Kim found themselves alone on a pavement in a strange city, with little traffic and few people about. She guessed that many people had fled from the invasion and had not yet returned.

She watched a passing cyclist and longed for a bicycle. She liked cycling and had once had a bicycle. It would be a good form of transport now. Kim could sit in a basket at the front and she would strap her case to a convenient rack behind the seat. It was no good. All she had now were her two feet. At least she was wearing suitable shoes and had a spare pair in her case.

She asked a passer-by for directions and went first to the station to see if any trains were running north. She discovered that there might be a train to Tours the next day. It seemed worth waiting around to find out, so she decided to spend some of her precious cash on a night in a cheap hotel. She found one by the station that would take a dog for no extra and booked a room. The Peyriacs had given her some food for herself and Kim, and she sat on a roadside bench to eat.

She was in a city where, even more than Bordeaux, she knew no one. It was then that she had the idea of writing a diary. She would use the sketchbook in her case. Back in the hotel, she took it out and spent the evening sitting on the bed in her room, writing about the journey from Bordeaux. She was oblivious to the shabbiness of the room and the sounds of plumbing, but later she slept badly in the lumpy bed. She woke in the morning bitten by fleas and keen to move on.

At the station, Nicole discovered that there was nothing for Tours that day. A fast train was going to Paris, but the purchase of a ticket would have left her with no more than a few coins. It seemed too risky when she had nowhere to stay. The only buses were local ones, so there was no choice but to walk, carrying her handbag and her case and with Kim on his lead. At least the case was only heavy when she was tired.

She bought food for herself and Kim in a small grocery shop. The choice was limited. People heading south and now those returning had been to the shop before her and fresh supplies were held up. She made do with bread, cheese and some apples for herself and persuaded the shopkeeper to open a tin of dog food for Kim. She fed him half of it, then wrapped the rest for later in a piece of waxed paper that she had with her. She took the road for Poitiers, the next large town in the direction of Paris. She would need to find food and places to sleep, but at least the weather was warm.

She had no real plan except to reach Paris. She did not know how far it was and had no map. She only knew that she was walking back the way they had driven and so would pass through the same towns. She would aim for Poitiers, Tours, Chartres and then Paris by any means, always hoping for lifts, but she would not get into a car with a man on his own again.

Nicole barely thought about what would happen when she reached Paris, except that she would knock on the doors she knew. Her world shrank to the journey she was making and to memories. She became absorbed by the details of her view as she was walking, what she would do about their next meal and where they would sleep that night.

In the countryside north of Angoulême, warm August air swept across dry harvested fields. There was little traffic on the road, but Nicole was reassured by the presence of other walkers. Families were by her side, ahead and behind her. France was going home, as people began to understand that the armistice was in place and that the Nazis, at least at present, were not seeking to annihilate them.

She did not feel entirely safe on her own and Kim was too small to protect her, but he was good company and did not complain about much more walking than he was used to. People talked to a dog owner readily and she found it easier to ask for food and water for him than for herself. When she stopped at a farmhouse on the first day, she was rewarded with a cup of milk for herself as well as a bowl of water for Kim.

That night, with the permission of a farmer, she stayed in a barn with haystacks for a bed and Kim by her side. A family of at least three generations had taken over the other end of the barn. She said hello to them, was glad of their presence, their voices and laughter in the growing dark. There were three women, a mother and her two adult daughters. The older daughter, who had no idea of the whereabouts of her soldier husband, had their three children in tow.

Nicole did not mind answering their questions about why a young girl was travelling alone, without her family. She learned that they came from Tours and had fled south to relatives to escape the invasion, but they were returning home now that things had quietened down. They were hoping for lifts on the road, but so far with no luck.

'May I walk with you tomorrow?' Nicole asked, finding them friendly.

'Of course, unless we get a lift. Perhaps we'll all squeeze into a farm truck,' the older daughter said. 'Anyway, you're mad to travel alone. There's safety in numbers, with all sorts of thieves and bad types about.'

'I know,' Nicole said, telling them about Benoit and continuing to feel relief at her escape from him.

The younger daughter, Céline, had a violin, which she played after everyone had eaten. Nicole was cheered by lively tunes. She had only heard the occasional busker on the streets of Bordeaux or music on the *pension* wireless in recent weeks and she clapped appreciatively.

Nicole fed herself and Kim that evening on her supply of food and an outside tap provided water for washing and drinking. She slept in her clothes. They awoke with the dawn and were on the road early the next morning.

Progress was slow with three young children and the uncertainty of finding food and places to stay, but Nicole was glad of the company. Among the people on the road, she found a spirit of camaraderie, as the fear of the enemy was dissolving. She noticed few men among the travellers because most of them had been conscripted. The only sign of the invasion came from occasional Nazi cars passing. People scattered out of the way to let them through.

Nicole became friendly with Céline, who was a music teacher in Tours of about her age. She had stopped giving lessons when her family had decided to flee the city, but she wanted to be back at work by the beginning of the autumn term.

'I couldn't have left it behind,' she said of her violin.

'It's just as well that you don't play the cello,' Nicole said, laughing.

The older woman had a basket on wheels with food for the journey from a family farm. She insisted on sharing the food. Nicole took as little as possible, grateful for the generosity because she needed her money for the train journey to Paris from Tours.

The reaction of local people to the travellers varied. Some were friendly and hospitable, giving them food in exchange for a few francs and allowing them to stay in outbuildings. Others turned silently away. One man complained of too many beggars on the road since the invasion.

One day, the small group stopped at a farm to ask for water, expecting to see the farmer's wife. A scraggy man answered the door. His mouth turned down at Nicole's request. She would have to pay.

Nicole was astonished. She would have refused for herself, but Kim and the children were thirsty. She offered some coins, wanting to help the family after they had shared their food. The man showed them an outside tap and everyone had a drink, also filling water bottles they had with them.

Every evening, when they had found somewhere to sleep, Nicole added to her diary, describing people and places, filling her fountain pen from a small bottle of ink she carried. She enjoyed writing and was glad of the evening daylight hours. She included sketches and filled the pages easily.

A week of walking all day brought them to Tours. Nicole's shoes were worn beyond repair by then and she left them in a rubbish bin. She began to wear her spare pair. Her feet were sore from so much walking and she had blisters.

In Tours, she said a fond goodbye to her companions on the road. They gave her directions to the station, where she discovered to her relief that a train to Chartres was leaving later that afternoon. She would have to change there for Paris, but at least she could afford the shorter journey. She bought a ticket and found a corner seat in the train. A middle-aged woman in the same compartment started talking to her straightaway.

'Hello, dear. You look as if you need to sit down. Have you come a long way?'

Nicole was feeling scruffy and could only hope that the woman did not notice that she was less than clean and sweet-smelling. She explained that she had come from Bordeaux.

'I left home in Chartres for fear of the invasion, but I'm going back now. My husband's away in the army and I've been to stay with cousins just outside Tours. I thought it would be safer south of the Loire, but now that's occupied too, there's no point in staying on.' Her travelling companion, Louise, was smartly dressed and spoke with assurance, but she smiled in a friendly way.

'I'm doing the same, trying to get back to Paris where I was living until all this happened,' Nicole said.

Prompted by questions, she talked about her journey from Paris and her stay in Bordeaux. After the slowness of walking, she was thrilled with the speed of the train. Louise had food with her and shared it willingly with Nicole and Kim. They were almost in Chartres when she suggested that Nicole might stay with her.

'There'll be trains to Paris soon, I hope. If you're stuck for somewhere to stay in Chartres, come to me. Your dog is welcome, too.'

'Thank you. I can't pay you anything...'

'Oh, be my guest.'

Nicole accepted with relief. When they arrived in Chartres, with no trains on to Paris that day, Louise shepherded them to her house in the centre of the city. With so many people on the move, she had been worried about squatters and was relieved to find the house untouched.

Nicole understood that Louise had been lonely in a large house on her own, with her husband away and her two adult children now living elsewhere. She did her best to be good company in return for her bed and board, and took the chance to explore Chartres Cathedral. She wanted to tell someone that she was on her way back to Paris, but she dared not spend money on paper and stamps or telephone calls, and was reluctant to ask her generous host for extra favours.

Going to the station every day to find out about trains, she was rewarded for her persistence one morning a few days after her arrival by the news that a train would be leaving the next day. She bought a ticket with almost the last of her money, relieved to be on the move without having to find a lift or walk to Paris.

She said a grateful goodbye to Louise and promised to write. The journey from Chartres was easy and she arrived with Kim at Montparnasse Station in Paris early on a gloomy evening in August. From there, she took the metro to Iéna. She could not go home, but friends nearby might take her in.

Nicole found it disquieting that the metro station lacked its usual early evening bustle. Outside, she noticed street signs in German, enormous Nazi flags hanging from buildings and soldiers in uniform. The presence of the occupier in Paris, the city of her childhood, was even more of an imposition than it had been in Bordeaux.

As they left the Place d'Iéna, Kim turned in the direction of home, but Nicole pulled him towards Marcel's flat at one end of a nearby street. Hope flared as she reached his building and rang the bell.

No one came. She rang again and was about to walk away when it occurred to her to try the concierge. She might know something. She rang the bell and an old woman opened the door, surveying Nicole suspiciously.

'Do you know where the Duponts are? They're not answering,' Nicole said. She was tired by now and more worried. On the last leg of her convoluted journey from Bordeaux, even though uncertain about it, she had buoyed herself up with the thought of seeing Marcel soon. Yet he was clearly not there.

'No idea. Mme Dupont went to stay with relatives somewhere,' the old woman said. 'I haven't anywhere to go or I'd have gone, too, even though I'm supposed to look after the flats.'

Nicole was disheartened but not surprised and it was obvious what to do next. Yvette's flat was slightly nearer than Miriam's and so she tried there. No one was in and no one, not even the concierge, answered the door when she rang other bells. Yvette might have been out, rather than away in Rennes as planned, but Nicole did not want to wait around until late at night to find out. Only Miriam remained.

With heavy steps, she turned towards Miriam's flat at the other end of the street. Miriam was her last and best hope. She had said that her family would stay in Paris because they had no relatives elsewhere in France. What she would do if Miriam and her family had left Paris, she had no idea. She was relying on them to be at home.

PART THREE

PART THREE

ONE

REFUGE

Nicole and Miriam had walked to school together every day for years. Miriam would always appear as soon as Nicole rang the bell of her flat. The Weiss family – consisting of two parents, Miriam and her younger brother, Louis – lived on the first floor of a block of flats not far from Nicole's Steps.

On meeting every school day, the two girls would walk together to where Yvette lived with her parents. Miriam grew to be half a head taller than Nicole, as their morning shadows on the pavement revealed in their later years at school. At Yvette's block, variations of the same scene always took place. Miriam or Nicole pressed the bell. Silence followed. Yvette, a placid girl, was slower to move than the other two, and always had to be dug out in the morning. They pressed the bell a second time and Miriam gave a mock grimace as she turned towards Nicole, calling out, 'Late again!' in her clear voice.

The two girls would then look through the window of the inner door of the block to see Yvette slowly descending the stairs, still talking to her mother, who could not be seen.

'Come on, slowcoach!' Miriam said as Yvette emerged. 'You'll make us late and then we'll all be in detention after school.'

Another morning, Miriam had said, 'Why can't you be ready to spring out of the door in the morning, like a young gazelle in the forest?' She gave a little jump in the air as the three girls laughed.

The daily journey took them to school on quiet streets, avoiding the heavy traffic of the grand avenues that flowed down from the Arc de Triomphe. The walk had begun in their first year at the school, at the age of twelve, after Miriam worked out where they all lived and decided it would be more fun to have company on the walk to and from school than to go alone.

On the way home, the three girls would stop at Yvette's flat, teasing and laughing as they said goodbye, and then Nicole and Miriam would continue. This routine had given them time alone together twice a day and they had become particularly close. Miriam had been the leader and Nicole had felt strengthened by the company of her bolder friend.

After saying goodbye to Miriam every school-day afternoon, Nicole would reach the top of her steps and run down, going faster and faster, or slide down the railing on one side, enjoying more gymnastics than her mother would have thought acceptable. She then crossed the road to her block, behind which rose the tall, slender shape of the Eiffel Tower. She liked to imagine that it was waiting to welcome her home.

***

Reaching Miriam's flat, Nicole rang the bell and waited, with Kim flopped at her feet. She did not have to wait long. When the door opened to her friend's surprised face, she felt relieved and joyous. She could not have stood a third closed door.

'Nicole? But I thought you'd gone to England!'

'Miriam! Oh, what a relief that you're here.'

'Come in. You look as if you're about to collapse.'

Miriam gave Nicole a hug, took her case and led her indoors. Nicole sank into a chair in the sitting room and Miriam and her family surrounded her, bringing her a cold drink and a bowl of water for Kim, who refused to leave her side even for the possibilities of a kitchen. They listened to her story.

'There's no one at Marcel's flat. Then I rang Yvette's bell, but there was no answer,' Nicole said as she finished a quick summary.

'You must stay with us,' Miriam's mother, Sonia, said. She was a pale, elegant woman in her late forties, who lacked Miriam's sparkle, but Nicole knew her to be kind.

'Thank you. I should love to, but there's Kim as well.'

'Oh, he'll be no problem,' Sonia said.

Nicole was grateful. Miriam took her to a spare bedroom where they made up a bed and Nicole unpacked her case, hanging her few, creased clothes in the wardrobe.

'You can't imagine how delighted I am to find you in,' she said, feeling a rush of fondness for her friend.

'I'm just as pleased to see you! Now, you're tired and need a good meal. It'll be ready soon.'

'Will there be enough for me as well? I've crashed in on you, but I didn't know what else to do.'

'Don't worry. Food is scarcer now, but *Maman* is a genius at stretching meals. Now, do you need anything else?' Miriam said as she was leaving the room.

'Yes. Could I ring my parents? I tried before, but couldn't get through and I wrote. I'd love to speak to my mother.'

'Oh, yes, you must. The phone is in the hall. Go ahead.'

Nicole found Jessie's phone number and spoke to an operator who told her that telephone contact with Britain, cut at the start of the occupation, had not been resumed. She put the phone down, disappointed but not surprised.

Nicole knew from her many visits in the past that Miriam's parents were generous and hospitable. Sonia had welcomed a surprise guest and was only concerned that Nicole should eat well enough to make up for the privations of her journey. Nor did Miriam's parents question her plans in the way that her father would have done. She was grateful for that. She was not sure that she yet had any plans and was still living with her journey.

'What's it like in Paris now?' Nicole asked as they began eating.

Miriam's father, Daniel, was a doctor at the Pitié-Salpêtrière Hospital near the Gare d'Austerlitz. He was an affable man with a courteous manner. 'Well, to start with, it all happened too easily. Barely a shot was fired and then they took over, just as if they know Paris as well as we do,' he said.

'Hitler even came one day and drove around the city, trying to be the conquering hero,' Miriam said with a grimace, but then she laughed. 'But he was so early that no one saw him. And he couldn't go up the Eiffel Tower. Someone had cut the cables!'

'It felt strange and unsafe here at first when the government had gone, leaving the police in charge, but the occupation was peaceful. We didn't even know that Paris had been declared an open city until the day before they came. And they've taken over the hospital where I work for their wounded,' Daniel said. 'I get the impression they had prepared for this in meticulous detail. But day to day, it's not so bad, not yet anyway. They're reasonably polite on the street.'

'It was like that in Bordeaux after they occupied the city,' Nicole said. 'It was awful seeing them arrive, but I kept out of their way.'

'They like military music. They have bands playing for marching soldiers,' Louis said.

'There'll be more food rationing, I'm sure, because they're sending so much French food off to Germany that there are shortages already, like cheese and garlic,' Sonia said.

'I can do without cheese, but I must have garlic!' Miriam was laughing again, but quickly became more serious. 'Papa is right that it's not so bad, but it's different from before. It's so dark and so quiet. There's the blackout and electricity cuts and so little traffic on the streets, due to the petrol shortage. It's hard to forget what's happened, especially around here, where so many of them are living because of the nice flats,' she said. 'It makes me feel I'm less of a person than I was. It's a sort of constraint. We've lost some of our freedom and we don't know what's going to happen.'

'I agree,' Nicole said. 'On the road, I've met people of all kinds, but I haven't felt free. I enjoyed it in some ways, but I've been worried all the time about where to sleep at night and about getting enough to eat and I haven't always felt safe.'

She learned during the meal of the anxiety that the Weiss family felt about the occupation. In Paris, there had been no physical violence against Jews, but the Nazis had already stripped plenty of Jewish homes of their contents. The Weiss family were leading a reasonable life, but they clearly feared for their future. Nicole asked if they had thought of leaving France like her parents.

'It's different for us,' Daniel said. He and Sonia both spoke French with a Polish accent, unlike Miriam and Louis who had been born in Paris. 'We've lost nearly all our ties to Poland now that our parents are dead. I was an only child and Sonia has a sister in America. Our home, our work, all our lives have been here since we left Poland and we couldn't go back there now it's under Nazi control. And we trust France. Don't forget the French Revolution brought about great changes, including full citizenship for Jews. As French citizens, we should be all right.'

'We thought about going to England, but it would have been difficult starting all over again in a new country. Miriam has been helping with Jewish refugees, collecting food for them from restaurants and finding bedding. They see France as a place of safety,' Sonia said.

'I belong to Solidarity, which was set up to defend Jewish people in Paris. We're active in our defence. We're not victims,' Miriam said.

Nicole nodded. She would not have expected anything less from her friend. She enjoyed the meal, but she refused second helpings, knowing food to be scarce now. The warm welcome from the family relaxed her. Later that evening, she showed Miriam the diary she had kept on her journey home.

'I haven't written up the journey from Paris to Bordeaux, but it was extraordinary. Everyone was leaving, not just in cars, but on bicycles and carts or walking. Carrying babies and pushing grannies on handcarts. And taking so much with them, not only ordinary luggage, but cooking pots and mattresses. I've never seen anything like it! And it was terrifying when they shot at us.'

'How dreadful. You should write it up, Nicole, but let me read this anyway,' Miriam said. She took the diary to bed with her that night.

Nicole slept well, with Kim once again at her feet. She awoke feeling refreshed and even hopeful. She had a quick breakfast with Miriam, who returned her diary.

'I read it all last night. It's good, Nicole. Meet me for lunch and we'll talk about it more. My treat and there's a place near my office on the Boulevard St Michel,' Miriam said, scribbling down an address and handing it to Nicole as she left for work.

Miriam had finished a degree in French literature at the Sorbonne in June and was now training as a journalist on *La Presse Parisienne*, the newspaper that Nicole remembered had employed Marcel's friend, Paul. Daniel had already left for the hospital. Louis, a student at the Sorbonne, too young to be a soldier in 1939, had already left for classes.

Nicole spent the rest of the morning talking to Sonia, whom she had known as Miriam's mother for many years.

Sonia invited her to live with their family for as long as she wished and Nicole accepted gratefully. Life under the occupation would be much better living with friends than alone.

Sonia offered to look after Kim while Nicole was meeting Miriam for lunch, but he whimpered as she tried to leave without him, so she took him with her. They crossed the Seine to the metro station at Pont de L'Alma. On the way, Nicole noticed empty streets and cafés. Many shops were boarded up and there was little traffic. The middle of a working day lacked the normal bustle of the big city and seemed more like an early Sunday morning. It was her home and yet seemed so different. Most people had left the city, although some, like her, were returning. She loved to hear the cheeping of sparrows and she was quick to notice a lack of birdsong. Feeling apprehensive, she averted her eyes from armed Nazi soldiers.

Dogs were running around the streets alone, clearly abandoned by owners fleeing Paris. A big dog came up to inspect Kim and she drew him away. She had never wished to abandon him. He would have been hungry and frightened and might not have survived as a stray in all the tumult of a city fearing invasion and besieged by refugees. She would not have been able to forget leaving him on the streets of Paris or the quayside in Bordeaux.

Despite the occupation, her mood was lighter. She was feeling rested and much safer now that Miriam's family had taken her in. Leaving the metro at Luxembourg, she turned north up the Boulevard St Michel. She passed a newspaper kiosk and stopped to look at the headlines. There was one paper she had never seen before. It was called *Pariser*

Zeitung and it was in German. They were not wasting time in taking over the life of her city.

'They're here, trampling all over the city and what are we doing to stop them?' the newsagent was saying to a customer.

'Nothing,' the customer said in disgust, stamping on a cigarette end. 'Nor are the wretched British.'

Sensitive as she was to comments about the British, Nicole did not linger to hear more. She pressed on to the café and found Miriam already there. Her friend waved as Nicole came in, motioning her towards the small table she had chosen. Kim settled at Nicole's feet.

'So many places have closed, but this stayed open. Now, they make great omelettes and it's my treat because I dragged you here,' Miriam said.

'You're spoiling me,' Nicole said with a smile.

Miriam lowered her voice. 'Before I forget, be careful what you say. You don't know who might be listening. They are everywhere and plenty of people are ready to inform on anyone.'

'I know – it was the same in Bordeaux,' Nicole said, quietly.

Miriam offered Nicole a cigarette after they had ordered and Nicole, once the cigarettes were lit, looked around her. Like the streets, the café was almost empty, with only one or two other customers.

'Yes, it's different,' Miriam said, noticing her friend's glance and resuming her normal voice. 'Everyone's gone, including some of our staff. We're struggling to get the paper together, so I must be quick. It won't be a proper lunchtime!'

'Never mind. Twenty-four hours ago, I didn't even know that I would find anyone in Paris. I'm so lucky you and your family are here, but Paris is strange,' Nicole said.

'It's not our Paris anymore,' Miriam said and they talked about how different it felt, until Miriam asked Nicole if she knew what she was going to do now that she was here.

'I need a job, but I must find Marcel. He was with the army in the north, but he should have returned to Paris by now. His mother was going to relatives in the south somewhere and maybe he's tried to join her,' Nicole said.

'What can you do, then?'

'Wait in Paris and see if he turns up or try to remember where Mme Dupont was going. I think it was Toulouse.'

Miriam laughed. 'Don't go chasing off when you don't know where Marcel is. Let him come to you.'

Nicole shook her head. 'He won't do that. He thinks I'm in England.'

'You're in love, that's the trouble. I wouldn't run across the country after a man!'

They laughed and Miriam added, 'I do want to move away from home, but now isn't the right time.'

Their food arrived and they began to eat. 'Marcel may still be on his way back to Paris, but I wish I could do something to find him. I feel so useless,' Nicole said.

'He would be back by now. It's weeks since France was defeated,' Miriam said.

'He might have been taken prisoner.'

'I hope not, but it's possible. I'm so glad you've turned up. I was beginning to think I had no friends left with Paris being so empty. There's David, of course...'

'Who's David?' Nicole was smiling at the thought of a

boyfriend. Miriam had high standards in that direction.

'I've been seeing him. He works for *La Presse Parisienne* as well. My parents like him more than I do, though.'

'Well, I look forward to meeting him, if you don't give him up first!'

'Oh, I expect you'll meet him,' Miriam said and then lowered her voice. 'As for a job, I can't offer you any money, but we need help with an underground paper. You're a good writer, Nicole. Your diary is so vivid.'

Miriam went on to explain that because their employer could not be critical of the Vichy government, she and David had formed a group with other like-minded people and started a newspaper as a form of resistance. They were looking for news and articles.

'Your experience on the roads is just what we want, but what we're doing is against the law and we could be arrested and possibly imprisoned if we were discovered. I've told my parents, but we don't talk about it,' Miriam said.

'So I won't be paid and might end up in prison! You make it sound so attractive!' Nicole said. 'And my diary isn't about resistance. It's just a journey.'

'I know, but it's about the impact of the occupation on your life. People want to read about that sort of thing, I promise you.'

'The occupation has certainly made a difference to me,' Nicole said. 'It's turned my life upside down in the past few weeks. I'll never forget being shot at and I'd like to do something to help get rid of them. But I need to find a job as soon as possible. I hated it when Papa wanted me to do secretarial training, but it'll be useful now.'

'No rush. I can lend you money, so settle in first,' Miriam said. 'If you decide to let us have your diary, I'll introduce you to David. You could come and see our office!'

'All right. Now, tell me, where are all the sparrows? I didn't hear any on my way to see you today. It's strange without them.'

'They disappeared when oil and gas tanks were set on fire during the invasion. Soot fell on all the trees and must have choked them. I hope they come back.'

Miriam had to go back to work and Nicole, seeing military vehicles advancing down the street, decided not to wander around Paris alone. She took Kim back to the flat, thinking on the way that she wanted to help Miriam, despite the dangers, but that she must find a job first.

TWO

PAUL

They had arrived in the dark on the previous evening, with no chance to look around them. In the grey light of the morning, Paul could see that the prison camp had been hastily thrown together. The buildings were makeshift huts and there was no perimeter wall, only a wooden fence festooned with barbed wire and guarded by men with large dogs. He was hungry after a meagre breakfast and was determined not to sit out the rest of the war as a prisoner. Looking around, he thought that escape might be possible, but it would need careful planning.

Pouring into France from Belgium in May 1940, the Nazi army and air force had overwhelmed French troops. The Nazis had surged through the gap between the northern end of the Maginot Line and the French and British forces along the coast. They had swept through Ardennes Forest, crossing the River Meuse at Sedan. Many

French soldiers had been killed trying and failing to hold the Nazis back.

Paul had been a soldier in the French 9th army, positioned south of the River Meuse and just north of the city of Laon, as part of the Allied forces. His infantry regiment had met a Nazi Panzer division, but had been too weak to contain a mainly motorised force. His regiment had fought strenuously against the Nazi invasion, but to no avail. The Battle of France had been over in a few weeks and, by the end of May, the Allies had drawn back to Dunkirk.

Paul had been surrounded by enemy soldiers when he and a small group quickly became detached from the main body of their regiment in the face of the Nazi onslaught. They had been taken prisoner, herded into trucks with dozens of other men and locked up for some hours, without food or water. They had been released from the trucks only to spend weeks in a barbed-wire compound with little to eat or drink. No chance had arisen to escape before he and fellow soldiers had been driven in a convoy to a prison camp in eastern Germany.

During the early days in the German camp, excited talk arose among the prisoners about a mass breakout, but Paul was sceptical. Even if they could breach the perimeter fence, they would be shot before they could get far. He had no alternative suggestion, but he was on the lookout for possibilities, talking to the other prisoners, thinking something might come up.

One morning, two of the French prisoners approached him. Stéphane was a seasoned professional soldier some years older than Paul. Philippe, shorter than Stéphane, but more muscular, his upper lip hidden beneath a luxuriant moustache, was also a professional soldier.

'We'd like you to team up with us,' Stéphane said.

'Good idea. Just the three of us, then?' Paul said.

'Yes. Keep quiet about it. Don't tell anyone else,' Stéphane said.

Paul did not need to wonder why they had chosen him. Having studied German at school and at the Sorbonne, he spoke it well. He was picking up new words at the camp, taking every chance to chat to guards and beginning to be used as an interpreter. This wasn't just for something to do. Speaking German was the key to escape. Stéphane knew some German, but Philippe only spoke French.

'I'll make up for not speaking German once we get out of here,' Philippe said. 'Brute strength will do it.'

He flexed his arms and the moustache quivered as they all laughed. He liked showing off his physical strength. He had grown up on a farm in Normandy and was used to hard manual work. He claimed to resemble the oxen who did the ploughing on his farm. Paul liked Philippe and found his strength reassuring.

Together, they would make a good team. Paul would speak German, Philippe would provide physical strength and good company, and they would need Stéphane's experience and cool head.

'The nearest foreign country not under Nazi control is the Soviet Union. We'll escape from the camp and travel by train to seek asylum there. We'll pass ourselves off as German civilians on the journey,' Stéphane said.

Philippe was grinning. 'I'll shave off my moustache and pass for a *boche*.'

The plan was audacious, but Paul was prepared to try it. 'How will we get out of here, though?' he said.

'Something will occur to us,' Stéphane said, with heartening confidence. 'We'll need money and civilian clothes first.'

'Money! I'm broke. They took it all off me.' Philippe turned out an empty trouser pocket to prove his point and they laughed again. Everything had been taken from them except their French army uniforms.

'We'll get what we need. Keep your eyes open,' Stéphane said. 'I overheard something about putting us to work. We might be able to take advantage of it.'

The work turned out to be building permanent structures at the camp. The men were put to digging foundations and bricklaying. The hard labour took its toll of their uniforms, which began to look torn and ragged. The camp authorities, not wishing anything to stand in the way of the construction work, supplied extra clothes in a variety of shapes and sizes. Stéphane, Philippe and Paul secreted enough civilian clothes under their mattresses for each of them to have an outfit suitable for wearing outside the camp. Paul felt excited about the prospect of freedom, even though he knew it required considerable luck, as well as resources.

The next question was money. There was no surplus food to try and sell, but the camp gave out cigarettes, under the control of a guard who kept his supply under lock and key. The three prisoners saved their cigarette allowance and even increased it by swapping food for cigarettes with non-smokers. They sold the cigarettes cheaply to civilian camp cooks and cleaners. Philippe was not a smoker, saying he did not want to set his moustache on fire, so he sold all his cigarette allowance. Paul and Stéphane both gave up smoking for the escape.

'It's murder, not smoking, when it's the only pleasure in this place,' Paul said one day as they stopped work and he watched others lighting up. He had not smoked much in Paris, but it had become a consolation in the army and in prison. He felt in his pocket and drew out a cigarette.

'Put it away. The quicker we save, the sooner we'll be out of here,' Stéphane said, seeing him waver.

Returning the cigarette to his pocket, Paul sighed. Stéphane was right. The escape came first. Deprivation was the order of the day now. It was not simply lack of cigarettes or good food or freedom. One or two episodes with women since he had joined the army now seemed a long time ago. It was awful to be banged up in a foreign prison without a woman in sight, except cooks and cleaners who were out of reach.

The three men used every chance to add to their stash of clothes and money for their escape, squirrelling away their gains in different places so that, when they were searched, nothing much was found.

'It's taking too long. We need another way of getting money,' Stéphane said one day.

'This place is lax, so there must be something else we can do,' Philippe said.

The three men watched what was going on around them, always with an eye to taking advantage of their captors. Paul set up a small business selling the clothes supplied for the prisoners to one of the camp staff he was cultivating and who turned out to have a market stall in the nearest town. It made more money than selling cigarettes and was easy to do as the clothes supply was loosely guarded.

They also adopted Nazi-style short haircuts and Philippe did as he had promised and shaved off his moustache to resemble a German civilian. He did this some weeks before they would try to escape in order not to arouse suspicion. Once they calculated that they had enough money for train fares to the Russian border, they were alert to the chance of escaping at any time. In an apparently casual conversation with the member of the camp staff who bought clothes from him, Paul found out how to reach the nearest railway station.

Meanwhile, the other prisoners continued to discuss possibilities for escape. Using some of the shovels, spades and pickaxes they had been given for the building work, they began to excavate under the perimeter fence of the camp, from the hut nearest to it. They worked at night, hiding the entrance under a pile of wooden planks and disposing of the soil here and there. The tunnel was going to allow all of them to escape and hopes for it were high. Paul, Stéphane and Philippe joined in with the work, not wishing anyone to guess they had other plans.

When a guard noticed the pile of planks and some loose soil, he discovered the entrance to the tunnel. The prisoners were at work at the time, but they soon found out what had happened. All the occupants of the hut were summoned to appear before the camp *führer*. Few of them understood his icy lecture, but the outcome was clear enough. They were deprived of food for twenty-four hours and made to fill in the tunnel. The pile of wooden planks was removed.

Undeterred, the prisoners began work on another tunnel in a different hut, locating the entrance under one of their beds. Waiting for the war to end was not enough. A plan for escape was essential, something to hope for, when the war might not end for years. Stéphane, Philippe and Paul helped to dig the new tunnel.

On a cold winter's day in February 1941, when the three men had been imprisoned for nine months and they were building permanent accommodation for the camp staff, one of the guards told them that they were to join the walk outside the camp that afternoon. This walk, escorted by Nazi sentries, had happened about once a week since their arrival. It had become less essential as a form of exercise after the prisoners had started work, but it continued as part of the regime. The prisoners were glad to escape their work for a couple of hours and have a change of scenery, however cold the day or how dull the landscape was outside the prison.

'We go today,' Stéphane said quietly to Paul and Philippe. 'We've got clothes and enough money. Put on as much as you can under overcoats and we'll place ourselves in the centre of the line, as far from the sentries as possible. When they're not looking, we'll throw off the coats and walk back along the line, past the sentries at the end. They'll just think we're civilians. The other prisoners will see us go, but they won't give us away. The road is well-used and no one will look at us twice. Stick with me and I'll give you the signal.'

Philippe agreed readily. Paul's initial reaction was to wait for warmer weather, as spring was not far off now, but fear of the other men's derision and the tantalising prospect of freedom silenced him and he nodded.

All three dressed up as best they could, putting on layers to combat the cold once their coats were discarded and filling their pockets with their savings. They had acquired thick jumpers as part of their prison outfits and their French army boots were still sturdy and waterproof.

Outside the camp, they walked in a column with sentries at the head and tail. The three were in the middle of the column, having placed themselves as far from the sentries as possible, so that they would be less likely to be seen dropping out of line. Full of anticipation, Paul and Philippe watched Stéphane closely. He was placed between them. After about twenty minutes, they heard his low voice.

'Let's go.'

In seconds, the three men had slipped off their coats, leaving them by the roadside. Side by side, they walked back, chatting with assumed nonchalance, alongside the column of prisoners, none of whom gave any indication of seeing an escape. Passing the sentries at the end of the column, Stéphane raised his right arm and said, "*Heil Hitler*," echoed only seconds later by Paul and Philippe. Paul was afraid that they would be seized on the spot, but, as Stéphane had promised, the sentries took them for German civilians.

The three men walked on, scarcely daring to believe their good fortune, but aware that plenty of risks awaited them. After two miles, they came to a small railway station, where Paul bought three single tickets for the nearest large town. Nazi officers and sentries from the camp, apparently on leave, boarded the same train.

'Keep your head down,' Stéphane said quietly, as they found seats together.

The three men were on tenterhooks, but they were not recognised, even though Paul, at least, was known to the Nazis in the camp as the interpreter. The soldiers were too busy laughing and joking among themselves to look around them. In civilian clothes, with their short hair, the three escapees once again passed for German.

With the aid of maps and timetables available at the larger station where they disembarked, they worked out a route to the Russian frontier. They changed trains several times, travelling via Danzig and Königsberg. Their confidence grew as the days passed and no one suspected them of being escaped prisoners. In between train journeys, they spent their time in station waiting rooms and cafés, among other travellers, eking out their dwindling funds with occasional cups of coffee and surviving on as little food and sleep as possible. Paul was good at acquiring plates of half-eaten food before any waiter noticed that the customer who had begun a hearty German meal had left something behind.

So that no one should try to talk to Philippe, he either pretended to be asleep most of the time or to be reading a German newspaper he had picked up in the first café and carried with him. Stéphane and Paul were always there to cover for him. The three men laughed quietly about notices saying, 'Don't talk. There are enemies in our midst'.

It took three days and three nights of train travel, waiting around for trains and snatching sleep where they could, before they reached the frontier. They walked from the last station before the border and eventually came to wire fencing and signs that told them they had reached the Soviet Union.

When he attempted to wriggle underneath the fence, with Paul and Philippe watching and waiting their turn, Stéphane set off an alarm. He swore. Flares appeared overhead and they heard the frantic barking of dogs. Stéphane hurriedly disentangled himself and they ran back towards the town and what they desperately hoped would be safety. They quickly became lost among the townspeople and hid until the following evening, cold and hungry, with almost no money, but more determined than ever to escape.

At twilight, they emerged from the town and walked to the border again. With extreme care, they slid under the fence without touching any wires. Standing up on the other side of the German border, they found themselves in a kind of no man's land. Silence stretched around them, but there were lights at intervals. Fearful of being spotted and shot down, they sought darkness immediately, becoming invisible to border guards.

They had no idea how wide the no man's land would prove to be, nor what would greet them on the other side. In the teeth of a biting February wind, they set off into the snow, thankful for the army boots that had seen them through their escape so far but missing the greatcoats they had discarded as they escaped.

The snow was deep and Paul, not as strong as the others, was soon struggling behind Stéphane and Philippe. He longed for the journey to end as he placed each foot mechanically before the other, feeling as if he were trudging to the North Pole. He was worried that if he stumbled and fell, he would not get up again and would be buried in snow until the spring thaw revealed his frozen body.

He would not allow himself to call out. In the dark, he could barely see the others ahead of him as the distance widened between them. He had never felt so cold. He was beginning to shiver and despair of his strength when Philippe turned round and came back towards him. Without a word, Philippe threw an arm around him and half carried him onwards, lending Paul some of the strength that he had promised months ago to contribute to the team effort.

They trudged for an hour across deep snow, in temperatures that they later learned were about twenty degrees below zero. Paul was frozen and weak, but grateful that it was not snowing. At last, they saw ahead of them the lights and fencing of the Russian border post. The sight gave him the extra strength needed to reach it.

They stood now in the brightest patch of light that they could find, with their arms out to show they had no weapons. They called out *'Nous sommes trois français!'* at the tops of their voices into the silence.

There was no response at first, but after some minutes of shouting and gesticulating, they could see guards descending from their post. To their great relief, no shots were being fired. The three French soldiers were now safe. They hugged and kissed each other with delight as the guards approached them. Realising that they were not dealing with an invasion, but only a simple plea for rescue, the guards took the starving and exhausted men into custody.

THREE

OCCUPATION

Living with a Jewish family held no surprises for Nicole, who had visited Miriam on many occasions during her schooldays. The family belonged to a liberal Jewish tradition and did not observe a kosher diet. Sonia's cooking included traditional Jewish recipes, but shortages meant that people were eating food they might not have liked before. Daniel and Sonia sometimes used Yiddish words in conversation, just as Nicole's family used French words when speaking English. Nicole, who had accompanied her parents to church on Sundays throughout her childhood, had been confirmed as a Protestant at the age of fifteen, but no longer regularly went to church.

Some paintings on the walls of the flat, depicting scenes of Polish life in cities and countryside, indicated Daniel and Sonia's background. Nicole, as a lover of art, also noticed several works by French painters. Miriam explained that her parents had put their savings into paintings, which gave them far more pleasure than putting money into a bank.

One urgent problem remained. Nicole could not expect the family to feed Kim. She thought of Thibaud, her family's butcher for years. He had seen her grow up and had often given her scraps for Kim when she went to collect meat that her mother had ordered. She took Kim with her to the butcher's shop on the Place d'Iéna the day after her arrival in Paris. There was much less meat on display than she remembered, but the butcher, a muscular man who ran the business with a son and daughter, greeted her in a friendly manner.

'Ah, Nicole! Another customer returned. Business has been bad since they came, with half of Paris leaving home.'

'I've come to beg a favour for my dog, Monsieur Thibaud,' Nicole said. 'You were always kind to him before. Could you let me have something for him every week?'

'He can have what we're throwing out. Take something now.'

Nicole tried not to quail at the sight of lungs and intestines as she watched Monsieur Thibaud wrapping up a parcel for her. He secured it with string and handed it to her with a smile. She thanked him and bundled it into her shopping bag. The contents of the parcel did not look so awful once she had chopped up enough for a meal, which Kim ate eagerly. She put the rest into a bowl, which she placed in the larder. Sonia also shopped at Thibaud's and offered to help with picking up Kim's parcel every week.

Nicole needed a job before her money ran out. She took Kim along to the art school on the Rue du Dragon and sought out Sandrine, the secretary, whom she knew from her time as a student. Sandrine, a blonde woman, always stylishly dressed, took no nonsense from anyone despite a delicate appearance. She had been in her post for a long time and knew everyone there so well that people said the art school revolved around her.

'We lost a typist because of the invasion and haven't been able to replace her yet. I don't think she'll be coming back now, but you'll have to be fast enough,' Sandrine said when Nicole requested a typing job.

She tested Nicole's typing skills there and then and pronounced her suitable, even though it was months since Nicole had touched a typewriter. She would be working full-time, including Saturday mornings. Securing the job meant that she would be able to give Sonia money for rent and food, and put something aside each week for her return to the art school as a student. She wanted to have a plan and not merely survive the occupation.

Miriam had a bicycle, which stood in the entrance to the flat. She had registered it with the authorities as required under the occupation. She encouraged Nicole to share it with her, as metro stations could be closed unpredictably now. When Sonia offered to help with looking after Kim, Nicole was able to ride the bicycle to work sometimes.

The work itself posed no difficulties, but Nicole quickly became aware of an art teacher who made her feel uncomfortable. He was a middle-aged man called Serge who taught art history and made a point of asking her to type what appeared to be an inexhaustible supply of lecture notes in difficult handwriting. Nicole could cope with that, but it was not long before he began to comment on her appearance and her manner. She shrugged him off and did her best to minimise contact with him.

Sandrine noticed his attentions. 'He's a nuisance. It's your age. You'll be all right when you're older and men take less notice of you.'

Nicole took little comfort from that. There was nothing for it but to keep her distance from the odious man.

She was glad of her French citizenship. Being British under the occupation did not lead to the internment she had feared, but it would have meant registering daily at a local police station. That would have made her feel like a foreigner or, at any rate, less than a citizen of the country in which she had grown up. As Jews, Miriam and her family took their daily registration in their stride, but it was demeaning.

***

Nicole slipped out of the Weiss's flat with Kim, down the single flight of stairs to the ground floor and stood on the street, wondering where to take him for a walk. On this warm Saturday afternoon in September, she had finished her first week's work. She did not intend to go to her family flat, not wanting to know that it was occupied by Nazis, but Kim was in no doubt about the way home. He set off and Nicole found herself walking along the Avenue du Président Wilson towards where she used to live.

As they descended Nicole's Steps, she was facing the Eiffel Tower. Coming close to it for the first time since her return to Paris, she was disgusted to see a swastika banner hanging there.

She neared her old home. She had not seen her parents for many weeks. Irritation she had felt at her mother's supervision, or at some of her father's views, had disappeared as if it had never existed. She wanted to see them, but there was no telling how long the occupation would last. It would certainly not be over at any time soon. The Nazis were digging themselves into Paris as if they owned it and the occupation could continue for years. War could be a long, slow business, as people said the last one had shown.

She stopped as she reached the lower steps and looked across the street, with a feeling of shock. Her family flat, on the first floor, was occupied. A tall blond man was standing in the frame of the open living room window where she often used to stand. He was smoking a pipe and appeared to be talking to someone in the room behind him. Nicole heard a great bellow of laughter and a stream of what sounded like German. Like many people she knew, Nicole smoked occasionally, but never in the flat because her mother disliked the smell. How dare they not only occupy her home, but also be smoking there. When her parents returned, her mother's nose would wrinkle in disgust as soon as she walked in.

She dared not stand there any longer for fear of attracting attention, so she descended to the street below and crossed to the main door of the building. Kim aimed for the stairs, but Nicole pulled him away and instead knocked at the door of the concierge.

M. Lebrun answered, his grim expression changing to one of surprise as he saw who was standing there.

'Good afternoon, Nicole. What are you doing here? I thought you were in England.'

'Good afternoon, M. Lebrun. My parents are there, but I missed the boat at Bordeaux because they wouldn't let me on with Kim.'

'Hah! A dog is always a nuisance, if you ask me.'

'I'm staying with a friend now, but I came to see how you are these days.'

'Well, I'm not too bad, but they are making themselves at home where you should be. They demanded the keys of empty flats when they came looking for places to stay, so I had no choice but to hand them over. I would have let your flat to French tenants, but with Paris so empty now, no one decent wants a place to live.'

'It's all right, M. Lebrun. You couldn't refuse. I hope they're treating you well.'

'I keep out of their way. Some of them speak a few words of French, but they only bother with me when they want something. I'd like to see the back of them, because they're taking the cream off the milk, but there's no saying when they'll be gone.'

Nicole chatted with M. Lebrun for a few minutes longer. She was pleased to see this old man she had known for years. Familiarity mattered more in unwelcome times.

'Can I leave you my address in case anyone asks for me?'

'If you like. No one's asked so far, but you never know. Your young man might come calling one day, if he ever returns from the army. Or is he back?' M. Lebrun kept a sharp eye on the comings and goings in his block and knew the regular visitors, as well as the residents.

'No, there's no sign of him. I'm hoping he'll be back in Paris soon, though.'

'By the way, I posted your letters,' he said.

Nicole thanked him, remembering her last frantic moments in the flat in June. She wrote down her new address for M. Lebrun. Walking on beside the Seine, she started composing a diary piece in her head about a grumpy concierge, whose almost empty block had been taken over by Nazis and who had become even grumpier. She had grown used to her diary in her journey from Bordeaux and was continuing it in Paris.

**

Nicole and Miriam disappeared into Miriam's bedroom when they wanted to talk privately. This was something they had done for years. Often with Yvette, they had played with the contents of Miriam's jewellery box, which had been growing since childhood. Moonstone, coral and lapis lazuli necklaces jostled for space in the box with bracelets, rings and earrings. They had dressed up in the jewellery, taking on different characters and inventing stories until they had grown out of doing that. They had moved on to Miriam's bookcases where all her books were crammed, ignoring those they knew well and knowing always that there would be additions because Miriam loved reading. She had a good collection of volumes by Georges Sand, Alexandre Dumas, Victor Hugo and other French novelists. They treated Miriam's bookcase as a library, borrowing her novels and giving her books as presents to add to her collection.

'Do you ever feel afraid these days? I've been afraid since it all began, since we first heard that they had invaded

France and then there were all those news reports that they were getting nearer and nearer. When we fled, I was afraid they would catch us and since the occupation I've been afraid because they're here,' Nicole said to Miriam one evening as they sat in her friend's bedroom.

'Yes, Paris is frightening now, not only because of the occupier, but because the government accepts it all. The occupation is constantly on my mind. I might forget it for a moment, but then I remember it again, with a slight shock each time,' Miriam said.

'But I'm not just frightened. I'm angry about losing my home and family.'

'And angry about what has happened to France – the loss of lives, the fleeing from home, the destruction. I'm afraid of what they're doing to Jews in France. They've started already,' Miriam said.

'I wish you and your family had been able to leave.'

'Then we wouldn't have been able to answer the door to you when you came back to Paris!' Miriam's quick laugh died away. 'Tell me, what are you most afraid of now?'

'All kinds of things; for example, that this could last for years, so that I might not see my family again for ages, or that something awful could happen to me or you or anyone I know, like being imprisoned or killed. Most of all, I'm afraid for Marcel because he should have come back by now. When we were growing up, I felt so safe and unworried. We had money problems at home, but so did most people during the Depression. There was nothing like this.'

'No, this is the biggest thing that's ever happened to us. Have courage, Nicole. We'll survive and, one day, they'll leave. We'll have our country back and we'll feel safe again.'

Nicole liked hearing that, even as she wondered if her friend was trying to persuade herself more than anyone. She drew a deep breath. 'Do you remember suggesting your underground newspaper could publish my diary? I've been thinking about what you said. It's risky, in case I'm caught, but you're taking that risk and you have family here to worry about, whereas I don't. You're bolder than I am, Miriam, but I want to help you in any way I can.'

Miriam's face broke into a broad smile. 'Come along to our office tomorrow and meet David.'

'All right.' Nicole was not sure what she was getting into, but she felt strengthened by their friendship. Facing all the difficulties of her new life was so much easier with a friend beside her. The occupation made her feel closer to the people who mattered.

***

Miriam and Nicole met at the offices of *La Presse Parisienne* the following day. The underground newspaper was being produced from a room in the nearby Rue Soufflot, not far from the Sorbonne.

'Do you remember your essay about the Paris flood?' Nicole said to Miriam on the way there.

At school, Miriam had written an essay about the flood that had overwhelmed Paris before the Great War. She had impressed the teacher with her description of the swelling waters, the streets turned into canals, people desperate to save their possessions, the damage done to homes and shops, and the strenuous efforts made by the flood victims to restore their lives. Miriam had read her essay out to the class and each student had listened, caught up in the story. It had all happened before the pupils were born, but everyone had heard of the flood.

'Yes. What made you think of that?'

'Because I could see then that you were good at writing and now you're a proper writer.'

'So are you – your diary shows me. Now, David will want to know you can be trusted, but I'll vouch for you.'

'All right. What's the paper called?'

Miriam lowered her voice so that Nicole could barely hear her say the single word '*Valmy*'.

'Is it on the Cours Valmy? But that's not near here.' Nicole was almost whispering in turn.

'No, it's nothing to do with that. It's named after the Battle of Valmy.'

'Oh, yes, I've heard of that. Do you remember history lessons at school with Mme Plombier, with her golden bun and the endless notes we had to copy down from the blackboard?'

'Yes, wasn't she strict?'

Miriam reminded Nicole that Valmy was a village in the Marne area where a battle had been fought against the Prussians in 1792 – the first important battle in the French revolutionary wars. The victory had created a sense of national pride in the French for the first time.

'It's the name of the Resistance group I belong to. We also call our underground newspaper *Valmy*,' Miriam said.

'Sounds fine to me,' Nicole said. They were walking briskly along. 'I'd forgotten what a fast walker you are!'

'Here we are. We use a room at the Sorbonne because that's where the group began,' Miriam said, stopping in front of a large building. 'All kinds of people come and go, and no one knows who everyone is. That makes us feel safer.'

They descended a short flight of steps into a basement and walked along a corridor into a small room, lit by a single bulb and with one high window. The only occupant of the room was a young man sitting at a desk piled with papers, writing furiously. One or two other desks stood around the room. Nicole saw a massive old printing press out of the corner of her eye. The man at the desk, with a pale indoor face, was slim and neat in appearance. Seeing a stranger, he stopped writing and looked at Miriam with some alarm.

'It's all right. We're old friends,' Miriam said as she introduced Nicole to David. 'Nicole and I were at school together. She fled Paris with her family in June and has written a diary of her journey from Bordeaux back to Paris. I've read it and it's good. We could publish it in sections as a diary in *Valmy*.'

Nicole wanted to impress on David that she was not the vagrant roaming the roads of France that he might imagine, but someone with a real concern for her city and her country. When David passed her a copy of *Valmy*, she saw a single sheet, printed on both sides, its name in bold black characters. Headlines covered a variety of news stories about the impact of the occupation on people's lives, especially the shortage of food and fuel.

'Why are you producing this? Are there no other underground papers?' she asked.

'Good question,' David said, looking at her more closely. 'Yes, there are some. There's a network at the Museum of Mankind that has a newspaper called *Résistance*. There's also the Communist newspaper, *L'Humanité*. And other newspapers are springing up all the time, but we think the more the merrier to strengthen resistance.'

Nicole nodded. She was not sure that David would be a match for Miriam, but she liked his seriousness of purpose. Most people she had met since leaving Paris with her mother had simply been thinking of their own survival. She had felt the same at first, but now that she had come as close to home as possible, she was beginning to see other ways of dealing with the occupation. A newspaper could be important in building resistance.

'All right, you can have my diary, if you like it,' she said.

'Bring it in at this time tomorrow. If it's as good as Miriam says, we'll print it,' David said.

Nicole went home feeling that she had taken an important step. She was pleased, even though fearful of what it might lead to.

FOUR

VALMY

Nicole returned to the *Valmy* office with her diary the following day to find Miriam and David there. She was going to leave it on David's desk and go, but he invited her to sit down and he began to read there and then. Five minutes later, he looked up.

'It's good. Lively and amusing and I like the sketches. Let's start with your journey from Paris, though.'

'I haven't written about that,' Nicole said, flustered.

'Well, write it! Sit here and start now if you like. We've got paper and pen. We can publish the whole journey there and back in instalments. I've spoken to lots of people who left and have returned, but so far no one has written anything I can use.'

'All right. I'll write about being attacked.'

He grimaced. 'People need to know that. Now, you'll need a pseudonym. We all have one. And remember this is a free press. We want to be rid of the occupier and we're not afraid to say so. Don't forget that.'

'I took my pseudonym out of a book,' Miriam said.

Nicole was ready with a name. 'I'll be Michelle Laforte.'

'A good strong name!' Miriam said. 'And make sure not to say anything that can identify you in any way.'

***

Nicole soon learned that nearly all Parisians hated the occupation, were despairing of the armistice and wanted their freedom. The sight of the hated uniforms on the streets, of the flags and banners, the road signs in German and the Nazi propaganda were all dispiriting. Armed soldiers manned numerous checkpoints where identity cards had to be shown, but no one queried her foreign surname. Perhaps Seymour looked like a French name to a German speaker or even to a French policeman. She heard that a Nazi parade, with a band, marched along the Champs-Élysées several times a week, watched by people in the cafés that lined the wide boulevard, but she felt no need to see the spectacle. Identity checks and searches by French or German police or the Gestapo were a common occurrence on the street or in the metro, and she was stopped sometimes and made to produce her identity card, always grateful for her French rather than British nationality.

General de Gaulle, who broadcast from the BBC in England to the French people, stood for the Resistance. Nicole liked what he said about being French and about resisting, but she could not help thinking that he was not

in France and did not know what life was like under the
occupation.

The Nazis siphoned off food for themselves and were
sending more than half of French food and other produce
to Germany. A black market had grown quickly, but only
the rich could afford it. The grey market – the links that
people had or made with country people for obtaining food
– was beyond the reach of the Weiss family and Nicole,
without contacts in the countryside. Since August, there
had been no milk for adults. Real cheese, oil and coffee
were unobtainable, while rice and pasta were rare.

Rationing was extended not long after Nicole's return
to Paris. For a Jewish family, the ration card depended
on registering daily at the police station. Sonia spent long
hours queuing for food, shopping for Nicole as well as the
family because they were one household, and often came
away disappointed when things were out of stock. The meat
ration of a few grams a week per person had to be bought
on a certain day. If M. Thibaud had run out of meat, that
coupon could be useless. Cheese was low fat. Sugar, jam
and margarine were in short supply. Coffee substitute and
bread were rationed. Fish and eggs were rare. Vegetables
were scarce, perhaps carrots, turnips and potatoes, with a
few dried peas or beans. Soap was a luxury and Sonia saved
the ends of soap bars and stuck them together to extend
their use.

'There was an incident with Kim today,' she said to
Nicole one evening.

'Why, what's the matter? Did he misbehave?'

'No, he's no trouble at all. But I was collecting his parcel
at Thibaud's when a woman in the queue snarled at me that

there's no food in Paris for dogs when people are going hungry. She said I should get rid of him.'

'Oh, I couldn't bear to do that!'

'Don't worry. Thibaud came to my rescue. He showed the woman what he was giving me and asked if she would like it. She backed off quickly enough,' Sonia said.

***

Marcel's continuing absence from Paris was ominous. When Nicole enquired at the Paris headquarters of his regiment, all they could tell her was that he was not on the lists of those killed in the Battle of France. An official suggested that he may have been taken prisoner, but he had no evidence of that. Nicole then visited the Sorbonne, trying to find someone who had known him. The young men she had met through Marcel had all been called up together and would now be civilians, but they did not seem to have become students again. Many students had fled the occupied zone and the Sorbonne was a much quieter place than it had been before the war. She asked Miriam if Marcel's friend, Paul, had returned to *La Presse Parisienne* as he might know something, but there had been no sign of him.

Nicole wrote to the Peyriacs in Bordeaux and to Louise in Chartres, thanking them for helping her and explaining that she was staying with friends. She wondered how Céline and her family were doing now that they were back at home in Tours. They, too, would be living a constrained life under the occupation. Yet she had to give all her attention to surviving a Paris that she had never dreamed could exist, and her journey to Bordeaux and back, so all-consuming at the time, was beginning to recede in her mind.

***

Nicole cycled to the *Valmy* room early one evening to show David what she had written about her journey to Bordeaux. They would publish that story first, with sketches that Nicole had done, and the journey back to Paris would follow. She returned to the *Valmy* room again the following week and the week after that, encouraged by both Miriam and David.

Other people were involved in producing *Valmy*. Nicole was introduced to Gérard, who did the typesetting and printing, and Berthe, who had a day job at the police headquarters as a clerk and was able to supply useful information. She began to feel that she was among friends.

A student fly-posted a few copies of each edition. The *Valmy* group gave the rest to people they trusted to take to friendly cafés and even hand out on the street, always keeping a lookout for the authorities. *Valmy* was free and relied on everyone involved giving services, supplies and donations.

'Your journey has gone down well with readers,' David said to Nicole one day. 'Several people have mentioned it to me. I can't pay you as much as a franc, but will you write a regular diary of living in Paris under the occupation?'

'But everyone is doing that! They know what it's like and they won't want to read about me,' Nicole said immediately.

'Oh, they will. Look, nothing like this has ever happened to us before. Don't you feel that? We are less free now and your diary can talk about how to live and how to resist the occupation.'

'Well, if you put it that way...'

'It's not just me. Read this.'

He passed her a leaflet with an encouraging smile. Glancing at it, she saw pointers to people about how to deal with the Nazis on an everyday basis, being polite but not helpful. Whoever had written it understood that resistance could be more subtle than open warfare.

She was being drawn into *Valmy*, despite her earlier fears. Nicole agreed to let Miriam and David have the Paris diary that she had already started. She used an old typewriter in the *Valmy* room and continued to write under her pseudonym of Michelle Laforte. Miriam and David encouraged her.

Nicole kept the style of her diary pieces lively and amusing, thinking that her readers would want something to entertain and hearten them. She illustrated them with quick sketches. Praise from other members of the *Valmy* group filtered back to her. People did want to hear about life under the occupation, about not having enough to eat, not earning much and yet wanting to look attractive and to be successful in defiance. She included a grumpy caretaker in her diary.

'I like what you're doing for *Valmy* and your stories bring people to life,' David said one day. Nicole glowed with pleasure at the praise.

David did not belong to a political party, but he knew the different groups in French politics and he talked about them in a way that brought them alive. Through him, Nicole was acquiring a good understanding of the different factions that made up the emerging resistance. It was fragmented. The Communists seemed strongest, but they were tied to the Soviet Union in a way that was foreign to her. The Gaullists, led by the general who had opposed the occupation from the beginning, included people too conservative for her. She was not Catholic, and the socialists seemed weak and divided.

Nicole had known little about politics before the threat of invasion and since then she had been concentrating on escape rather than on playing a part in resistance. Since returning to Paris from Bordeaux, meeting Miriam again and talking to David, her mind had opened in a way that was new and stimulating. She no longer saw politics as her father's concern. The war had drawn her into a conflict that mattered to her.

David was well informed about the details of the occupation as well as politics. It was he who told her how the Nazis were using Paris. They did not stay in the barracks for fear of being bombed, but instead occupied hotels. They stored equipment in the Hotel d'Iéna, near where Nicole and Miriam lived. Their principal headquarters were in the Rue de Rivoli and one of the pavements there was forbidden to French people. They occupied the Hotel Majestic as well as many large houses in the Avenue Kléber and the Avenue Foch. The metro was always full of them.

Nicole, slowly becoming a trusted member of the group, began to help with the production of *Valmy* as well as writing for it. She could not take up her art studies until the following autumn and she had time to help *Valmy* after work and at weekends.

Berthe was slightly younger than Nicole, with thin features and dark, tangled hair. She lived with her Communist parents and worked at the police headquarters as a clerk, a job that was useful to *Valmy* when she heard of events, like arrests, in advance. Quick-thinking and fearless, she was knowledgeable about the mood and concerns of working-class districts of Paris.

Gérard, about the same age as Berthe, was an athletic young man with a confiding manner. Information spilled from his lips and his pen as he brought in stories about the Nazis, the police and the black market for each issue of *Valmy*. He was a student at the Sorbonne with a wide acquaintance. Like David, he had been in the army.

'I'll help with typesetting and printing, if you teach me how,' Nicole said to Gérard as he arrived one evening.

His eyes lit up as he pointed with a flourish to the massive old printer in the corner of the room. 'I'll give you a lesson now as we're printing the next issue today. Let me introduce you to Napoleon.'

Nicole laughed. 'Why do you call it that?'

'Well, I'm sure it's nineteenth century, even if not as old as the emperor himself.'

Gérard explained that Napoleon came with the room and that David had an arrangement with someone at *La Presse Parisienne* concerning paper and ink. Supplies were increasingly difficult to find so they could not always print as many copies of *Valmy* as they wished.

Gérard did the typesetting and printing of *Valmy* with Nicole's assistance. Setting the type was fiddly work, but she was quick-fingered and earned his approval. Moving the levers to apply the printing press required strength and sureness of touch. If anything went wrong, Gérard and Nicole would find themselves splattered with black ink.

'*Merde!*' Nicole said one evening, examining an ink stain on her skirt after a difficult session with Napoleon. The stain would be impossible to remove. It was a nuisance when she had few clothes and no money or coupons for a new skirt.

'Think of it as a badge of honour,' Gérard said.

'I'll try,' she said, feeling only slightly better.

***

So many men were absent in the army or had been taken prisoner that Paris had become a city mainly of women. Miriam and Nicole aimed their writing largely at women and were critical of the Vichy government's socially conservative policies. Neither of them had any patience with being told to stay at home and bring up children. Yet they were careful in their travels around Paris and fearful of being viewed with suspicion. It was common knowledge that people were being reported to the authorities for all kinds of reasons by anyone who felt like it. A conventional appearance helped to allay suspicion and Nicole was grateful, as never before, for being a tailor's daughter, even one with an ink-stained skirt.

I have only one hat, but I've seen many women on the streets of Paris with hats that draw attention, taunting the soldiers, defying the occupation. All credit to the women of Paris for continuing their flair for fashion under such trying circumstances. This is a matter of pride and helps morale. Elegance is part of resistance.

There was freedom in being able to print the truth, while the official press was under the control of the Vichy government and the Nazi authorities. The constant fear of discovery was not enough to deter Miriam, David, Gérard or Berthe. Nicole, striving to overcome her fears, was proud of doing something, however small, aimed at freeing her chosen country. She was thinking and talking about how to win people over to resistance and what kind of country she wanted to live in rather than simply keeping her head down.

Have you noticed not merely their soldiers in grey-green uniforms, but that women are arriving from Germany to support them? Their women in uniform, that we call grey mice, seem to be as numerous as the soldiers. They work as typists, telephonists and postal employees. Their many nurses have a section of their own in every Paris hospital. Then there are the wives of Nazi officers and officials. Bringing women here is a clever move, because it helps to make the occupation look settled, but it's taking work from French women.

In writing diary entries for *Valmy* of her life in Paris, Nicole hesitated over Kim. On the one hand, Sonia's experience in the butcher's queue and comments Nicole had sometimes overheard on the street showed that owning a dog made some people angry during a shortage of food. Few people had dogs in Paris now and people might not want to read about a dog, while mentioning Kim might help to identify her. Yet he had been a key figure in her diary of the journey to Bordeaux and back, and the story of missing the boat. No one had thought of that when publishing the account of her journey in *Valmy*, so Kim appeared from time to time in Nicole's Paris diary.

Under Miriam and David's leadership, *Valmy* joined other resistance newspapers like *Combat*, *Libération* and *L'Humanité* in Paris calling for action. People liked the bravery of the Resistance papers and their encouragement to readers to avoid the collaborationist press. It made readers feel better to see some resistance to the occupation, but these newspapers were making enemies. Miriam stressed the need for secrecy about *Valmy* to everyone involved. The group did not need telling, but the distributors were more loosely connected to them. Miriam was always careful to vet anyone before allowing them to help with *Valmy*. Informers were everywhere and were often impossible to detect.

***

Miriam told Nicole about the Resistance group behind *Valmy*. It was collecting information to give to the Allies, rescuing Allied airmen stranded in France and had begun to talk about harder forms of resistance like sabotage. She invited Nicole, now a regular contributor to *Valmy*, to attend a meeting of the wider group. They met weekly to exchange news and make plans.

Nicole accepted the invitation, although not sure what she would be getting into. The meeting was held in the

Valmy office one evening and included people Nicole had not met before. A discussion began about the Battle of Britain, which was stirring the hopes of occupied France.

'Why do you think that the British aren't invading the coast of northern France the way they did with Norway?' a young man called Pierre said.

He looked directly at Nicole for an answer, clearly knowing of her British background. Nicole groaned inwardly. As in Bordeaux, people she did not know well, but who knew of her connections, expected her to answer for the British military as if she were Churchill's chief of staff. Almost everyone hoped for a British victory now that France was no longer at war, but it wouldn't be easy.

The British had failed to defeat the Nazi invasion of Norway and Nicole lost no time in pointing this out. 'Anyway, the British have just rescued their army from Dunkirk, so invading France in the north probably wouldn't work now. The *boches* are too dug in there,' she added.

'It's time they invaded France to end the occupation instead of blocking our food supply,' Pierre said angrily, referring to the blockade that the British had recently imposed on imports to France and which was adding to the shortage of food.

'I'm French, despite my British parents. I don't know what the British military are planning, but I imagine they're busy defending themselves from bombing raids,' Nicole said, sharply.

David rescued her by changing the subject to the group's plans for action. Some members were interested in acts of sabotage and Nicole found herself growing anxious as she listened.

'I don't think this is for me,' she said to Miriam afterwards. 'I'll stick to *Valmy* the news-sheet and let *Valmy* the group go its own way, at least for the time being.'

'I hope Pierre didn't put you off. He shouldn't have jumped on you like that,' Miriam said.

'It's a waste of time pointing out that I'm a French citizen when people want to be angry with the British,' Nicole said. 'He annoyed me, but it wasn't just that. I'm not suited to weapons and sabotage and so on. It's all a bit frightening.'

PART FOUR

ONE

NEWS

Nicole attached Kim to his lead and set off. On a September afternoon, the air was crisp with a hint of autumn. It was Saturday and she was on her way to her father's shop. She was curious to see how it was surviving and he would be eager for any news. She did not know if her parents had ever heard from her, but she continued to write to them in hope.

She had been an occasional visitor to the shop, which was near her old home, for much of her life. She crossed the Place d'Iéna and arrived, noticing afresh how much she liked the entrance, where panes of glass curved to meet a central door above a patterned tiled floor giving the name of her father's business – J. Seymour and Sons, Tailors. Suits and shirts were displayed in the windows and she could see from movement inside that the shop was open. She rang the bell and went in.

At first sight, nothing had changed. There were the familiar wooden counters and storage units with glass fronts for shirts and ties, and the racks of off-the-peg suits for sale that her father had been saying lately were the future, with bespoke tailoring in decline. There were the tailor's dummies that he used and the metres of wool cloth and bales of Scottish tweed.

She breathed in the familiar scent, a mixture of cloth and wood, remembering how much her brother, Christopher, had hated tailoring and how glad he had been to go off to war to escape it. She hoped he was safe in the RAF, but she could not imagine that he liked the military life. Unlike her breezy elder brother, Ralph, Christopher was dreamy and quiet. Unable to return to her old home, she felt closer to her family in the shop since her return to Paris and was sharply aware in that moment of a feeling that was usually more in the background. She missed her family.

'Nicole!'

The sound of her name brought her back to the present. It was Pascal, a cutter whom she knew and could see working behind the counter. Like M. Lebrun, he was surprised to see her. She greeted him and looked across the shop to see Patrick McGrath, the Irishman who was managing it in her father's absence. He was wearing a well-cut suit and had a good haircut. He looked prosperous and there was no hint in his appearance of suffering under the occupation.

'I thought you were in England!' Patrick McGrath said. He had a strong Irish accent.

'My parents and brothers have gone, but I'm still living here, so I thought I'd call in to say hello,' Nicole said.

She did not want to explain any further, not knowing him well. His manner was not friendly. Did he think her father had sent her to spy on him? She looked at Pascal again and noticed that he was wielding his large scissors on a bolt of the grey-green material used for Nazi uniforms. Just behind him was a tailor's dummy with a nearly completed uniform draped over it, including swastikas.

'Are you making uniforms for them?' she said incredulously.

'Why, yes. We have to keep going somehow and no one wants a new suit these days,' Patrick McGrath said.

Nicole was horrified. The man was a collaborator. What would her father say? Patrick McGrath must have been aware of what was going through her mind because he continued to justify himself.

'Ireland isn't at war with Germany, you know. We're a neutral country.'

'This is a French business. You are collaborating,' Nicole said furiously.

'Be realistic. Shops all over Paris are selling to them and your father left no instructions about that. I must do the best I can when all our usual customers seem to have left Paris. Would you like me to tell Pascal here that I can't pay him any longer? He has a family to support. Do you want them to starve?'

'No, of course not. Look, I must go. I only came to say hello,' Nicole said, shaken and stumbling over her words. She waved to Pascal and left the shop in a state of confusion, pulling at Kim's lead. He knew the shop and was reluctant to leave.

At home that evening, she told Miriam about the encounter. 'It's my father's shop and I hated seeing that material being made into Nazi uniforms, but supposing Patrick McGrath is right and it's that or starve because the old customers have gone?'

'Perhaps we are all collaborators if we have no choice but to live here. But it depends on how far you take it. Maybe he's not right. I know your father is a men's tailor, but I expect they could make clothes for French women or children rather than making Nazi uniforms. After all, people need new clothes and some people must be able to afford them, but maybe he doesn't care. And if he's Irish, he may want the British to lose the war,' Miriam said.

'I won't go back there. I don't need to,' Nicole said, to quell her feeling of discomfort.

What upset her the most was that it was possible to see the Irishman's point of view. She wanted the argument for and against collaboration to be as clear-cut as one of her father's suits, but she was learning that life was not like that under the occupation.

***

Nicole made a point of passing Marcel's block every so often, to see if his mother had returned, but the concierge always told her the same thing – no one was there. She left a note with her new address in Mme Dupont's letterbox in the entrance of her block. She wanted to know that Marcel was all right, but it was increasingly likely that he was in prison.

One day, she came home from work to find a letter waiting for her. It had been hand-delivered, presumably to avoid using the government's required format for post, which involved ticking various boxes on a card. It was the only personal letter she had received since returning to Paris and she opened it with a feeling of anticipation, although she did not recognise the handwriting on the envelope.

Sept 10th 1940

Dear Nicole,

I've come back to Paris and the concierge says you have been calling on me. Please come and see me at the shop when you have a moment.

Best wishes from Denise Dupont

Nicole felt a mixture of dread and excitement. This could mean news of Marcel at last, but why hadn't Mme Dupont said anything about him in her letter? The next day after work, she cycled to the typewriter shop on the Rue Raymond Losserand. She locked the bicycle to a railing because bicycles were a valued form of transport now that petrol was so scarce and expensive. Entering the shop, she saw Mme Dupont talking to a customer. She greeted Nicole with a brief smile.

Nicole felt apprehensive as she wandered among the printers and typewriters, waiting for Mme Dupont to be free. She remembered her first visit to the shop, years ago, with Marcel, in all the excitement of falling in love. Mme Dupont finished with the customer and disappeared into a room behind the counter. She returned with a jug of coffee and two small madeleines, apologising for her meagre offer. Her rations would not stretch to anything more and she could barely feed herself. She poured two small cups of the steaming liquid before she said anything and then she looked at Nicole.

'Nicole, it's terrible news. There's no other way to say it. Marcel was killed in battle in May.'

It was unbelievable. 'But the regiment told me he wasn't on the list of deaths,' Nicole said.

'They made a mistake. That's what they told me to start with, but the National Archives told me he is on their list of men killed in battle. Drink your coffee. It's getting cold.'

Nicole hardly tasted the coffee. She had been bracing herself for news that Marcel was in prison, because he had not returned, but she had not allowed herself to think that he might have been killed.

'I wrote to the regimental headquarters before I left Paris in June, but I heard nothing,' Mme Dupont said. 'When I came back here, I went to see them and they told me what they told you. But then someone here said that the National Archives are providing information about missing soldiers, so I went there the other day. They're going to make sure that the regiment corrects their records.'

Mme Dupont was much the same as Nicole remembered her – a fussy, voluble woman. Marcel had often complained about his mother's inquisitiveness. How trivial that seemed now.

'I'm so sorry. How awful.' Nicole got up from her seat to give Mme Dupont a hug and they clung to each other. 'Do you know any more about what happened to him?' she said as they drew apart.

'No, but I expect to hear from his commanding officer soon and maybe he'll be able to say what happened.'

Nicole nodded as she sat down again. She felt numb, as if she were a machine. 'Please let me know when you hear anything.'

'Of course, my dear. I'm so sorry to lose my baby and I was looking forward to your wedding,' Mme Dupont said.

'What about Jean?' Nicole said, remembering Marcel's older brother.

'He's in North Africa with the army. As far as I know he's all right, but I don't hear often. He writes when he can, but I've lost both my boys to the war and I pray every day for Jean's return,' Mme Dupont said.

The fingers of one hand played with a crucifix around her neck. She was dry-eyed, but Nicole was not deceived. Mme Dupont looked as if she had been crying, but she did not give way then, instead asking Nicole for her story. In as few sentences as possible, Nicole told her about the journey to Bordeaux and back.

'You should have left that dog on the quayside. Oh, your poor mother! What will you do now?' Mme Dupont said.

'I'm working as a secretary at my old art school and I live with my friend, Miriam, and her family.'

'Miriam? Is she Jewish?'

'Yes.'

'It's terrible what they are doing to the Jews, even here in Paris.'

'I know. They have to register every day and some people have been stripped of possessions, but so far Miriam and her family are all right,' Nicole said.

'Hmm – so far,' Mme Dupont said.

Her disbelieving tone made Nicole feel apprehensive as well as numb with grief. She wanted to be alone to think about Marcel, but Mme Dupont obviously needed company. The shop was empty of customers for the moment, allowing them to talk more about Marcel before Mme Dupont turned to her most immediate problem.

'I must get the business going again, but it's difficult on my own. I hate being in Paris now, with this awful news and with them crawling around everywhere. At least Toulouse is still properly French, but I couldn't stay there. This is my life and Jean will expect me to be here.'

'Who is there to help you?' Nicole said.

'I have some relatives here and one or two friends. Don't worry about me.'

'I'm so sorry about Marcel and, of course, I'll come and see you again soon.'

'I'm easy to find and thank you for coming over, my dear. I am so sorry to give you bad news.'

At home, the Weiss family commiserated with Nicole. After the evening meal, she retreated to her room, refusing an offer by Miriam to keep her company. It was only months since she had last seen Marcel and he was so alive in her memory still that she could hardly believe he had gone. She remembered so much about him, from their first meeting at the dance class to saying goodbye during his last leave. Snatches of conversation came into her mind, declarations of love, their running joke about whether she was French or English, his unravelled look, the passionate embraces, the sex. Jumbled as they were, her memories were all she would ever have of the man she had planned to marry. What a stupid war to snatch someone like Marcel – clever, amusing and totally harmless – and simply destroy him. She cried herself to sleep and tossed and turned all night.

There was no post between occupied France and Britain. When a neighbour mentioned that he was planning a journey to the unoccupied zone, Nicole asked him to post a letter to England for her. She kept a letter to her parents in her bag in case anyone she met would be able to post it. The neighbour hesitated. What if he were caught with a letter addressed in handwriting not his own to someone he did not know? In the end, he shook his head and refused. Fortunately, Nicole then ran into an old school friend, who was going to visit relatives in the unoccupied zone and seemed to relish the idea of a secret mission. She agreed to post the letter to Nicole's parents.

The arrival of one letter would go a long way to putting her parents' minds at rest. They had other problems, apart from a missing daughter. London was still suffering the Battle of Britain, with bombing raids on most nights. Nicole was more worried about her parents' safety than about her own and yet they would not be able to write to her until the war was over. She doubted that they knew anyone in the unoccupied zone who would be able to pass news to her. There was no way that they could reach her.

***

Nicole and Miriam scarcely needed to say that they were keeping away from the Nazis as much as possible. If they had to speak to them, they, like most people, avoided looking them in the eye. But one problem would bring Nicole closer to the occupier than she wanted to go. Apart from a cardigan, the suitcase that she had taken to Bordeaux contained only summer clothes. As September advanced and days grew chillier, she needed warmer clothes, but regular expenses and trying to save for her art course put new clothes beyond the reach of her purse. Instead, she found herself thinking about the winter clothes in her bedroom at her family home.

She devised a plan, telling no one. Miriam would only offer her own clothes and the family had been generous enough to her already. It was a daring plan and she had to screw up her courage, but alongside any fear was a sense of injustice about being deprived of her own possessions and anger at the senselessness of Marcel's death.

One afternoon, she left work early, promising to make up the time the next day, and went to see Monsieur Lebrun, leaving Kim at home and taking her suitcase with her.

'Good afternoon, Monsieur Lebrun. Do you have a master key to our flat here?' she said when he answered the door. It was fortunate that he always seemed to be in.

'You know I do. Why do you ask?'

'I need my winter clothes. If no one's there, let me in to the flat, please. It won't take long.'

She waved a note at him as she spoke. She half-expected him to refuse outright, but instead he was looking at the money and she knew that he would welcome a small victory over the *boches*, even one they would never know about.

He cleared his throat. 'There'll be trouble for both of us if you're caught.'

'Two minutes is all I need. It's getting cold and I can't afford new clothes.'

'All right,' he said, taking a set of keys from the wooden board on the wall behind him. 'They're out all day, every day. I know that much. I'll let you in, but you're on your own after that, so don't forget to shut the door behind you.'

Nicole handed M. Lebrun the note, which vanished into a pocket. They walked upstairs together. On the first floor, he unlocked the front door of the flat and Nicole went swiftly in. It was quiet inside. Wasting no time on being in her own home for the first time in months or seeing what changes the occupier had made, she dashed to her room with the suitcase. She tried not to look at anything except what she wanted, but out of the corner of her eye, she saw a man's shoes by her bed. Opening the bottom drawer of her dressing table, where her winter clothes should be, she was relieved to see that everything was there. She thrust what she could into her case. In the wardrobe, pushed to one end of the railing to make room for a man's clothes, was her winter coat and, underneath it, her boots. She put the coat on over her light jacket and squashed the boots into the case.

She was almost ready to leave when footsteps sounded along the corridor to her room. Her heart leaped. Snapping shut the fastenings of her case, she stood up and turned round. A man was standing in the doorway, a man in a grey-green uniform – a Nazi soldier, much taller than she was and not young. He was not smoking, but she smelled smoke on him. It was the man with blond hair she had seen standing in the window of the sitting room, smoking, the day that Kim had dragged her to her old home. He was looking astonished.

Terrified, Nicole found she could speak. 'I needed my clothes,' she said, holding up her case as proof. 'Excuse me, please.'

He smiled then, understanding why she was there. 'Of course, *mademoiselle*,' he said in accented French and stood aside to let her pass.

She moved fast, clicking the door shut behind her and scrambling down the stairs. There was no sign of M. Lebrun, but a twitching net curtain as she passed his ground-floor flat told her he was watching. She hoped he would not be in trouble with the soldier, but there was nothing she could do about it. He could always claim he knew nothing; that she must have kept a key.

Trembling, she climbed the steps away from her old home faster than ever before, even with the heavy case. By the time she reached the top, her fear had evaporated. She was safe and even gleeful at her audacity. That evening, she told Miriam what she had done.

'You took a terrible risk! Anything could have happened to you. Why didn't you ask me? I have clothes to spare,' Miriam said, exactly as Nicole had thought she would.

'Because you've helped me so much already and, anyway, they're my clothes and I kept thinking about them.'

'Well, you're brave, but what if...'

'I know, he could have arrested me or... worse. What was he doing coming back in the afternoon anyway? Surely they have work to do?'

'That was bad luck. What a mad escapade and it's not at all like you!' Despite her rebuke, Miriam was smiling with admiration.

'Isn't it? Well, life is a bit mad these days,' Nicole said. 'But don't worry. I won't do it again.'

***

Nicole began to spend more and more of her spare time writing for *Valmy*. She did not feel part of a movement, but she wanted to help bring an end to the war that had caused Marcel's death and dashed her hopes for the future. She was writing her diary early one autumn evening when Miriam arrived at the *Valmy* office. It was obvious from her tight-lipped expression that something was wrong. She sank into a chair with the news that she and David had been sacked. A recent decree had barred Jewish people from many jobs and allowed their property to be seized. The police had been given powers to intern them in special camps.

'The editor said he was sorry, but he has no choice. They'll be shut down otherwise,' Miriam said.

Nicole grimaced. 'That's dreadful! What will you do?'

'Find another job. I can't live off my parents and I'm worried now for my father. He could lose his job as well. At least there's still *Valmy*, even though it doesn't pay anything,' Miriam said with a grim satisfaction.

Nicole was reminded of what Mme Dupont had said about Jews and her own response that the Weiss family were all right. How naïve she had been.

David found a job in an ironmonger's shop in the Marais district of Paris, selling to customers. Miriam took longer to find work. All the jobs she applied for were well below her level of education and skill now that any professional work was barred to her, but she never seemed to be invited to an interview. Just as she was beginning to despair, Sonia found a position for her as a companion and helper to an elderly Jewish woman of her acquaintance, Mme Verrier. Miriam was reluctant to take it at first. It did not suit her lively spirit to be tied to someone Sonia admitted was irritable and exacting. After some days of indecision, she accepted the post because nothing else was coming her way. She refused to complain about the demeaning loss of her professional work, but she was entertaining about the crankiness of her employer.

There was more; that autumn, an edict repealed the naturalisation granted to Jews after 1927. Daniel and Sonia Weiss lost their French citizenship.

TWO

THEFT

'It's getting worse. Our identity cards are stamped in red with *"Juive"*. The wireless and newspapers attack our culture. Jewish shops must carry a sign saying they're Jewish. Some people are going underground and Solidarity is now providing false underground identities,' Miriam said. 'And do you know the latest thing? We couldn't even move if we wanted to. We've left it too late. Another decree prevents Jews from moving home.'

On a Saturday afternoon, Nicole and Miriam were at home, talking in the sitting room. Daniel and Louis were out and Sonia was resting in her bedroom.

'My parents are just reassuring themselves. They explain away every restriction imposed on us. They think it'll be all right as long as we obey all these hateful decrees,' Miriam said. Her face, as so often now, was taut.

'But if you don't obey them, what then?'

'I don't know. A fine or imprisonment, I suppose. But that's not the main thing.'

'What do you mean?' Nicole shifted in her seat and looked at Miriam with a feeling of alarm that was growing more familiar.

'What's bothering me is what will happen even though we do obey them? They won't stop at anything and the government is giving in to them all the time,' Miriam said.

'It's awful to have to say so, but the government supports the persecution,' Nicole said. She did not feel safe either, because she feared her British background showed too easily, but that was different. She avoided bothering Miriam with her fears these days. 'What will happen next? Some sort of imprisonment of Jews?'

Miriam laughed. 'It would be impossible to imprison all of us in the occupied zone! Even in Paris, there are thousands of Jews.'

Nicole jumped up. 'This won't do! We're being too gloomy. Let's take Kim for a walk. It'll clear the air.' She fetched his lead and they set off, with Kim eager to be out.

***

The Weiss family and Nicole were brought face to face with the occupation on one Saturday morning during the late autumn. It happened at breakfast time. They were gathered round the table where Sonia had poured *ersatz* coffee from a steaming jug. It was the chicory substitute that most people drank now, using the German word that had crept into the French language with the occupation. Louis was talking about a student assignment he was doing when conversation was halted by a loud knock at the door. Miriam leaped up to answer it and returned almost immediately, her face pale.

'There are two soldiers here. They want to speak to you, Papa.'

Her father swallowed his coffee and went to the front door without a word. Nicole could not hear what was being said, but through the open dining-room door, she saw two Nazi soldiers, wearing the now familiar grey-green uniform.

Daniel returned with the soldiers. Sonia went to his side. Miriam, Louis and Nicole sat still, not moving or speaking. The clock on the mantelpiece ticked loudly. Kim barked at the sight of strangers and Nicole quietened him.

The soldiers said something in bad French about looking around and Daniel nodded. They went from one room to another as if they were in an antique shop deciding what to buy. They said little except to ask about a piece of furniture here, a painting there. When they had finished their tour of the flat, they pointed to several pictures and ornaments, as well as to an exquisite small chest of drawers inlaid with marquetry.

'We should like to buy these things and will pay you,' one of them said, naming a price. Nicole, aghast at the effrontery, knew that the price being offered was risible. She was too frightened to do more than sit in silence, not even looking at Miriam. When she tried to sip her coffee, it was cold and muddy. Her cup clinked loudly in the saucer as she put it down.

Daniel nodded at the offer. He had scarcely said a word since the entrance of the soldiers. In silence, he and Sonia swiftly cleared the chest of drawers of its contents. Within minutes, the chosen furniture, pictures and ornaments had gone with the Nazis. In their place was a small pile of coins.

Daniel watched from the window. 'There's a van outside, big enough to take a lot more than what they have stolen from us. They'll be going to other Jewish families,' he said, turning to face the others.

'More coffee?' Sonia spoke too brightly.

No one wanted anything more and Miriam and Nicole cleared the table in silence.

'They would have taken those things anyway, even more, if I hadn't agreed. I've heard several stories about this sort of thing. They seem to know who to call on,' Daniel said.

'At least they didn't take my favourite vase.' Sonia picked up a small ceramic vase with a swirling art nouveau pattern. 'Daniel gave it to me for our first wedding anniversary.' She attempted a smile, but she looked shocked. Daniel put his arm around her.

Nicole made a quick excuse and went to her room. She tidied her things, hardly noticing what she was doing. She was embarrassed that she had seen the family humiliated and felt furious at what had happened.

She needed a walk, so she went out with Kim, anxious to give the family time to themselves. She went to see her school friend, Charlotte, the one who had taken a letter for her parents, and was pleased to hear that she had posted it from Lyon.

She spent the day with Charlotte, coming back late in the afternoon to find that the only sign of the morning's disturbance was a quietness of demeanour and empty spaces where objects had been looted. She followed the family's lead and made no mention of the gaps on the walls of the flat or the missing chest of drawers. At the evening meal, Daniel and Sonia tried to make ordinary conversation, as if the incident had not happened. The young people played along, but later Nicole spoke to Miriam alone.

'I felt I was intruding this morning, being there when those soldiers came. I also wanted to jump up and tell them to leave, that they had no right to burst in and steal from you, but I was afraid.'

Miriam cut across her. 'Don't think that, Nicole. There was nothing any of us could have done. If we had protested, they would have come back with more soldiers and stripped our flat. My father did the only thing possible to get rid of them without endangering us.'

'That's what they'll do to my parents' flat, except that there'll be no one to pretend to ask,' Nicole said, thinking of the furniture and paintings that her parents had collected and had had to leave behind.

Miriam nodded. 'From what I've heard, they're stealing anything they like, but it's not the same, because you're not Jewish. Oh, I wish I could say that's all that will happen to us, but I'm more nervous now. They're the intruders, not you, Nicole.'

Miriam wrote an article for *Valmy*, suitably disguised, based on the thefts from her family home. It appeared in the next edition under her pen name. Much to everyone's relief, no further visits from Nazi soldiers occurred, but everyone now felt anxious at the sound of a knock on the door. Daniel filled the blank spaces on the walls of the flat with other pictures and placed a side table where the chest of drawers had stood. Sonia tried to say that they had had too much furniture and more space was welcome in the flat, but Nicole did not believe her.

'It's more than theft,' Miriam said to Nicole when they were talking a few days later. 'It's a violation of our privacy.'

'Yes, you're right. Now, I know it's different, but did you hear there was a round-up of British citizens here? Gérard told me. He always knows what's going on. People were arrested at home and taken away. I don't know if they've been sent to prison or to labour camps in Germany, but I'm relieved that my parents are in England and that I have French citizenship.'

'Yes, your parents did the right thing in leaving Paris,' Miriam said with feeling.

***

Encouraged by the underground newspapers, the mood in Paris began to change from one of acceptance of the occupation towards resistance. When the Nazis executed an innocent Frenchman in Paris for the first time, people responded by tearing down Nazi posters about his death or placing flowers around them. 'V for Victory' signs sprang up and anti-Nazi slogans were pasted here and there, while posters in German were torn down. Metro tickets were folded into a V shape and dropped on the ground.

For the first time in her life, Nicole had no Christmas that year. Their British origins meant that her family had always celebrated Christmas in the traditional style. She missed her family even more as the season approached and wished that she knew her parents had received at least one of her letters. She managed to smuggle another to England with someone who was going to the unoccupied zone on business, but there was nothing else that she could do. She was grateful to Sonia for inviting her to join in when the family lit candles for Chanukah. It was not their normal practice to observe religious festivals, but Sonia felt the need, under the occupation, to affirm their Jewishness.

Nicole sometimes found it difficult to believe in Marcel's death when he still seemed so alive in her mind and there had been no funeral. Her days were busy, but he was never far from her thoughts and, alone at night, she remembered him. She told him about her life now, longing for his touch. Mme Dupont had received a letter from Marcel's commanding officer commending his bravery and regretting the loss.

'It doesn't say anything in detail about what happened, but at least it acknowledges the part he played in the Battle of France,' she said, bringing out the letter on Nicole's next visit to the typewriter shop. 'He's been buried in a military cemetery somewhere in the north. I'll go and see his grave one day, with Jean, when he comes home. Perhaps you would like to come with us?'

'Yes, I would,' Nicole said.

Much of her reason for returning to Paris had concerned Marcel, but the future she had imagined for herself had disappeared with his death. Yet here she was, in Paris, and managing to survive day to day. Writing for *Valmy* and taking part in the Resistance was what she most wanted to do now that she knew about Marcel and had seen the Nazis in action for herself. She was feeling less nervous about taking part in the Resistance now. Marcel's death and the treatment of the Weiss family had made a difference to that.

The winter of 1941 was colder than any that Nicole could remember. There was little heating. The combination of privation and the short days of the season made the occupation seem endless. Nicole endured every day, wishing the war to be over. It had been over for France since the signing of the armistice in June the previous year, but it would not be over for her, or for most French people, until the Nazis were defeated. No one could say how long that would take, but she was certain that defeat would come about one day. She needed to believe that.

Paris, known the world over as the city of light, was in darkness now and much poorer. Streetlights were dim and electricity supplies uncertain. Many clubs and restaurants were closed, except for those patronised by the occupier. Coal, which was rationed, remained scarce for the same reason that had led to the scarcity of petrol and food: supplies were going to Germany. Few homes were heated except those the Nazis inhabited. There was heating in the form of giant old radiators at the art school, but it was not always on, and *Valmy's* small room had only a fireplace, which no one was able to supply with fuel. At home, apart from the warmth of the kitchen stove, the only heating was a fire in the sitting room in the evening if there was enough coal. Everyone took a ceramic hot-water bottle to bed. Miriam and Nicole, sometimes with Louis or David, went to the cinema as often as possible to keep warm, as much as for the escape that films offered from the daily grind.

Miriam fetched *La Presse Parisienne* from a newspaper kiosk every day and took it to Mme Verrier, who expected her to read out the main news items. Miriam did not mind that task and was able to keep the paper afterwards as Mme Verrier's eyesight was too poor for reading. She would read snippets of news aloud in the evening at home.

'The death rate has gone up and children are getting rickets,' she said one day, pointing to an article. 'It doesn't say so here, but it's because of the occupation, especially poor diet.'

Everyone could see that fuel was scarce and traffic was less and less motorised, except for the vehicles of the occupier. Old bicycles were brought out of storage to join modern ones. The appearance of more carts on the streets gave the impression that time was going backwards.

***

Nicole had taken to dropping in on the typewriter shop now and then to see Mme Dupont and talk to her about Marcel. She was pleased to discover that Mme Dupont supported the idea of resistance to the occupation.

'This is a resistance newspaper I contribute to,' Nicole said one day, flourishing the latest edition of *Valmy*, confident that her new friend would not betray her to the authorities.

Mme Dupont took the single sheet, closely printed on both sides, and began to read it. Nicole pointed out her diary entry and read some of it aloud:

When I needed a new pair of shoes, what a performance! First, I had to apply to the local Mairie, producing the old pair as proof. Months later, when the soles on my old pair were so thin that I could feel the street beneath them, I was granted permission for a new pair. The new soles are wooden, of course.

'I'm glad you're doing this,' Mme Dupont said. 'It makes me feel less alone to see some sort of resistance to what we have to put up with.'

She went over to the shelf where she kept stationery supplies for sale and returned with a hardback scrapbook with a cloth binding, which she gave to Nicole. 'Keep a record of your contributions to your newspaper. It might come in useful one day,' she said.

Nicole began to paste in clippings of her pieces of journalism for *Valmy*, including the diary of her journey to Bordeaux and back, and of her life in Paris now.

***

'Nicole, can you help distribute *Valmy* today? We don't have enough people and I want to get it moving. I'll give you the nearest ones,' Gérard said one Saturday afternoon, as they finished stacking the copies of a fresh edition into separate piles for deliverers.

'All right. Kim would enjoy the walk,' Nicole said, attaching his lead.

Nicole had not previously helped distribute *Valmy*. Gérard gave her a list of cafés on the Boulevard St Michel and other nearby streets that would take the copies he gave her. She departed, leaving Gérard to wait for other deliverers to come for their copies.

It was a sunny afternoon in early spring. Trees were coming out, bringing life to the streets. Little traffic, apart from military vehicles and the occasional bicycle or cart, was in evidence. Gérard had told her to leave a few copies in each of the cafés, giving them to the manager who would know who to pass them onto. This went well and the stack of papers that Nicole was carrying was soon much lighter.

At one point, Kim, straining on his lead, wandered into the road to inspect some rubbish. Nicole pulled him away with a mild reprimand. Hearing a click, she looked up to see a man lowering his camera. Only then did she notice to her consternation that she was holding the copies of *Valmy* in a way that displayed the name.

The photographer might have guessed that she was doing something forbidden, so she stopped, not knowing whether to confront him and ask for the film or carry on as if nothing had happened. He looked nondescript and did not seem frightening in any way. He even gave her a slight smile and a nod, as if thanking her for the picture. No photographer would willingly waste a roll of film and asking him to give it to her could arouse suspicion, so she said nothing. She continued with her round, taking the copies to each café in turn and being discreet about the bold headline of *VALMY*.

When she next saw David, she told him what had happened. He looked serious.

'Do you have any idea of who he was?'

'No idea at all, except that he looked French. He wasn't one of them.'

'Well, there's nothing you can do now. Try to forget it and let's hope that he was simply just a man with a camera taking a picture of a pretty girl.' He glanced at Kim, adding, 'Get someone else to take Kim out for a while. If he's in the picture, that could be a way of identifying you.'

He turned back to his work. Nicole appreciated the compliment that made light of her mistake, but she felt embarrassed about her carelessness. The regular deliverers would not have been so foolish. She might have imperilled not only her own safety so easily, but that of everyone working on *Valmy* and within the wider group of that name. She settled down to write her next diary piece, omitting the incident of the photo. It was better forgotten.

THREE

TRIO

The arrival of spring in 1941 brought good news when Yvette wrote to Miriam from Rennes. She and her mother were about to return to Paris for the first time since leaving the previous June. With no sign of an end to the occupation, they wanted to come home.

'Thank goodness she's coming back,' Miriam said. 'It will be so nice to see her and it means we can all meet on May 19th on our bench without missing a year.'

'Oh, of course. How long is it since we began doing that?' Nicole said.

'Seven years without a break, if Yvette comes back in time. Do you remember that we even met last year before the invasion?'

Nicole nodded. She had the impression these days that Miriam was trying to reassure herself in the face of danger, just as she had said her parents were doing, but she did not say so.

***

The thought of seeing Yvette again reminded Nicole that in their later years at school, the three friends had enjoyed exploring Paris. Journeys to and from school had led to longer walks. One afternoon had found them in the Luxembourg Gardens. Arriving there in the warmth of an early summer's day, flower beds even more brightly coloured than their cotton dresses greeted them. They had sat on the metal chairs that were always to be found in the gardens and Miriam had complained about her parents.

'They were arguing this morning over something stupid. My father wanted to have some boring people to dinner and my mother was against it. I'm never going to get married. Marriage is such a prison.'

'Will you live on your own all the time then?' Yvette had been alarmed. Her blonde hair and substantial figure had contrasted with Miriam's dark colouring and slim build.

'Oh, I don't know. but I'm not going to live like my parents, at least not like my mother – at home all day with only shopping to do and friends to see. I'm going to be a journalist and travel abroad all the time and write about exciting places. I'll speak English as well as Nicole and I'll go to the United States. I'll have affairs with foreign men.' Miriam's laugh had rung out as she finished speaking.

'I'm going to be a nurse,' Yvette had said, after a slight gasp at Miriam's last statement. Nursing had been her plan for a long time, ever since she had played at nursing her dolls.

'Yes, we know,' Miriam had said. 'You'll be mopping up blood and wiping bottoms. Ugh!' She laughed again, but not in an unkind way, and the others joined in.

'I'll get married as well,' Yvette had said.

'You haven't found anyone yet!'

Meeting boys had been difficult as they attended a girls' school. Brothers had not quite counted, although Nicole's brothers, Ralph and Christopher, had sometimes joined the girls at tennis. Miriam had disliked sport as much as dancing and had spent her spare time either reading and playing the piano at home, or meeting friends in parks and cafés. Louis had been a keen tennis player, but with his own set of friends and tennis partners.

'What about you, Nicole?' Yvette had asked. 'What are you going to do when you leave school?'

Yvette had been planning a further year at school, followed by nurse training. Miriam was going to stay on to take the *baccalauréat* and then wanted to go to the Sorbonne.

'I know what I want to do,' Nicole had said. 'You know I like drawing, but the art teacher says I need more training than she can give me. I'd like to go to an art school, but my father will have to agree. My parents want me to get married and have a family, but I don't know if I want to do that. It might get in the way of being an artist.'

'So, are you leaving school at the same time as me?' Yvette had asked.

'I don't know yet. I need to talk to my parents. Oh, look at that dog in the water!'

In the ornamental pond nearby, a dog, whose owner was ignoring a 'No Swimming' sign, had been splashing about. Nicole, at fifteen, liked dogs and wanted to have one.

'I'll get married as well as being a nurse. I want lots of babies!' Yvette had said.

'Two or three will be enough for me. I'll teach them to play the piano and to draw, if I have any,' Nicole had said.

'I don't want babies. They're noisy, messy things. All right, I've got an idea. We're fifteen now. Let's swear to meet on this day by the pond in ten years' time, no matter how much we see each other before then. We'll be twenty-five, a whole quarter of a century. Then we'll see who's doing what. It's May 19th today so that will be our date in 1944,' Miriam had said.

'You might not be able to, travelling as a journalist. Our foreign correspondent,' Yvette had said.

'You've forgotten to say what time. I don't want to arrive at the wrong time and miss you both,' Nicole had said, visualising three sophisticated, glamorous women, in ten years' time, telling each other stories about their exciting lives.

'Noon!' Miriam said. 'And I'll find a way of being here. You two can bring your babies and I'll buy them all an ice cream.' She had waved towards an ice-cream kiosk nearby. 'Let's have one now. I'm starving.'

Standing up, they had watched the little dog struggle out of the water and shake itself, before they wandered over to the kiosk to buy ice creams and then walked around the park, licking, making faces and giggling, until it was time to leave. They had then gone to Yvette's flat where her mother, as so often, had served them with a generous slice of *gateau* each. Not wishing to wait ten years, they had met every year on May 19th by the pond in the Luxembourg Gardens, as well as on many other occasions.

***

Yvette was already there when Miriam and Nicole arrived at a café that they all knew well on the Place d'Iéna, early one evening in April 1941. They greeted each other with affection, heightened by absence and by the occupation.

'You're a bit thinner, but not much. I'm surprised you're not skinny, with so little food around,' Miriam said, looking Yvette's still substantial figure up and down.

'I'm naturally a comfortable shape!' Yvette said, laughing.

The year since they had met seemed to slip away as the three friends began talking. Miriam and Nicole began by pressing Yvette for her news.

'We left before they came and my father drove us to Rennes, where my grandparents live. It took days to get there because the roads were jammed with people leaving Paris, but at least we weren't attacked. My father left us then, to join the army. He wanted to sign up, although he was older than conscription age. It was something to do with being too young to fight in the last war. My mother begged him not to, but he went ahead and then we heard he'd been killed in action.'

Yvette stopped, looking tearful, while Miriam and Nicole, who had both known her father and were saddened by the news, said how sorry they were. Nicole was conscious, as always, of her loss of Marcel. Yvette took a deep breath and continued.

'It's been a terrible shock for us both. That was one reason for coming back, to be where my father lived and where all his things are. Rennes is occupied like Paris, so there's no reason to stay there. We're in the same flat as before. Our concierge said it wasn't available when they came looking for vacancies last summer. She told them we were about to come back even then.'

'Were you working in Rennes?' Miriam asked.

'Yes, as an assistant nurse. I'm hoping to start training now I'm back in Paris. That's enough about me. Nicole, I thought you were in England and might never come back! What have you been up to?' Yvette said.

Nicole told her story and Yvette sympathised with her loss of Marcel, whom she remembered well. Miriam talked about her family and losing her job.

'You lost your job because you're Jewish? I wondered what it would be like for you now, Miriam. What a horrible world we're living in,' Yvette said.

'Well, it's nice that you're back and we're all together again. We can help each other out,' Miriam said.

Yvette had met a man she liked in Rennes. He had been discharged from the army after the Battle of France and had returned home. She had been torn between coming back to Paris to suit her mother and staying in Rennes for her boyfriend. Miriam made fun of her relationship with David, who persisted with her, even though she kept him at a certain distance.

Without naming any names, Miriam explained that she and Nicole were involved in the Resistance. There was no doubting that Yvette could be trusted, although she drew back from any idea of joining her friends. Thanks to information she provided, *Valmy* reported that the Nazis printed French money at a factory in Rennes so they could buy what they wanted in French shops. The Bank of France had to provide the paper. The three friends talked for a long time and made plans to meet again soon.

***

'There were arrests in Paris last night,' David was saying as Nicole arrived at the *Valmy* office late one afternoon in the middle of May. 'Arrests and internment of Jews.'

'You're not safe,' Nicole said, alarmed by the news and thinking also of Miriam and her family. 'What are you going to do, David?'

'I don't know yet, but I'm thinking about getting away. Either that, or I'll go into hiding and live underground like a badger!'

His light tone did not deceive Nicole. That evening, she raised the subject at home.

'There's no need to worry about us. They were immigrants. I don't like the sound of it, but they would stop short of doing anything like that with French citizens,' Daniel said.

'The immigrants who were rounded up before were sent back to Poland. That's where most of them came from,' Sonia said.

'Some of them were the refugees I've been helping, but I'm sure they're capable of rounding up French Jews,' Miriam said.

Daniel and Sonia disagreed strongly and Miriam avoided arguing with her parents. Clearly Daniel and Sonia did not think of themselves as immigrants, because, like Nicole, they had acquired French nationality. They made no mention now of the fact that it had been taken from them by a decree the previous year.

***

In 1941, the annual reunion of the three friends took place on a Monday. Miriam and Nicole were free in the late afternoon to meet Yvette, who had not yet started work as a nurse. They all went to the Luxembourg Gardens together, just as they had done before the war. They sat down on chairs near the pond, but as they looked around, Miriam stood up.

'I can't sit here looking at that all the time,' she said, taking off her glasses to blur the sight. They were facing an enormous red flag with its black swastika, draped over the Luxembourg Palace. 'Let's find somewhere else.'

They moved to a view of trees and Miriam put her glasses on again. Fewer people were strolling around or sitting down in the park than before the war and it was not hard to find a seat.

'All the flowers have gone,' Nicole said, looking around.

They had heard that the flower borders had been dug up in favour of the planting of vegetables, so acute was the shortage of food. They recognised carrot and beetroot tops, runner beans and tomatoes.

'What are those?' Nicole said, pointing to a large patch of leafy plants.

'Potatoes,' Yvette said. 'I know that because my grandfather has an allotment in Rennes.'

'They've done the same in the gardens of the Invalides and the Tuileries,' Miriam said.

'My mother still makes a cake now and then.' Yvette drew a package wrapped in greaseproof paper from her bag.

Miriam's eyes lit up. 'Oh, I remember your mother's cake!'

Yvette unwrapped the package and handed around pieces of cake. It was plain, but the more delicious for being a rare treat now. Sparrows pecked at the few crumbs that fell to the ground.

'You see, they came back,' Miriam said to Nicole as they watched one little bird flying off with its prize. She told Yvette about the sparrows missing after the invasion.

'What a treat! Do thank your mother,' Nicole said, finishing her piece of cake.

Miriam, licking fingers, echoed her.

Not only were French police stationed around the park, but Nazi soldiers were wandering about like tourists. It was discomforting to see them, but no one bothered the three friends who sat and talked for a couple of hours in the spring sunshine. Among other things, they discussed Yvette's boyfriend and her dilemma about returning to Paris.

'That's just like me,' Nicole said. 'Do you remember I had to leave Paris with my mother when I wanted to stay and wait for Marcel to come back from the army?'

'Yes, but you found a way back to Paris. Did you miss that boat on purpose?' Miriam said, squeezing Nicole's hand affectionately.

Nicole laughed. 'It was a shock at the time, so if it was on purpose, it was a secret even from me!'

Miriam assured Yvette that her boyfriend would pursue her if he were worth anything and that it would not do to be too available. The others teased Miriam for keeping David at arm's length. He had even suggested marriage, but she had rebuffed him. She did not want to marry anyone, at least not yet. The three friends left the gardens feeling heartened by their conversation.

***

Signs of resistance to the occupation were growing. Nicole was pleased to see Parisians wearing black ribbons and ties on 14th June, the first anniversary of the occupation of their city. She and Miriam took Kim for a walk that evening, wearing black ribbons that Miriam had found in Sonia's sewing box. Nicole tied one to Kim's collar.

A week later, Parisians were joyful when the Soviet Union entered the war against Germany. Hope that the Allies would turn the tide against the Nazis began to grow. On Bastille Day, 14th July, the wearing of red, white and blue colours together led to some arrests.

The mood darkened when a German naval cadet was shot by a Frenchman in August. The Nazis responded harshly by putting six hostages to death. They introduced a new policy of creating a pool of hostages to be shot in reprisal.

At the same time, the persecution of Jews in Paris was increasing. Berthe told the *Valmy* team that people were writing in droves to the police about individuals they disliked or had a grudge against, and that many of the letters denounced Jews who would then be visited, arrested and sometimes disappear. After the big round-up in May, thousands of Jews were taken to camps outside Paris. Miriam did not mention this at home, but Nicole knew that she and David were disturbed by the news and *Valmy* covered it.

A further turn of the screw came when Louis had to leave the Sorbonne because of a decree excluding Jewish students. Every Gentile was required to carry a certificate stating the holder did not belong to the Jewish race. A new census was introduced; curfews were tightened and could be changed at any time. The use of public places by Jews was curtailed.

The Weiss family had ignored the decree prohibiting French people from listening to the BBC at home. Nicole tuned in to hear about the war in Britain, especially anything that might affect her family. London was still suffering bombing raids. The Free French, based in London, had been given five minutes on the BBC every night at 9pm to broadcast to French people.

The family had to turn in their wireless in the summer of 1941 when another decree forbade Jewish people from possessing one. They dared not disobey for fear of being found out and penalised. Nicole took to visiting Yvette and her mother, Jacqueline, to listen to the BBC. She wanted the benefit of unbiased reporting both for herself and for *Valmy*. News items about the persecution of Jews and other groups or indicating growth in French resistance would appear in the next edition.

August saw another round-up of Jews in Paris. 'They were French Jews, not just immigrants and refugees. My parents know about it, but we're not talking about it. They don't want to believe it's happening,' Miriam said to Nicole.

'I know they're keeping their heads down,' Nicole said. If only Miriam would try to escape from Paris, but she would never leave her parents and they would never disobey the decree that prevented Jews from moving.

Miriam nodded. 'We're left with hoping that things will be all right.'

The propaganda campaign that the Vichy government was conducting against Jews continued. Nicole saw a poster for an exhibition called "*Le Juif et la France*" on her way home from work one day and the exhibition opened at the Palais Berlitz in September. *Valmy* denounced it, but people flocked to see it and Jews were even more vilified in the mainstream press as a result. Nicole became increasingly worried for her Jewish friends.

FOUR

JOURNEY

Paul, Stéphane and Philippe were interned for seven months in a prison in the Soviet Union. They were treated well enough, but they were left idle. Philippe let his moustache grow back and he and Stéphane concentrated on keeping fit. Paul did his best to learn Russian from prison guards.

The three men found themselves among French soldiers who had escaped from Germany alone or in small groups, leaving their prison camps and journeying together by train or in stolen cars, covering long distances to the Soviet Union. It was clear from the conversations that took place when they were allowed out of their cells for exercise or meals that many of the men had shown extraordinary courage in drawing enemy fire or carrying wounded comrades for incredible distances, just as Philippe had virtually carried Paul at the end of their escape. They knew they were the lucky ones. Stories circulated about small parties of escaped prisoners discovered by Nazi soldiers and shot or recaptured.

Their release came with the entry of the Soviet Union into the war after the Nazi invasion of their country in June 1941. The prisoners, including Stéphane, Philippe and Paul, were sent by train to Murmansk and then travelled by boat to Liverpool. They were in a group of two hundred French officers and men who had similarly been captured in the Battle of France and escaped from German prison camps into the Soviet Union.

Arriving eventually at Euston Station in London, the men were greeted by Free French Forces. The station platform was festooned with the Union Jack and the French *Tricolore*. Toughened by hardship and wearing a motley collection of battledress, sheepskin coats, fur and woollen hats, and their well-worn boots, the two hundred men marched down the platform smoking a gift of cigars, while French nurses served plates of sandwiches. The nurses were almost the first women Paul had spoken to since his capture in May the previous year. Their welcoming smiles and words in French touched his heart and he enjoyed a feeling of real freedom for the first time in sixteen months.

During the reception, the men were offered billets in London.

'What do you say to sticking together if we can?' Stéphane said to Philippe and Paul.

'No need to break up the team,' Philippe said. Paul nodded in agreement.

Stéphane went up to the man in charge of billeting and asked if anyone was offering space for three men. After some thought, they were offered what turned out to be a large house in Notting Hill, the home of a wealthy French couple, Thierry and Sylvie, who were anxious to be of help to escaped French prisoners of war. Sylvie, who was at the reception at Euston station, took the men home and settled them in. That night, Thierry came home from work with a copy of the *London Evening News*, complete with an article about the Frenchmen who had escaped from Germany into Russia and had been sent to London.

The three men revelled in the change from prison life to staying in a large and comfortable London house with heating, hot baths and enough food. Thierry was too busy to spend much time with them, but Sylvie made sure they were well looked after.

A charming and resourceful woman in her middle-thirties, she managed to convey French chic in drab, wartime London. They had no children and Sylvie had plenty of time for her various charitable endeavours and her support for the Free French. She found suitable second-hand clothes for her guests, who had traded their Nazi prison camp garb for ill-fitting Russian clothing in prison. She gave them money to cover their stay in London as they had none. Paul enjoyed talking to her, not simply because they could speak in French, but also because she took a real interest in the progress of the war and was able to give her three guests much of the news that they had missed during their spell of over a year in prisons of one kind and another.

Paul had never been to London before and wanted to see the centre. He went on his own one day when Stéphane and Philippe were busy trying to link up with their regiment. Armed with directions from Sylvie and a map, he took the underground to the City of London. Even though he knew about them, he was shocked by the sight of bombsites. He stood in the late summer sun, taking in the tumble of bombed buildings around St Paul's Cathedral and noticing how weeds were flourishing among the ruins. Sylvie had told them about the Blitz, but no description could match the impact of looking at the damage for himself. He had seen nothing like it in France, Germany or Russia. He knew from Sylvie about the spirit of Londoners in coping with the losses and deprivation of the bombing, but he could also guess at despair and grief alongside humour and stoutness of heart. Back at Sylvie's house in Notting Hill, he found her talking to Stéphane and Philippe. Thierry was away on business.

'There's news. Our regiment has been posted to North Africa and we'll be going there to join it,' Stéphane said to Paul. 'Why don't you come with us? You can sign up as a regular soldier when we get there. I'll vouch for you.'

As a conscript and with the Franco-German armistice in place, Paul was no longer required to serve in the military. He was free to go to France and pick up the threads of his life there, which was what he wanted to do. He had been unable to contact his family for over a year and was worried about their safety under Nazi rule. Some resistance would be developing to the occupation of France and he would fight the Nazis from within.

'No thanks, Stéphane. I must see my family in Dijon and then I'd like to go back to Paris. I'll join the Resistance there,' Paul said.

'How will you get to Paris if that's what you decide to do? There's no direct way nowadays. The Golden Arrow is closed,' Sylvie said.

'I'll find a boat going to Lisbon and make my way through Spain and across the Pyrenees,' Paul said. He had been thinking about routes home since his arrival in England.

'I'll ring the shipping companies and see if there is a boat going that takes passengers,' Sylvie said.

She did not delay. Paul, Stéphane and Philippe left England from Southampton at the end of September 1941 on a small boat bound for South America via Lisbon. They were three of only twelve passengers. Sylvie not only arranged passage for the three of them and paid for their tickets, but even gave them money each for their travels. Philippe joked that it was the best way of getting rid of them, but Paul appreciated the help. Sylvie also supplied rucksacks and warm clothing as it would soon be winter.

They were travelling in convoy with other shipping and with a military escort. They were fortunate not to meet any Nazi warships, but there was a storm in the Bay of Biscay. Without any stabilisers, the boat pitched and rolled. Passengers were confined by seasickness to their cabins and Paul discovered that he was not a good sailor. Groaning on his bunk, he joked grimly to the others that seasickness was worse than being taken prisoner by the Nazis or being interned in a Soviet prison.

The storm subsided after a day. On a calm morning, under an innocent sky, their boat travelled down the coast of Portugal and entered the harbour at Lisbon. Stéphane and Philippe were planning their journey to North Africa, where the Allies were attacking the Nazi siege of Tobruk. The group of three men who had lived so closely together since their capture in May 1940 was about to break up.

They sought lifts from Lisbon that same day. They were all going to Spain, but Paul was travelling north and the others were heading south. Portugal was neutral in the war, but close to Britain. Spain was also neutral, but it was more dangerous for the three men, who might be caught and imprisoned by Franco's government. It was a danger they had to face. Stéphane and Philippe, aiming for a boat from a port in southern Spain, stood on one side of a hot, dusty road out of Lisbon. Paul, on his way to France, was on the other side.

Paul wondered if he would ever again see these two men who had become his good friends. They had all exchanged addresses and promised to be in touch, but Paul had learned from the war how it flung people apart. When a truck stopped for Stéphane and Philippe, he watched them clamber aboard. He waved and the others waved back before they disappeared.

Watching the truck recede into the distance, Paul became aware of the emptiness of the road. He had never felt so alone. In the army and then the prison camp, in Russia and then London, he had been surrounded by people all the time. Now he must rely on his wits. He waited in silence. Lisbon was a capital city, but traffic appeared thin.

When a car stopped an hour later, he was on his way. He hitchhiked through Portugal to Salamanca in Spain, then to Valladolid and Burgos, and from there, seeking advice from people he met on the road, to the border with unoccupied France. He spoke a few words of Spanish and quickly learned more. He offered his labour to farms in return for food and a bed for the night, keeping well clear of anyone who looked official. The harvest was long over, but farmers found him jobs to do.

Near the border with France, Paul stopped. The next stage of his journey would be much more difficult. He had no papers to enable him to cross. Although he thought it unlikely, he could not dismiss the fear that Vichy government officials might have the names of Frenchmen, especially Jews, who had escaped from German prison camps and were trying to return home. The last thing he wanted was to spend the rest of the war in another prison camp. That would be if he were lucky. He could easily be shot for escaping.

Careful enquiry in village bars led him to a Spaniard, who agreed to include him in a group that would shortly be entering France through the Pyrenees, avoiding border patrols. He had changed his dwindling store of cash into pesetas during his journey and was able to pay his guide. A trustworthy guide was vital as people could easily get lost on their own, even in the early autumn.

It was still October and not yet cold, but as they rose into the mountains, along mule paths, he was glad of the warm clothing that he had brought with him. The climb was gruelling – one foot in front of the other; eyes fixed on the boots of the guide ahead of him and only occasionally lifting to take in the mountain scenery. It was not as difficult as the walk through the snow at the Russian border, but no one was looking out for him now.

They crossed the border into France at the Col de Mantet, avoiding officials, and made their way towards the French town of Prades. Once there, Paul said goodbye to his guide and the others in the group, and hitched lifts alone through southern France to Toulouse. By then, he was almost penniless, but farmers took him up on his offer to work and he did not starve.

South of Toulouse, when traffic was thin, Paul found himself standing near a Spaniard – a man of about his age. He was poorly dressed and did not look clean, but he was friendly. His name was Jorge. He spoke reasonable French and Paul, with his gift for languages, by then knew enough Spanish for a simple conversation. He told Jorge about escaping from a German prison camp.

'I've escaped from a French prison near here,' Jorge said.

'Whereabouts?'

'Not far enough from here. It's called Le Vernet. I got out yesterday, with some others. They're going back to Spain, but I don't want to be there under Franco. I came to France after our republic collapsed. I'm going to stay in Toulouse for a while.'

Jorge described a large field, full of huts containing hundreds of men who had poured into France from Spain – refugees like him from the Spanish civil war, but also men from other countries, displaced by the Nazi war. They had been brought there by train.

Just like Paul in Germany, they had been forced to build their own barracks. Conditions were inadequate with poor sanitation, insufficient food and a harsh regime. Jorge had escaped with a group of others by tunnelling under the perimeter fence, exactly as Paul's fellow prisoners had failed to do in Germany, at least while he was with them. Jorge was hoping to find work in France.

The two men hitched a ride together and headed for Toulouse, arriving in the early afternoon. Paul did not know the city at all, but he was relieved to have reached safety. He knew from Sylvie about the different zones of France under the occupation. As an escaped prisoner, he had only the French police to fear in Toulouse, if anyone. His money had nearly all vanished on the journey of several weeks to France, so he needed to live as cheaply as possible and to stay in Toulouse at least until he could travel to Paris. Jorge, a waiter by trade, was destitute and they were both looking for work.

In Toulouse, despite the lateness of the season, the weather was warm and sunny. People were hurrying about their business through streets of pink brick buildings. Toulouse had become a melting pot of refugees, particularly from Spain, and included many Jewish refugees from the occupied zone, but they noticed few Nazis. Paul did not want to stay long, but he knew that he would need a permit, either genuine or forged, to enter the occupied zone and return to Paris. He would stay in Toulouse until he had sufficient money for the next stage of his journey and a permit.

Thanks to Jorge's experience as a waiter, from which Paul benefited simply by association, they found jobs in a café on the Place du Capitole and were able to stay in rooms above. Asking around discreetly, Paul discovered a Jewish organisation that provided him with false papers so he could enter the occupied zone. It was a better idea than acquiring a permit in his own name, given that he was an escaped prisoner. He did not think of staying in the unoccupied zone. It would have been easier and safer, but he needed to see his family. By December 1941, he had enough money for the journey to Dijon. If his parents were well, he would then go to Paris to try and reclaim his job as a journalist at *La Presse Parisienne*. Hearing that month of the Japanese bombing of Pearl Harbor, he hoped, like everyone around him, that the USA would soon join the war and the Nazis would be defeated, but the end of the occupation was not yet in sight.

Paul said goodbye to Jorge and made for the station with his rucksack. There, he bought a ticket for Paris. When the train arrived, he took the last seat in a crowded compartment. Reaching the border between the zones, the train stopped. Nazi soldiers came aboard to check papers.

Passengers in the compartment where Paul was sitting held out their papers to the soldier who came along to check them. He was young and brusque in his manner, scrutinising the papers with concentration before returning them. Paul's mouth was dry as he handed over his forged identity card and *ausweis*. The soldier frowned as he checked Paul's documents and abruptly left the compartment, taking them with him.

Paul was horrified. The soldier must suspect he was travelling under a false identity. He considered making a run for it, but the train was standing in a station crowded with people, several of whom were Nazi soldiers. He would have no chance, so he sat still, his heart thumping in his chest.

The compartment was quiet as everyone realised that something was wrong. An old man seated next to him had a small dog at his feet. For something to do, Paul stroked the dog. When it growled and snapped, Paul withdrew his hand quickly.

'He thought you were going to attack him,' the old man said, chuckling.

The atmosphere in the compartment relaxed as people chimed in with advice about not touching strange dogs.

The soldier returned and handed Paul his papers without a word. A few minutes later, the train moved on, but the incident with the dog had broken the ice and people continued talking.

'You're the only young man here, so he thought you might be good material for a labour camp in Germany,' said one man, who was middle-aged and had an air of authority.

Paul managed a smile. 'It looks as if I'm not good enough, but I can't say I mind about that!'

'It must be a relief, young man. No one wants to be sent off there, surely,' said an elderly woman, with a sympathetic smile.

Paul agreed. Neither the soldiers nor the train passengers had realised his papers were false. He said a silent thank you to the forgers in Toulouse.

The rest of the journey was uneventful. The train arrived at the Gare Montparnasse in Paris in the early evening. Paul crossed the city to where he knew his friend, David, had lived, hoping he would be there. As journalists at *La Presse Parisienne* before the war, they had become friends. He was in luck and was invited to stay with David and his mother, telling them of his adventures since being captured and listening to David's story of losing his job and working in an ironmonger's shop while editing a resistance newspaper.

'That means *La Presse Parisienne* won't take me back, but I want to come back to Paris once I've seen my family,' Paul said.

'Stay with us when you do, if you like, until you find somewhere of your own,' David's mother said.

'Yes. If you like, you can help with the news-sheet,' David said. 'It's the only kind of journalism open to us these days, but I wouldn't want to have to follow the government line.'

The next morning, Paul took a train for Dijon. As it was also in the occupied zone, he did not need to show his papers again. He had written to his family from Toulouse and they were expecting him. They were relieved to see him after an absence of eighteen months and he was reassured that, although their lives were increasingly restricted, his parents were well. His brother, who lived nearby, was on hand to help them. After a week, Paul felt able to return to Paris. He could not reclaim his old job, but Paris, even occupied Paris, was where he had begun his working life before the war and where he wanted to be now.

FIVE

PAUL

Nicole and Miriam arrived at the *Valmy* office after finishing work one day in December, as they often did. To their surprise, the door was locked.

'That's odd. David's meant to be here today,' Miriam said, unlocking the door.

'Oh, what's happened?' Nicole said as they saw chairs flung about and pieces of type scattered on the floor.

'David left a whole edition here last night for distribution today, but there's no sign of it. My guess is a police raid,' Miriam said. 'Let's see if we can find him.'

David was not hard to find. He was sitting in his favourite café almost next door, looking dispirited. Nicole and Miriam joined him.

'It was the police. The concierge said that they arrived last night with a copy of *Valmy* and made him open our room. They've seized the latest edition,' David said.

'How did they know where to find it?' Nicole said.

'I don't know. Someone has informed on us, but I've no idea who it is. Anyway, they're after us now, so we'll have to find somewhere else. And we'll need another printer. I can't think of anyone who can offer us space. Have you got any ideas?'

'I might be able to help,' Nicole said.

'Save the day, Nicole!' David flashed a smile at her.

'I need to ask first, but I know someone who sells typewriters and that sort of thing. She may be able to help. She's nearby. I'll go and see her now.'

'All right. I'll be here same time tomorrow, after work,' David said.

***

In the typewriter shop on the Rue Raymond Losserand, Mme Dupont was pleased to see Nicole, who called on her now and then. They enjoyed each other's company and they both liked talking about Marcel. Nicole explained what had happened about *Valmy*.

'Oh, I hope you're going to carry on with *Valmy* – I rely on it now,' Mme Dupont said.

'Well, I hope so, but we must find somewhere else. Do you know anyone who has a room and a printing machine that we could use? It's not just for *Valmy*. There's the group as well. They have regular meetings,' Nicole said. She did not want to ask outright and make a refusal difficult, but she need not have worried.

'I have a duplicator and there is a spare room at the back here.'

Mme Dupont led the way to the back of the shop, showing Nicole a room about the size of their existing office with its own exit independent of the shop. Old machines and papers were lying about. It looked like a storeroom.

'You can have this room. The duplicating machine will need strong young men to move it in here. I have skins for it, because I sometimes do small jobs for people, but you'll have to pay for them and supply your own paper and ink. And I'm afraid there's no heating,' she said.

'Oh, thank you, Mme Dupont. We'll provide our own supplies and we already manage without heating. But you know it's risky, don't you? *Valmy* is an underground newspaper and if the police find out what you're doing, you could be arrested.'

Mme Dupont clenched her fists. 'I'd like to do something to help the Resistance, because of Marcel. I want to see the back of the murderers of my son. Now, you'll have your own exit with a key, so my customers won't see you coming and going. If they do notice anything, I'll just say you're doing some printing jobs for me.'

'That's excellent! I'll tell David and Miriam. Can they come and see you, Mme Dupont?'

'Yes, at any time during opening hours. And that's enough of Mme Dupont. Please call me Denise.'

Nicole agreed and gave Denise a hug before she left, cheered by her success. The next day, David and Miriam welcomed the plan and Nicole thought Denise would relish her new role as landlady to a resistance group. They went to the shop straightaway to meet her and they arranged to use the spare room immediately. David and Gérard moved the duplicator and Denise gave them a key to the outside door.

'This way you won't meet any customers and there'll be less risk of being reported to the police,' she said.

***

It was not long after that event that David announced that a friend of his had arrived in Paris and would like to help with *Valmy*.

'His name is Paul Lévy and he was a journalist at *La Presse Parisienne* with me before the war, but he didn't come back. He was captured in the Battle of France and has had all sorts of adventures since, including escaping from a German prison camp. And I trust him completely. He could write for *Valmy*,' David said.

'Miriam and I knew someone of that name,' Nicole said, smiling. 'He was a friend of Marcel's before the war and he used to come to our dancing class.'

Paul Lévy came to the typewriter shop one evening with David. By chance, everyone who worked on the *Valmy* news-sheet was there. Nicole and Miriam recognised him immediately and he was pleased to meet them again, although saddened by the news of Marcel.

Paul told them he had grown up in Dijon, where his father was the editor of a provincial newspaper. His parents, like Miriam's, had come from Poland. His older brother, another journalist, also lived in Dijon. Paul had begun his working life as a reporter on his father's paper and had come to Paris before the war to attend courses at the Sorbonne and later to work for *La Presse Parisienne*, where he had met David. He had been conscripted, like other young men, in 1939 and had fought in the Battle of France.

The *Valmy* team were fascinated by Paul's story of his capture and life in a German prison camp, his escape with two other soldiers, their journey by train across Germany and escape into Russia, their time in prison there, the boat journey to England and Paul's return to Paris the long way round through Portugal and Spain, while his fellow escapees went off to North Africa to join their regiment.

Paul was now living on the fifth floor of a block on the Rue Daguerre near *Valmy*'s new office. He joked that his tiny flat was too small, but that the scarcity of food was shrinking him, so he might one day fit in. He had found a job as a waiter in a café in Saint-Germain-des-Prés. He explained that he had worked as a waiter in Toulouse, on his way back to Paris. It was his alternative profession. Now that Paul was back in Paris, with work as a journalist closed to him, he would help with *Valmy* in his spare time.

Paul began by writing articles for *Valmy* about his escape from the German prison camp and his journey back to France. He was learning about the restrictions placed on Jews in France and their increasing feeling of being unsafe, but now that he had returned, he wanted to make a go of it. His was a reassuring presence and he inspired confidence in others.

Nicole saw that Paul fitted easily into the group and she was pleased to find him in Denise's shop when she arrived to write her diary or work on an article for *Valmy*. She liked him for his sense of purpose, his good humour and consideration of others.

Walking along the Rue Daguerre one cold winter's day, on her way home from *Valmy*'s new office, Nicole looked up at the flats behind the shops along the street. She had not seen Paul that evening and was wondering where he lived. It was gloomy and few lights were on anywhere, so it was hard to see anything.

'Are you daydreaming?' a familiar voice said to her from behind.

Nicole turned around and saw Paul, obviously on his way home. She blushed and realised that she had stopped and had been standing there looking up at the flats. Not daring to tell him the truth, but not wanting to lie, she avoided the question and merely said hello.

He did not press her, but instead invited her to come with him to a café he knew across the road, where the owner would discreetly give copies of *Valmy* to customers. Nicole assented and they went inside.

'I've been reading David's back copies of *Valmy*, including your diary. You certainly had some adventures! Tell me more about it all,' he said, as they sat down with their coffee.

Nicole told him about her flight from Paris and her journey back from Bordeaux, and he listened quietly, complimenting her at the end on how she had dealt with difficulties. She asked about his escape from prison in Germany and he told her the story in greater detail than he had given the *Valmy* group when they first met him. Time passed and Nicole looked up at one point and realised it was getting late.

'Oh, I must get back. They'll be wondering where I am.'

'Don't go back on your own in the dark. It's not safe. You might be spirited away. Let me come with you,' he said.

Paul escorted her home, much to Nicole's relief because the dimly lit Paris streets were unnerving at night. She was glowing as she entered the flat and Miriam began teasing her about a secret liaison.

'I ran into Paul on my way home and we went to a café. Then it was dark, so he saw me home,' Nicole said.

'Oh, I *see!*' Miriam was laughing.

***

One spring evening, Nicole finished her work for the day and called in at *Valmy*'s office on her way home. Kim was with her that day because Sonia had not been able to look after him. Paul was there, writing an article about food shortages in Paris.

'I'm writing with feeling because I'm always hungry these days,' he said.

Nicole laughed and offered him a biscuit. Someone at work had been passing them round that day and had given her two. 'I saved them for later and this is later,' she said.

Paul took one gratefully and they worked in silence for a while. Nicole finished writing her diary for the next issue with an item about the requisitioning of leather coats.

I've been visiting the great department stores like the Samaritaine. Few goods remain now. Not content with emptying Paris department stores, they've requisitioned all leather coats, that popular winter wear, to send to the Russian front. Armed soldiers placed at the gates of several factories are ordering any man wearing a leather coat to remove it. Anyone who refuses is arrested.

As she put away her pen and paper, Paul looked up.

'That biscuit whetted my appetite. Do you fancy a bite to eat? I know a place nearby. Don't expect much. Rabbit stew might be the best available and I'll see you home afterwards.'

He made it sound like an adventure and Nicole laughed. 'I like rabbit and Kim will want a taste of it.'

They went to a small bistro on a narrow side street near the typewriter shop, taking with them sufficient ration coupons. Nicole gave most of hers to Sonia but kept some back, as she did not always eat with the family.

The bistro was a modest place with a bar on one side and small tables with red-checked tablecloths. Net curtains drooped at the windows and bare light bulbs were hanging from the ceiling. The tables were almost all taken. Nicole sat down opposite Paul, after he had guided her to a table and tied Kim to her chair. Paul had been careful to choose a place that allowed dogs.

'At least none of *them* are here,' Nicole said, looking around her.

'None in uniform, anyway. No, I'm sure you're right. It's too small and obscure a place,' Paul said.

While they were waiting for their food to arrive, Paul asked her how she felt about being in Paris in the occupation.

'Probably the same as a lot of people. I almost don't know where to begin, because it's been a shock, but I suppose I'm getting used to it after over a year. I wish that the Nazis were the only people to dislike. It's never as simple as that because there are also collaborators.'

'Yes, like the French police who round up Jews,' Paul said.

'Or the tailor looking after my father's shop, who makes uniforms for them,' Nicole said. She told Paul about the visit to her father's shop and how disconcerting it had been to find the tailors making Nazi uniforms.

'The occupation is bringing out the worst in some people and it's difficult to know who to trust,' Paul said.

'A few weeks ago, I was carrying some copies of *Valmy* and someone took my picture. I was stupidly displaying the name and sometimes I worry about it,' Nicole said.

'You think the photograph will surface one day as evidence against you?'

'Yes, but I don't know who he was and there's nothing I can do about it.'

Nicole felt comfortable with Paul and did not mind admitting to him her mistake in carrying *Valmy* with the name exposed. When he asked about her job, she found herself telling him about Serge, who was becoming more and more of a pest. She was at his mercy because her desk was in a large space that also acted as a corridor, through which people, including Serge, passed all the time. Paul suggested she find another job as an escape from the nuisance and Nicole agreed that she might have to do that, although the job suited her in every other way.

'Tell me, why did you come back to Paris?' she said. 'It's no place for Jewish people now. I wish Miriam and her family had left before the occupation. Things are getting worse for them.'

'Because it's where I want to be a journalist, but I must admit I didn't realise how bad things had become in France for Jews.'

'Will you stay?'

'For the moment, yes.'

She was pleased to hear that because she liked him increasingly. He asked her about her family. He knew of her British origin and he wanted to hear more. She told him about her father bringing his family to Paris from London before the Great War and working as a tailor. When the meal arrived, both ate hungrily before Nicole looked up, smiling.

'This is chicken, but you promised me rabbit stew.'

'Never mind. They taste similar, so you have nothing to complain about. I shall aim to invite you for rabbit stew another time,' he said.

Nicole liked the idea of another time. The chicken was tough and probably old, but she did not care. She could not remember the last time she had tasted chicken. She slipped some of her portion to Kim under the table and he thumped his tail on the floor in appreciation.

Paul did not recognise a yellow mashed vegetable on their plates. 'What's this?' he said, grimacing as he prodded it with his fork. He had a naturally strong voice and Nicole was amused by his attempts to speak quietly in public.

'It's swede,' Nicole said, tasting it. 'I've had it in England. This is plain, but served with butter and seasoned, it's not bad. I buy one sometimes in the market, because it's one of the few vegetables I can find. Sonia makes it into soup or I mash it up with scraps from the butcher for Kim.'

'So, the British eat animal food,' Paul said with disgust, but he was too hungry to refuse it and his plate was soon clear. Like everyone else, other than the occupiers or the favoured few who could afford the black market, he was thinner than he had been before the war and hungry much of the time.

'Yes, but the French eat quite a few things that the British wouldn't touch. Snails spring to mind.'

Paul laughed at the mock horror on Nicole's face. 'Maybe you're not as French as you like to think.'

After the meal, Paul suggested taking Kim for a walk around a small park nearby. Nicole agreed, but they did not get far. When Paul took her arm and tucked it into his, Kim started barking and they sprang apart.

'I hope I didn't tread on him!' Paul said. 'No, he thinks I'm attacking you!'

'Kim, stop it!' Nicole said.

They laughed and moved on, with Kim now trotting quietly beside Nicole. Paul took Nicole home, as he had promised. He walked by her side, joking that he did not dare take her arm again. Outside her flat, he said goodnight quickly and Kim trotted upstairs quietly with Nicole.

Miriam was in the kitchen at home making a drink. When Nicole told her about the evening, Miriam's eyes gleamed.

'It might have been a friendly gesture in the dark, taking your arm, but it could have been the start of something. Paul obviously likes you! I've seen the way he looks at you.'

'I like him as a friend,' Nicole said. Then, she laughed. 'Oh, you won't let David close to you, but you think Paul would suit me!'

SIX

PERSECUTION

Nicole had no idea how long the occupation would last. It had seeped into every corner of her life and, after two years, it was beginning to feel permanent. She and Miriam followed the news about the war as closely as possible, but it did not help them know the future. Like many French people, they longed for an Allied invasion to restore their country, but there was never any indication of when, or even if, that might happen. Even though what they now thought of as the Resistance was growing in strength, it would not be enough to overcome the occupier. They began to slip into thinking of the occupation as permanent because it dictated so much of their lives. It was mundane and yet it was also terrifying because the persecution of the Jews was worsening all the time. Living with a Jewish family, Nicole was constantly aware of that.

At home, one evening late in 1941, Miriam described

a disturbing scene that she had witnessed earlier that day. They were talking in the kitchen while clearing up after the family evening meal. Daniel was working late. Sonia and Louis were huddled around a small fire that Sonia had lit in the sitting room, after managing to obtain some coal.

'I had to deliver a message to someone today. I went upstairs to a room overlooking the courtyard of the local *mairie*. From the window, I saw a group of people, obviously Jews, including children, standing in the courtyard in front of the building. It was bitterly cold. They were being guarded by soldiers with fixed bayonets. Someone made a move and was struck with the butt end of a rifle. It was so distressing. I hated not being able to do anything.'

'You might only have made things worse, for yourself and for them,' Nicole said.

Miriam nodded. They both knew that was true, but also that it was hard to witness ill treatment and not be able to do anything.

***

'Hundreds of Jews were dragged out of bed two nights ago, packed into trucks and taken to Drancy,' Miriam said a few weeks later, referring to a suburb of Paris.

'How do you know?' Nicole said. She and Miriam were alone in the *Valmy* office late one afternoon.

'Berthe told me. She heard about it at work. There hasn't been anything in the papers. Apparently, there's no food. They must be starving.'

Miriam made sure that *Valmy* carried what news she could uncover of that round-up in January 1942. In March, coming to the end of another cold winter, they heard that Jews were being deported to Germany. Miriam was aware that they included French as well as foreign Jews. Again, *Valmy* reported the news. Daniel and Sonia clung to their belief that they would be all right if only they kept their heads down, but Miriam was openly perturbed.

'Look at this,' she said, thrusting a leaflet at Nicole one evening.

They were in the sitting room of the flat, tempted to leave the warmth of the kitchen by an unusually mild spring evening. Nicole glanced at the leaflet and then began to read. It was badly written and printed, but it was not for those reasons that it caught her attention. The leaflet claimed that Jewish people were being taken to Poland and Germany and killed by being gassed.

'Is this really happening?' Nicole was shocked. If it were true, not only Miriam and her family but all Jewish people in the occupied zone and even elsewhere in France were in grave danger.

'This is the second leaflet I've seen saying this. I ignored the first one, because it seemed so incredible. I thought it must be a hoax. But this is a different one. I'm afraid it might be true.'

'It's terrible, like mass murder!'

'Yes. You know my father tells me not to worry, that only foreign Jews are being rounded up and that we'll be all right, but this is devastating. And not only that, but Berthe is saying now that it's French police who are doing it.'

Miriam's *sangfroid* seemed to have deserted her and it was that, as much as the discussion, disturbing though it was, that worried Nicole. She wanted Miriam to dismiss the leaflet with some superior information of her own. Her belief in the ability of her capable friend to survive the ordeal of the occupation was fraying and Nicole struggled to think of how she could help.

'Miriam, you must escape from Paris,' she said.

'How can I? We're not allowed to move.'

'Go into hiding, then.'

'I can't see my parents doing that. We're trapped, Nicole.'

Nicole knew that Miriam's worst nightmare these days was that the family would be taken away one night. 'If I found a flat, you could hide there,' she said. 'I mean it, Miriam. I can afford rent with my salary and flats aren't difficult to find these days.'

'But it wouldn't be just me. I can't possibly desert my parents and Louis. Even if you found a flat big enough for all of us, we couldn't get ration stamps if we were in hiding and we couldn't all live on your rations. I'm always hungry as it is! And someone would give us away. You don't know who you can trust these days. No, you're a dear friend to suggest it, but it wouldn't work. The only thing to do now is to stay put and hope things won't be so bad.'

Nicole could not think of a reply. She and her family were in nothing like the danger facing Miriam's family. After a short silence, Miriam spoke again.

'David wants to leave Paris and go to somewhere like Toulouse, in the unoccupied zone.'

'That's a good idea – to escape the occupation altogether.'

'He's pleaded with me to escape with him, but I won't.'

Miriam leaned forwards in her seat, folding her arms emphatically. Nicole knew better than to argue with her.

'Paul should go, too,' she said.

'He's staying because of you, isn't he?' Miriam asked. Her face lightened and she smiled, to Nicole's relief.

'I don't know. He's just a friend and we don't talk about that sort of thing. I don't want him to stay here for me.'

Nicole had suggested to Paul that he leave Paris. He had agreed that there were dangers in staying, that he had not foreseen such persecution of the Jews on his return to France, but he showed no sign of leaving.

Miriam wrote an article for *Valmy* about Jewish people being deported and killed, but she stopped bringing home frightening leaflets and the question of the family's safety was hardly discussed. Everyone concentrated on living day to day, in the hope – which surfaced now and then – that the Allies would invade France and rid their country of the occupier.

David asked Nicole to go to the Gare de l'Est on her arrival at the *Valmy* office one summer's day when she had been able to leave work early. He wanted her to report on the arrival of Nazi wounded. She watched the arrival of a train and talked to station staff. Back in the *Valmy* office, she began to write an article.

A hospital train arrived at the Gare de l'Est this afternoon, bringing their wounded from the Russian front. Long lines of ambulances took the wounded the short distance to the hospital they have requisitioned near the Gare du Nord. Nazis who aren't even stationed in Paris are depriving Parisians of vital hospital care. Does this mean they're losing their war with the Soviet Union?

'They are losing the war,' Miriam said, reading Nicole's question over her shoulder as she was typing. 'They've sent all the young soldiers who came here in 1940 to the east. Have you noticed their soldiers are either just boys or quite old men these days? They come to Paris as civilians and they're put into uniforms here.'

She and Nicole were in the *Valmy* office with David, discussing the news that the occupation troops in Paris had been reduced from three divisions to two.

'Uniforms made by Patrick McGrath in my father's shop,' Nicole said, knowing that the shop was still open. She walked past sometimes, but never went in. She added a few sentences about the change in the soldiers and about their uniforms to her article as they were talking.

'If only British troops would land in France and defeat them. Failing that, we need more British propaganda to support the Resistance,' David said.

The clandestine papers were helping with the formation of small Resistance groups in Paris and David remained certain that *Valmy* was useful in providing information and helping to keep up morale. Yet the chance of defeating the Nazis looked remote.

***

Nicole was increasingly aware that life was becoming more and more difficult for the Weiss family and for Jewish people everywhere in the occupied zone. But, despite Miriam's fears, Daniel kept his position at the hospital where he was well liked and valued. Sonia did her best with the provision of meals and Louis ran errands for people and did any odd jobs that he could find. Miriam carried on as a companion to Mme Verrier.

Nicole's problem with Serge at the art school continued. It was minor in comparison with what the Weiss family were enduring, but she kept Miriam in the picture to take her friend's mind off her own fears.

'Serge has taken to stopping at my desk and chatting for too long. I'm busy and need to finish my work before I leave the office. And I don't like him. He's much older than me and he's married. He's just on the lookout for extra on the side.'

'Oh, he sounds like a pest. Give him the cold shoulder,' Miriam said.

'I do, but he carries on annoying me. Yesterday he tried to persuade me to come to a bar for a drink with him at lunchtime. I told him I don't have time for drinks during the day.'

'What did he say?'

'He suggested the evening! He knows a small bar nearby where nobody asks questions. I refused.'

'It sounds as if you know how to see him off,' Miriam said.

'I do hope so, but he's persistent.'

Miriam took an interest in Nicole's problem and asked her about it from time to time. At the art college, Serge became more aggressive.

'What are you so busy with? You're not married, are you? Doesn't a pretty girl like you need a bit of fun, especially now all the boys have gone?' he said to Nicole one day, placing a hand on her shoulder. She hated his touch.

Serge was a good-looking man of about forty, who gave the impression that he expected to have his way with women. He had the reputation, according to Sandrine, of sympathising with the Vichy government and might well have been rewarded in some way for his views. Nicole hated the weight of his hand on her shoulder, creeping down to her breast, but she did not want to cause any trouble when her job suited her so well. Male attention was an accepted part of life for a young woman and complaining about it could cause difficulties.

'No, thank you,' she said. She shrugged off his straying hand and turned back with such determination to her work that Serge had no choice but to retreat.

***

'Nicole, May 19th is coming up again!' Miriam said one evening at home. The weather was warm enough by early May for them not to need heating and they were in the sitting room of the flat.

'Oh, yes. Let's meet up with Yvette in the Luxembourg Gardens.'

'I went round to see her today, but she wasn't there, so I left a note to remind her. This year will be eight years since we first met on our special day and then there will be only two years to go until our tenth anniversary!'

Miriam's cheerful voice did not deceive Nicole. She arranged with Yvette for them to meet in the early evening on May 19th. The gardens had not changed in the year since their last visit. An enormous flag with a swastika still hung over the Luxembourg Palace and, without needing to say so, they made sure to sit where they couldn't see it. Flower beds were still being used to grow vegetables.

They stayed and talked about their lives for almost two hours, despite the chill in the air. Yvette was training to be a hospital nurse and told stories about the strictness of the hospital regime and how she had to nurse Nazi soldiers brought back from the eastern front.

'I've been writing to my boyfriend in Rennes, just to prevent him from forgetting about me,' she said.

'Oh, your boyfriend! And when are we going to meet him? Is he coming to Paris?' Miriam's face lit up with the chance to tease.

'I don't think so. We have no plans to meet.'

Yvette sounded woebegone and the others sympathised.

Miriam entertained them with the idiosyncrasies of Mme Verrier, and Nicole, prompted by Miriam, talked about Paul. Her friends wanted her to have someone else after the death of Marcel and a long time on her own. She admitted to an increasing friendship with him and that these days, two years after his death, Marcel was beginning to slip into the past.

Yvette had brought some cake again and a flask of coffee to sustain them. Time fled and it was late when fading light told them they must leave. Nicole and Miriam escorted Yvette to her door before going to their flat. They continued to be careful about their safety on the Paris streets.

***

'Don't you hate wearing that?' Nicole said one day, looking at the yellow star on Miriam's dress as she prepared to go out.

'I'm proud to show I'm Jewish,' Miriam said, as if she would rise above whatever the Nazis tried to do to her.

In the summer of 1942, Jews over the age of six in occupied France were required to wear a yellow star. Some refused, but Miriam only made a face over hers the first time she pinned it to her dress and said that yellow did not suit her colouring. She and her family made sure to wear the star whenever any one of them went out. Paul and David had to do the same.

The yellow star allowed restrictions on Jewish people to be more easily enforced and more restrictions followed. Jews were forbidden to attend the theatre or cinema, to go to certain shops until late in the day or to use public phone booths and parks. The public were not told that Jews could only travel in the last carriage on the metro, so they were humiliated by being ordered out of other carriages until everyone knew about the new restriction. *Valmy* denounced the yellow star and Nicole felt ashamed to see it on her friends or to pass someone on the street wearing one.

***

Berthe came to Denise's shop early one evening in mid-July. Nicole, David, Gérard and Miriam were all there, about to print the next edition of *Valmy*. Paul was at work.

'I heard today there's going to be a big round-up of Jews early on the 17th,' she said, as soon as she arrived. 'At work, they're getting ready for it, making lists and assigning staff.'

'Did you manage to see who's on the lists, whether they're aiming for particular parts of the city?' David asked.

'No, it's nothing to do with me. This is just what I picked up in the canteen, but it seems to be wherever Jews are living and they're after thousands of people,' Berthe said.

'We'll publish a warning,' David said.

Miriam was pale, but she said nothing. *Valmy* was distributed with the warning two days in advance. Both David and Paul left home and went to stay with friends for a few nights as a precaution.

'Miriam, you should go to stay with friends, too,' Nicole could not help saying, even though she knew what the reply would be.

'Nicole, you're as bad as David. He spent half an hour trying to persuade me to do that. You know I'm not leaving my parents and there isn't anyone we can go to stay with,' Miriam said.

With no other suggestion to make, Nicole was silent. More restrictions had followed the imposition of the yellow star. Jews were forbidden the use of the telephone; a propaganda film, *Le Peril Juif*, was being shown in Paris cinemas; all books by Jewish authors were to be withdrawn from sale; Jews were not to go to cinemas or theatres and other public places; their access to shops was restricted; and they were not to attend any public establishment or entertainment.

Over the family meal that evening, Miriam told her parents about the proposed round-up of Jews.

'I fear they will be after any of us, not just immigrants and refugees,' Daniel said. He had never admitted that before.

Miriam's face was pale and serious as she spoke. 'You're

right, Papa. Isn't there someone we could go and stay with until it's over?'

Sonia, serving slices of a vegetable tart she had made, stopped what she was doing. 'Do you mean they will come for us? Surely not. Whatever are you saying, Miriam?'

'Stop it, Miriam. Now, don't say any more about it. You're upsetting your mother,' Daniel said, firmly.

Nicole had been wondering if Yvette and her mother could take the Weiss family in for a few days, but she dared not cut across Daniel and the conversation shifted to the amount of time Sonia had spent queuing for rations that day.

Nicole talked to Miriam later about the family going to Yvette for a few nights. She even secured Yvette's agreement to the plan on the following day, but when Miriam spoke to Daniel, he refused to consider it. Such a performance would not be necessary and he seemed to have retreated from his earlier admission that all Jews were vulnerable to a round-up.

SEVEN

ROUND-UP

On the night of 16th July, Nicole went to bed full of foreboding. She was dreaming about rocking backwards and forwards in a chair that was out of control when she awoke to find Miriam standing over her, shaking her shoulder and calling her name. Kim, who slept on the end of her bed, had woken up and jumped to the floor. A glance at her bedside clock showed that it was 5am.

'Miriam, what's the matter?' she said, relieved to be awake because the dream had been frightening.

'They've come for us. We've got to go. Not you, just us.' Miriam was dressed, her face pale, her hair in tangles and her words rushed.

Nicole sat up, wide awake now. 'You mean they're here, in the flat?' Fear unfurled and spread as Miriam nodded.

'Not them. French police. Two of them. You didn't hear the banging on the door?'

210

'I was dead to the world until you woke me up.' Nicole was out of bed and pulling on a dressing gown and slippers. In the hallway of the flat, Daniel, Sonia and Louis, all dressed, were waiting quietly. Sonia was carrying a shopping bag packed with food. She was pale and seemed breathless. Next to them stood two French policemen, one of them taller and older than the other, both wearing guns. Their impatient manner made it clear that they were intent on doing their job as quickly as possible.

Seeing strangers, Kim barked. One of the policemen aimed a kick at him, not quickly enough. He jumped out of the way, his feet scrabbling noisily on the wooden floor. Nicole moved to his side to protect him.

'Where are you taking us?' Daniel was asking.

Nicole could see that there was no point in refusing to go. It would have meant the indignity of being manhandled out of their home or, worse, being shot for resisting arrest.

The taller policeman answered. 'To the *mairie*. Get a move on. There's no time to waste.'

The town hall did not sound so bad, Nicole thought, desperate not to believe the worst. Yet where would they go from there? No one ever returned from round-ups. She knew what a refusal to comply would lead to, but she had to say something. She could not bear seeing the family taken away.

'What right have you to do this? This is a law-abiding family. They haven't done anything wrong.'

Neither policeman bothered to answer. They did not even look at her. She was not on the list of Jewish residents of the block that the smaller one was holding in one hand. The taller one opened the front door.

'We have no choice,' Miriam said, giving her friend a quick kiss. 'Look after the flat for us, Nicole.'

Within seconds they had gone, closing the door behind them. Nicole rushed to the window of the sitting room, which faced the street. Outside, a coach waited, its engine rumbling. Numb with horror, she watched the Weiss family, with a few other people, climb in, followed by the policemen. The coach set off and was soon lost in the pinkish grey summer dawn.

Nicole sat down and Kim padded over to her, his tail wagging, ready for a walk. He was disappointed. Nicole sat still, wide awake, in shock and anger. Although her worst fears had been realised, she could scarcely believe what had happened. She sat unmoving until, looking at her watch, she saw that it was nearly 6am. What was she thinking of, just sitting there? She would find them. She knew where the local town hall was. She would go there now, try to see the family, bringing them what food she could find, in the hope of catching them before they were taken elsewhere.

She went into the kitchen. Her ration stamps were lying on the kitchen table. Sonia must have left them out as she was packing the food, knowing Nicole would need them. She packed what she could find – cheese, a few apples, carrots and the remains of a cake. She added a bottle of water. She doubted there would be any supplies where the family were being taken, wherever it was.

It was light outside by then, but no shops were open, so Nicole could not add to her small bag of food. She left Kim in the flat, shutting the door against his whimpering. She rarely left him alone, but it was a crisis.

At the town hall, she saw a busload of people and walked round it, looking through the windows, but there was no sign of the Weiss family. She enquired inside. Staff seemed preoccupied and rushed, but someone stopped to tell her that everyone was being taken to the winter bicycle stadium, the Vélodrome d'Hiver.

She knew where the stadium was, on the other side of the river, in the Rue Nélaton. It was a short journey on the metro. She arrived there to see that police were everywhere. Made bold by her sense of terrible injustice, Nicole went straight up to the main gates and spoke to the nearest of the policemen guarding them.

'Please let me in. I've brought some food for my friends.'

He was about to refuse when his attention was caught by a large group of people who had disembarked from a coach and were being ushered in. The round-up was continuing. Nicole took the chance to slip in with them. Her fear had left her, replaced by a determination to see the Weiss family. She refused to accept what was happening.

Inside, the stadium was crowded, the ranks of seats full of people sitting and waiting. Children and even some adults were crying. Others sat huddled together, wordless or conversing in low tones. Nicole shrank back at the sight and could hardly believe that thousands of people must have been rounded up during the night. How would she ever find Miriam?

As she grew accustomed to the cacophony in the enormous space, she began to walk around, scanning the ranks of seating. She could feel the despair and there was an unpleasant smell.

She could not see Miriam or her family at first and she had made her way around almost half of the huge oval before she caught sight of them. They were sitting in a row above her head, Daniel with his arm round Sonia, Louis looking glum and Miriam waving a hand and calling out at the sight of her friend. Nicole climbed the nearest flight of steps and edged her way along.

'I've brought you some food and water.'

'Dearest Nicole, thank you. There's nothing here and we don't know how long we must stay. They told us to bring food and drink for three days, but we don't have enough,' Sonia said.

Nicole had last seen the Weiss family a matter of hours ago, but already they looked different. They were huddled together and seemed crushed. They were accepting whatever might happen to them when she wanted them to rage and fight. She wanted all the people in the stadium to get up and pour out of it. But then, she was free.

They talked quietly until Miriam suggested that she wanted a word with Nicole and the two friends moved away together.

'You see, my mother doesn't believe any harm will come to us, or she doesn't want to believe it,' Miriam said, quietly. 'So, Papa and Louis and I are pretending to her that things will be all right. We will go to a camp somewhere, Nicole. I don't know if we'll survive, but there's nothing more you can do to help us. It's so kind of you to bring us food, but you're putting yourself in danger. They might arrest you or even take you prisoner, too, if they find out you're British underneath. It's not just Jews who are being rounded up. Go now and don't come back. Promise me.'

Nicole knew when Miriam's mind was made up and she did not want what might be their last moment to be clouded by an argument. Her mind skated frantically, uselessly. Trying to walk out with them, the way she had walked in, would not work, especially as Miriam would never come with her alone. It would only cause distress and they might be shot. She and Miriam went back to the others and Nicole said goodbye. She tried to be calm like them and she avoided empty reassurance. The least that she could do was match their dignity.

As she left the family, her attention was caught by a swift movement. Someone was falling from the top of the stadium. It could have been an accident, but Nicole knew that it was much more likely to be a deliberate jump. People were desperate and some could not bear what was happening. She felt faint and rushed for the exit, desperate to get out.

Without knowing quite how she managed it, she found herself outside in the fresh morning air. There had been enough chaos in the huge round-up for her to slip in unnoticed and escape without being questioned. Miriam's last words came back to her, that she must not come and see them again. It was too dangerous. She did not want to go back there, yet she desperately wanted to help the family and that might mean ignoring Miriam's plea. On the way home, Nicole went over the horror of the last few hours. The Weiss family had never had a chance. They were as French as she was, but their French identity had offered them no protection.

In the flat, Kim was frantically pleased to see her. Nicole could not bear to leave him again and she took him with her to work. She arrived late, hardly caring what might happen. As she sat at her desk, slipping off the typewriter cover, Sandrine came over.

'You're late, Nicole. Make up for the time you've lost today and don't let it happen again. Now, Serge wants you to type this,' she said.

She thrust some papers at Nicole, whose heart sank at the sight of Serge's almost illegible handwriting. She began to type, but she made mistakes and had to start again. She found it hard to concentrate and Sandrine grew irritable when she twice found Nicole gazing into the distance.

In the late afternoon, Nicole ran into Paul at the *Valmy* office in Denise's shop. She was not surprised to see him, knowing that he had been staying with friends and so had missed the round-up. He was shocked by her news.

'They were French police,' Nicole said, as if she could not believe it.

'We need to find out more. I doubt there'll be much on the wireless or in the regular press, but Berthe might know something,' Paul said.

'I must find out where they're going and when they'll be taken away,' Nicole said. 'They won't be left in the Vel d'Hiv for long. It's too hot and insanitary and there's no food.'

'You don't want to go back to that flat tonight. Come and stay with me, on my sofa. You'll be quite safe and I'm going home now the round-up is over,' Paul said.

'Thank you, but I must go back there. Miriam's last words were to look after it.'

Nothing Paul could say would change Nicole's mind. He tried to explain that she was shocked and needed company, not to be alone in an empty flat that the family had been forced to leave, but she would not listen.

Although she was exhausted by the end of the day, Nicole could not rest. She went to see Yvette, who was horrified by the news and pleaded with her to stay the night rather than return alone to Miriam's flat. Nicole refused.

That night, alone with Kim, she straightened the beds the family had left so hurriedly. She fell asleep with Kim at the foot of her bed and dreamed that she and Miriam were sitting in the Luxembourg Gardens. Miriam was her normal self and Nicole woke to a fresh realisation of the horror of what had happened.

After work the next morning, a Saturday, she returned to the stadium again, this time with Kim, queuing for food with her ration stamps on the way. The stadium looked closed and was heavily guarded. She hesitated, but when she asked to be allowed in to see her friend, she was abruptly turned away by a policeman. The same thing happened the next day, Sunday. She saw Paul in the *Valmy* room at Denise's shop on both days and he took her to a café where they could talk quietly. David made sure that *Valmy* carried the news with headlines like *Massive Round-up of Jews by French Police: Jews packed in the Vel d'Hiv in atrocious conditions.*

Nicole was unable to gain entrance to the Vel d'Hiv again, although she went there every day after work, taking food with her. One day, the stadium looked different. There were no policemen and the place seemed deserted as far as she could tell from outside. She talked to boys who were kicking a football about nearby and learned that the people in the stadium had gone earlier that day. They had been taken away in coachloads and the building was empty now. The boys, who seemed well informed, knew that the prisoners had been taken to the Paris suburb of Drancy.

It was too late to go there that night. The next day, Nicole called the art school and explained that she would not be in that day. She then took Kim to Yvette's mother, explaining what had happened. Jacqueline was distressed at the latest news. She knew Miriam well and had seen her grow up.

'Can I leave Kim with you for the day? I'm going to take them some food,' Nicole said.

'Yes, of course. You must do what you can, my dear. What if it were Yvette or you in that position? But are you sure you're all right? You look a bit peaky,' Jacqueline said.

'I'm fine. I must go.'

'All right. Wait a second.'

Jacqueline disappeared indoors and returned with a slab of spice cake wrapped in paper and string to add to Nicole's parcel before ushering Kim indoors.

Consulting a map, Nicole took the metro and then a train to Bobigny, the nearest station to Drancy in the north-east of the city. Asking the way of a woman at Bobigny Station, she approached an enormous housing estate, which looked unfinished and was surrounded by barbed wire. Clutching her bag of food, to which she had added a bottle of water, Nicole approached armed guards standing at the entrance.

'No visitors,' one said curtly, hardly sparing her a glance.

'Please – I must see my friend. She's ill and she needs food and medicine.'

The lie came easily. The guard looked at her properly now and Nicole smiled persuasively.

'Please let me see her. I've had a long journey to get here.'

'No visitors allowed. Go away or you'll find yourself in trouble,' the policeman said, touching the gun at his waist and raising his voice.

Nicole could see from the set face in front of her that there would be no persuading him. She turned away and walked back to the station, feeling dreadful. Because she had seen Miriam and her family in the bicycle stadium, she had hoped to do the same at Drancy and she had clung to the thought that there might be some way of helping them escape. Now she saw how foolish she had been and that there was nothing, absolutely nothing, that she could do to help them. Miriam had been right.

She had not eaten that day and she was so hungry on the way home that she ate all the food she was carrying. She could almost hear her mother reminding her that a well-brought-up girl did not eat on the metro and certainly not out of a paper bag. She did not care about that, but it hurt her that she was eating food meant for the Weiss family, as if she were taking it away from them when they were starving.

She went to collect Kim. It was the afternoon by then on the kind of warm and sunny July day that lifted spirits, but Nicole barely noticed the weather. Yvette and Jacqueline were at home and listened in silence as she explained what had happened. They were upset and begged Nicole to stay with them rather than return alone to the flat.

'No, I can't do that. Miriam's last words to me were to look after the flat. I must stay there. The police might think it's empty and come to rifle it. Or anyone could break in,' Nicole said.

'What could you do to stop them if they did? And you would be safer here,' Yvette said.

'I don't know, but I must be there. I would be betraying the family by leaving.'

'But Nicole, that's nonsense. They've gone. Terrible as it is, you can't change that now. Please stay with us. You must be suffering from shock or you wouldn't be so obstinate. Anyway, you look pale,' Yvette said.

Nothing that either of them said would change Nicole's mind. Jacqueline made coffee and served some of the spice cake from which she had earlier given Nicole a slab. Nicole ate her piece of cake so quickly that Yvette's eyes narrowed.

'When did you last eat, Nicole?'

'Oh, I don't know. Coming back from Drancy, I ate the food meant for Miriam. Some bread and an apple and Jacqueline's cake.'

'That's not enough. And what about yesterday and the day before?'

'Oh, I can't remember. Just snacks here and there. But I made sure Kim was fed.'

'You matter more than a dog. You're not looking after yourself. You obviously haven't had a decent meal for days.'

Nicole had to promise, if she were going back home, that she would take proper care of herself. More than that, Yvette insisted on giving her bread and a small portion of cheese before she left. Nicole ate obediently, knowing that she was taking from Jacqueline and Yvette's meagre supplies, but lacking the strength to refuse.

PART FIVE

ONE

LOSS

Nicole was exhausted and went straight to bed when she reached home that night. She saw nobody on the Sunday and only took Kim for a walk in the afternoon, thinking all the time about the Weiss family, how frightened and hungry they must be in what seemed to be a prison and how her efforts to help them had been so useless.

On Monday morning, she returned to work, explaining to Sandrine why she had been absent on the Saturday.

'Well, I'm sorry about what's happened, but you should have known better than to go. It was a waste of time that would have been better spent here,' Sandrine said, heaping work onto Nicole's desk.

Later that afternoon, Nicole went to Denise's shop. David and Paul were there, working on *Valmy*. They all listened to Nicole's news and Denise gave her a consoling hug.

'It's dreadful, but you couldn't have done more,' Paul said reassuringly.

'I've just heard from Berthe that a train left Drancy this morning. Miriam and her family were probably on it,' David said gloomily.

In the *Valmy* room with David and Paul, Nicole sank onto a chair and put her head in her hands. She felt the mixture of hopelessness and anger that had been with her since the round-up. The three of them were silent for a moment and then David spoke again.

'I can't stay in Paris anymore. I've managed to get some permits and I'm going to take my mother to relatives in Chateauroux, in the unoccupied zone, and then I might go to Toulouse. It's becoming a centre for resistance. So *Valmy* will need a new editor. Will you do it, Paul, if you're staying?'

'You should go, too, Paul. Neither of you is safe,' Nicole said.

'I'm not going, not yet, anyway,' Paul said.

'So will you edit *Valmy*?' David said, looking at Paul.

'Nicole has been involved with it for longer than me and could do it just as well,' Paul said.

'Nicole's good, but you're a journalist,' David said.

'I'm happy for you to do it, Paul, if you're staying in Paris,' Nicole said. It had never occurred to her to take charge of *Valmy*.

'All right,' Paul said.

David was pleased to hear that. He said goodbye to them both and left quickly.

'Nicole, I'm so sorry,' Paul said, as soon as they were alone. He put his arm around her and hugged her as she clung to him. He did not try to pretend things would be all right. They both assumed that prospects for everyone who had been rounded up were bleak.

'I feel terrible that there's nothing we can do except report what has happened. I might be the editor now, but *Valmy* seems so useless,' he said.

She nodded and raised her head, looking around the room as if not knowing where she was. 'I'm going home now. I can't do anything for *Valmy* today.'

'I don't like to think of you going back to that empty flat. Won't you come and stay with me? You can have my bedroom and I'll sleep on the sofa.'

She smiled briefly. 'No. I must go back to the flat. Miriam asked me to look after it and it's all I can do for them now.'

He did not try to persuade her further. Using what Nicole reported, as well as making his own investigations, Paul publicised the round-up through *Valmy* with big black headlines: *Jews taken to Drancy, Pithiviers and Beaune-la-Rolande and Left Starving for Days* and *Thousands of Jews Deported to Death Camps in Germany or Poland.* The police would be more determined than ever to destroy *Valmy* and arrest its staff, and Paul warned everyone to be extra secretive and vigilant, but he would not hold back.

'Michelle Laforte can't write her diary for *Valmy* anymore,' Nicole said to Paul in the typewriter shop the next day. She had been writing the diary regularly for nearly two years and it had an assured place as a popular column.

'Because of what's happened?' He was looking up at her from a desk as she stood in front of him.

225

She nodded. 'I feel too wretched for that breezy style.'

'Well, give it a break until you feel like doing it again. I hope you won't abandon it completely, though, because it helps to keep up morale,' he said.

'I don't want to be idle. I need things to do.'

He gave her some events to report on instead. They were less personal than the diary. He said several times how sorry he was for what had happened to Miriam.

'You're not safe either, Paul. You might not escape the next round-up,' Nicole said bleakly.

***

When Paul next invited Nicole to his flat, she accepted. She was feeling wretched and lonely and in need of consolation. It was only for a Saturday afternoon as he was working a late shift that night. They bought some food in a grocery nearby and took it with them. Kim was with Nicole as there was no one to look after him anymore and she would not leave him alone in the flat.

There was no lift. They climbed flight after flight of stairs until they reached the fifth floor. Paul's flat was certainly small, Nicole thought, catching her breath as she surveyed the tiny living room and kitchen.

'I know. It's just a *pied-à-terre*,' he said, seeing her glance.

'It's fine. It feels safe, away from the outside world,' Nicole said.

She knew that Paul, like all Jews, had registered with the local *mairie*, but she felt safe in his presence. They ate the food they had brought with them. It was only bread and fruit, but it was enough. Nicole gave some of her share to Kim. Paul asked Nicole to tell him about her friendship with Miriam.

'She's like a sister to me,' Nicole said. She told Paul about the walks to and from school every day; the visits to the Luxembourg Gardens; and the young woman, full of life and spirit, who had rescued her from the street in the summer of 1940. 'I can't help imagining where they are and what might be happening to them. Whatever it is will be bad.'

'The Nazis won't show any mercy to Jews or anyone else on the trains from France. The best that they can hope for will be prison or forced labour,' Paul said.

'I feel so angry about the injustice of it all that I want to do something dramatic and noisy.'

'Like burst into Nazi headquarters with a gun, but what then?' he said, with a grin.

'I can't imagine myself with a gun. I've no idea of how to use one. No, I'm not going to do anything senseless.'

'It would only lead to reprisals against more innocent people. They have to be defeated, but in the right way.'

'Where are the Allies when they're needed?' Nicole said.

This was a constant cry in Paris. She had followed the progress of the war and, like most Parisians, hoped for an attack on the Nazis in France, but the occupation had dragged on for over two years now and still there was no sign of its ending.

They talked for the rest of the afternoon. Nicole felt comforted by Paul, glad that he realised she only wanted to talk and that he did not try to take advantage of her presence in his flat. They left together with Kim when Paul had to go to work.

***

Abandoning the bicycle, Nicole took Kim to work and to the *Valmy* office every day. No one complained. She was glad of his company. She did not have to explain anything to him; he was always affectionate and his need for a walk every day helped her in her distress. At the art school, he settled down quietly under her desk and in Denise's shop, he stayed close to Nicole. He seemed to sense that Denise was not a dog lover and Nicole was glad that she, at least, tolerated him.

Kim had unwittingly been responsible for so much of what had happened to her. Did he miss the Weiss family? Sometimes he walked around the flat as if looking for them, glancing at her as if asking a question, but it was hard to tell if he was thinking of anything more than his next meal or a walk.

Alone in the flat with Kim at night, Nicole felt that it was full of ghosts. She could almost see Sonia in the kitchen, Daniel reading, Miriam talking or playing the piano and Louis busy with his studies, at least until he had had to give them up. She listened for sounds and jumped if she heard anything unexpected.

Once or twice, she awoke at night convinced that she had heard banging on the door. She would sit up and listen intently for a moment. Kim would be sound asleep at the foot of her bed, just as he had been on the night of the round-up. He was not a good guard dog, even though he was a consoling presence. She could have been wakened by a nightmare or a sound from elsewhere within the building or on the street outside. There was only silence. She would lie down and go back to sleep again.

She continued to try and follow Miriam's injunction to look after the flat and she visited Yvette and Jacqueline often, still refusing to live with them, but glad of their company.

'I feel guilty about not being able to save Miriam and her family,' she said to Yvette one evening after work.

'Nicole, you couldn't have done anything!'

'Shouldn't I have argued with those policemen who came to the flat, persuaded them to leave empty-handed or even suggested bribing them with the family jewels – anything to make them go away? Shouldn't I have walked out of the Vel d'Hiv with the family, speaking to the guards as if I had the authority to take them away?'

'What nonsense! You're just an ordinary person and you wouldn't have got away with it.'

'All right, then, should I have tried to get them released from the dreadful camp at Drancy instead of merely taking them food? If only I'd known people in authority, I might have been able to save them. I don't know many people anymore. There are people at the art school and there's the *Valmy* people and there's you.'

'It's too bad if I'm last on your list!'

Nicole smiled. 'Of course you're not, Yvette. I'm sorry. I'm not at my best.'

'You would have had to be on first-name terms with the chief of police to release a Jewish family from the round-up. It's futile even to think about it. Nicole, this is getting you down.'

In her better moments, Nicole knew that Yvette was right, but still she struggled, much of the time feeling useless, sad and angry. Weeks passed. One evening at the beginning of October, she was startled by a knock on the door. Her first feeling was one of fear, that it was the police. When the knock came again, not banging but normal, she answered and found the concierge of the block of flats standing there – a small woman, whom she knew only by sight.

'Good evening. I've come about the rent. It was due for the quarter on the 1st of October, but hasn't been paid,' the concierge said. She looked startled, as if she had not expected anyone to be there.

Nicole had been too preoccupied with the loss of the family to give any thought to rent. Looking at the closed face in front of her, she wondered if the concierge had taken part in the round-up, telling the police where to find the people on their list.

'Is it? But the Weiss family aren't here. There's only me now. Could I stay on here?'

If she could do that, not only would she have a home, but she would be able to fulfil Miriam's plea to look after the flat and the family would have a home to return to, should they ever come back.

'If you can pay their rent while they're away,' the concierge said, maintaining what Nicole was certain was a fiction – that she did not know what had happened. 'There would be papers to sign, of course.'

'How much is the rent?'

The concierge named a figure for the quarter that, even when reduced to a monthly amount, was several times Nicole's existing rent. It was completely out of her reach. It showed how little Daniel and Sonia had charged her. Nicole shook her head at the answer. 'I'll leave tomorrow,' she said.

The concierge nodded and reminded her to return her keys. She was turning to go when Nicole stopped her. 'Wait a minute. What will happen to all their things?'

'They can go into the store in the cellar. You don't need to do anything. I'll arrange it. They can collect them when they come back,' the concierge said quickly, as if she had anticipated the question.

Nicole knew that the family might not return, but she grasped at the possibility that they might. She did not know if the concierge was telling the truth about storing possessions. There was a store in the cellars of the building, but would she do what she had said, or would she sell everything and keep the money for herself? Almost everyone was hungry in Paris, increasingly so. Nicole knew enough of life under the occupation to realise that honesty was often limited to those who could afford it.

Yet there was nothing she could do. She could not pay the rent for the flat, nor the storage costs for furniture and possessions. For the hundredth time, she wished she knew influential or wealthy people in Paris, people to whom she could now turn. She went to see Yvette that evening and explained that she needed somewhere to live.

'Come and live here,' Yvette said, straightaway. She turned to Jacqueline. 'We've been talking about it, because we thought you wouldn't be able to stay on at Miriam's flat for long.'

'Of course, you must come and live with us now, Nicole,' Jacqueline said. 'You've been through enough.'

'Thanks, I will. What good friends you are,' Nicole said. 'But what about Kim?'

'Oh, he's welcome. I work part-time, so I can help look

after him. He'll be company for me. But we won't be able to feed him. We can barely manage on our rations,' Jacqueline said.

'I've made friends with Thibaud the butcher and Kim lives on scraps he can spare me, mixed with any vegetables I have,' Nicole said.

Jacqueline suggested a rent that Nicole could afford and invited her to move in the next day after work, bringing her few possessions and the bicycle.

Nicole did not think of going to stay with Paul, even though he had asked her again to do so. Apart from not wanting to share a flat with a man she was not married to, he needed to be free to leave Paris and she must not stand in his way. She hoped that he was not endangering himself by staying in Paris. She did not want anything more than friendship from him. She was glad that he seemed to understand that, although she had sometimes caught him looking at her as if he wanted more.

Returning to the Weiss family's flat, she wandered around. If only she could forget that people were being gassed in Nazi prison camps, but it was impossible when she had heard rumours from different sources. She packed suitcases with the family's clothes against the slim possibility of their return. If the concierge were telling the truth and would store the family's possessions rather than selling them, it would be helpful to have packed cases.

In Miriam's bedroom, she opened the jewellery box on her dressing table, feeling guilty as she did so. Necklaces and bracelets, rings and earrings showed how much Miriam had loved jewellery. Many of the pieces she recognised as ones that her friend had worn. She chose a simple necklace of lapis lazuli. It was one that had been a favourite and she packed it in her bag. If the Weiss family came back to find they had lost everything, Nicole would at least be able to give Miriam the necklace. Close to tears, she saw that, if Miriam did not return, it would be something to remember her by, even though she would never wear it.

In the kitchen, she packed perishable food into a small bag and tied it onto the handlebars of the bicycle. She strapped her suitcase and the extra clothes from her raid on her bedroom at home to the rack behind the bicycle seat. Like the necklace, the bicycle would be something to give Miriam if the family returned to find all their possessions gone. Her last task was to drop the keys off with the concierge.

'There's only one set here. There should be three, at least,' the concierge said.

'I don't have the other keys. They must have taken them with them,' Nicole said, shrugging and not even bothering to say that leaving in such distressing circumstances meant the family could not possibly have thought of something so trivial.

Wheeling the bicycle and with Kim on his lead, Nicole walked away from her home of the last two years. She felt sad, but also relieved to be going after the trauma of the round-up. These were not her only feelings. Paris was her home and the basis of her decision to be French. After what had happened to Miriam, she wanted to do more for the Resistance.

TWO

RESISTANCE

Nicole felt safer living with Yvette and Jacqueline than she had done for some time. The anxiety she had felt for the last two years for the Weiss family changed to a feeling of dread when she thought of them. There was nothing she could do for them now, but she could do more for the Resistance, which was growing in Paris. Using weapons did not appeal to her, but she wanted to do more than write for *Valmy*.

'I was put off by the one meeting of the group I attended when I first came back to Paris, but they are now more of an action group,' she said to Yvette, one evening.

'But you are part of *Valmy*.'

'I write for the newsletter, but there is a wider group doing more for the Resistance. Terrible things are happening at these camps in Germany. Miriam and her family are in danger. I feel increasingly that I must do everything I can.'

Yvette looked alarmed. 'The best thing I can do is become a good nurse. I'm not cut out for the Resistance, Nicole. So, what are you going to do?'

'I'll have to stay in my job, but I'll forget the art course for a while. I've missed getting a place for this autumn because of everything that's happened. I'm going to see what the *Valmy* group are doing.'

***

Nicole talked to Gérard, one evening, about what more she might do for the Resistance.

'You could be a courier. You'll need a cover story, of course,' he said.

Delivering messages was often safer than using a wireless transmitter, which the Nazis could easily locate. Nicole knew that the leader of the *Valmy* group used one, careful never to transmit from the same place twice, but that members of the group also acted as couriers.

'All right. I'm visiting a sick aunt, but I've forgotten to bring the address with me. I've been walking around trying to remember it and I don't know the area well. Will that do?'

'It's not bad.'

'And if I'm caught with a package?'

'Prison at the very least,' he said with a straight face and then he smiled. 'There are risks, Nicole.'

There would be risks, of course. She must not expect otherwise. She decided that she must not be caught. She did not need to be vetted by the wider *Valmy* group because they already knew and trusted her. Gérard gave Nicole a plain packet one Saturday afternoon, to take to an address near the Gare de Lyon, in the south-east of the city.

'Memorise the address, the journey from the station and the password, and make sure you get the right reply before you hand this over. And it's urgent, so go now,' he said, giving her the details.

Nicole placed the packet in her handbag and set off almost immediately, conscious of its presence and the responsibility of the job. On the journey, she kept her head down, wondering if anyone would guess what she was doing, but no one spoke to her. She found her way to the nondescript block of flats of the address and rang the bell. A scruffy young man appeared. She gave the password and he replied correctly. She handed over the packet without another word and scurried away. The journey back was more relaxing.

The next time, she felt more confident and was soon making two or three journeys a week with secret items or papers or urgent messages, juggling her work for *Valmy* with her new role. She was content not to know what any of the envelopes or packets contained. She moved quickly and confidently and was discreet, doing her best to look as French as possible and always leaving Kim at home with Jacqueline so that she could move fast if necessary.

'There's a job for you,' Gérard said to her, one evening in September. 'Something big has come up and we need your help urgently.'

'Why me?'

'You speak English and we need to move a British airman. He crashed north of Paris. He's not badly hurt, but he doesn't speak French and needs a guide. The safest way for him to travel is by bicycle, with someone else. He's less likely to be questioned that way. We'll make him some papers – he can be Flemish. You can pick him up in Clichy tomorrow and take him to Vanves.'

'I'll call in sick at work. Have you got a bicycle for him?' Nicole said. If she were caught with a British airman, they would both be imprisoned at the least, but her wish to help the Resistance urged her into action.

'Yes. I'll give you the address and a map and papers for him. It's a fair way, so set off early,' Gérard said.

It was autumn, but not yet cold. Nicole pumped up her tyres, oiled the bicycle and arranged that Jacqueline would look after Kim all day. She set off early, accepting Jacqueline's offer to call the art school for her. At the Place Clichy, she took the avenue of the same name, reaching the address that she had been given by mid-morning. Propping the bicycle against a wall, she knocked at the door. A woman answered and beckoned her in. Inside the cramped living room was a blond man who looked English, but who was wearing French clothes that had seen better days.

'That's the Englishman,' the woman said. 'I gave him my husband's cast-offs.'

Nicole spoke to him in English. He smiled, clearly relieved at hearing his language.

'I'm Harry. My plane was hit and so I bailed out and I was brought here. I'm OK, but I don't know where my crew are,' he said.

'I can't help you there,' Nicole said.

She had to focus on the job she was there to do. She gave him his false papers and told him he was Flemish and spoke only his own language. The story was that he was going to work on a farm just south of Paris and Nicole, who lived in Paris and was a cousin of the farmer, had offered to show him the way. Nicole could not think why a French farmer would need to hire a Fleming he had never met, but it was not for her to change the story.

'Go now, before anyone notices I have two visitors,' the woman said, anxiously.

Nicole waited for Harry to get on the bicycle that the woman produced and they set off. He rode behind her, burbling about cycling as a schoolboy on country lanes in England.

It was long journey to Vanves and Nicole had plotted the route. They rode one behind the other, with her in the lead. She wondered how Harry's plane had crashed and where, but there was no time for conversation because she wanted to be home before dark, not least because her bicycle had no lights. Nearing the centre of Paris, she slowed down to let him draw up beside her.

'This is the most dangerous part of the journey because we could be stopped at any time by French police or Nazi patrols,' she said. 'If we are, I'll do the talking.'

Used to being taken for a foreigner, she was worried that they both stood out as not looking French enough. They came to the Place de la Concorde, with more bicycles and carts about than cars. They had almost reached the other side when a tall French policeman put out his arm to stop them.

'Papers, please.'

Nicole stopped and produced her papers, while Harry did the same. Harry seemed calm and even bemused, while Nicole was slightly out of breath from the exercise and trembling with a fear she had not felt on the journey so far.

'Are you all right, *mam'selle*?' the policeman said, looking closely at her.

She did her best to smile divertingly. 'Just a bit out of breath. I should get more exercise.'

He questioned her and she told her prepared story. He barely glanced at Harry's papers. His eyes were on Nicole. 'Mind how you go, a pretty girl like you,' he said.

Nicole smiled again and thanked him as she took her papers back. They cycled on. Nicole was sure of the way until they reached the Porte de la Plaine, where she stopped to ask someone for directions. They arrived at the safe house in the late afternoon.

Nicole handed Harry over to the waiting resident with a sense of relief. She wished him *bon voyage*. She wanted to ask him to write to her parents if he reached England, but a Fleming could not be caught with an English address on him and there wasn't time for him to learn it off by heart. She would never know if he reached his destination. He was grateful for her guidance and seemed reluctant to leave her for someone who did not speak English, but there was no choice. Saying goodbye, she rode off and arrived home before dark, satisfied that she had done a good job and relieved not to have been caught.

***

Paul's sympathy and understanding over the loss of the Weiss family drew them closer as the weeks passed. His flat near the typewriter shop offered an escape for Nicole from the occupation and she enjoyed such visits there as they could manage. He never tried to change their friendship into something else. Nicole was grateful for that because she did not feel ready for a new relationship. There was no rush.

They talked again about whether Paul should leave Paris. Nicole encouraged him to go to the unoccupied zone to be safer or even to leave France. He had liked London. What about returning there?

She was finishing an article for *Valmy* late one afternoon in September, alone in the office in Denise's shop, when Paul arrived, with his rucksack. He was looking agitated.

'I've just been home and my flat was broken into today. Neighbours told me it was the Gestapo, not even French police. I was lucky not to be there at the time and there was nothing incriminating for them to find. I've managed to collect some things and I'm going to stay with friends until I can leave. I don't think it's a round-up. Someone must have betrayed me. I have no idea who it was, but it doesn't make sense for me to stay in Paris anymore,' he said.

Nicole did not want him to go, but she was not surprised at what had happened or at his decision. It was, after all, what she had encouraged him to do. Paul had been the driving force behind the *Valmy* news-sheet since David had left. Without him, it might go under or it would, at least, struggle. Yet Paris was no longer safe for him.

'It's the right decision, but I'm going to miss you. Where are you going?' she said.

He relaxed and smiled at her then. 'I'll miss you, too. I want to go via Spain and Portugal to join de Gaulle's forces in London.'

'Spain is dangerous. You might be caught and imprisoned.'

'There's no choice. There are no boats to England from France. You missed the last one, didn't you, in 1940?'

Nicole nodded, remembering Miriam's tease that she had missed the boat deliberately.

'First, I need to get into the unoccupied zone and then I'll go to the border and find a guide,' Paul said. 'I'll link up with David if I can and I might stay in Toulouse for a while. Now, let me tell you my plan. I want you to come with me, Nicole! After all, you meant to go to England.'

It was an appealing idea and Nicole felt a thrill at the prospect. There were so many reasons to accept. She would be in good company on the journey and she would have escaped from the occupation to a free country. Most of all, she would see her parents for the first time in over two years. She did not answer him immediately and he pressed her.

'Will you come? You can join the Free French, too. They'd welcome a strong-minded woman like you!'

Nicole snapped out of a fantasy about arriving in England. She had tried to leave France in 1940, but things were different in 1942. 'I've heard that they have a women's unit, but I'm not coming with you.'

It was his turn to be disappointed. 'Not because of Kim, surely? He's a great dog, but don't let an animal rule your life.'

'No. I could probably leave him with Yvette and her mother, as he's already living there.'

She looked down at where he lay beside her chair. Seeing her glance and hearing his name, he thumped his tail on the floor.

'It's because… well, lots of things, but mainly that I don't want to give up on what I'm doing. You need to go, you're doing the right thing, but I'm not under that kind of threat.'

'Are you sure? I would like us to go together. Will you think about it?'

She did not want to answer that question. 'When are you going?'

'As soon as I can get a permit for the Free Zone – forged if I can't get an official one.'

'Would you mind going to see my parents when you get to London?' Nicole said.

'Of course not.'

She told him the address and he repeated it, promising to learn it off by heart to avoid carrying an address.

'But what shall I tell them about why you wouldn't come with me?' he said.

'Say that I miss them, but I don't want to give up on being French. They'll remember the arguments we had about it,' Nicole said. There was more. She would not leave because she now felt she was part of a movement fighting for the liberation of her country. Hearing those words, he might have felt that he ought to stay, too, and then he would be rounded up like Miriam.

She changed the subject. 'Now, what will happen to *Valmy*?'

'I'm hoping it will continue. Will you take charge of it if you won't come with me? Gérard and Berthe will help you, but be careful.'

'All right,' Nicole said. She felt no hesitation. These days, she was looking for a challenge.

'Good. There's no need for *Valmy* to go under just because David and I aren't around. It's dangerous, of course, especially after what we said about the round-up. They'll be looking for *Valmy* and for Michelle Laforte even harder now.'

Nicole nodded, remembering the day that *Valmy*'s office had been vandalised by the police, forcing them to move.

'Be careful, Nicole. I want to find you when I come back to Paris! But don't forget I want you to come with me. And perhaps I should stay?'

His direct look into her eyes pleaded with her to change her mind, but she suppressed the temptation. Paris was where she wanted to be. She would love to know that her parents were all right, but they were much safer in London than they would have been in Paris, with their accented French.

'You aren't safe here, Paul. You must go,' she said.

Before he left, Paul cleared out the *Valmy* room in the typewriter shop, impressing on Nicole the need not to leave evidence lying around. Later, he took her to a café to say goodbye.

'I don't know when I'll be back, but my plan is to return to journalism in Paris as soon as this dreadful war is over, so don't think you've seen the last of me. I'll find you somehow, through Denise. I'll want to know all about what mischief you've been getting up to in my absence,' he said.

'Oh, yes. Denise will always know where I am,' Nicole said.

He repeated her parents' address in London, to show her how well he had learned it. Quelling a feeling of panic at losing him, she said that she had to go home. She was afraid that if he knew she wanted him to stay, he would do so and would eventually be arrested or rounded up. She felt confused about why she wanted him to stay and how much she liked him. Was it simply that his presence made her feel safer in the occupation or was there something more?

He took her home, as it was dark by then. He gave her a chaste kiss goodbye and hugged her. They parted near the door to Yvette's block and he turned away. She did the same, but after taking a few paces, she looked back to see Paul watching her. He waved and blew her a kiss. She waved back and watched as he disappeared into the distance. It would be some time before he arrived in England, given his circuitous route, and she had no address for him. She had no idea when, or if, she would see him again and could not help remembering her last farewell to Marcel.

Paul's departure made Nicole even more conscious of how many people she had lost because of the occupation – her parents, Marcel, the Weiss family and now Paul himself. She had stayed in Paris, trying to build a life that was always being torn apart, yet she remained determined on her new course of action.

Yvette was relieved that Nicole had not left Paris with Paul, but she did not like her plan to take charge of *Valmy*.

'Aren't you in enough danger already? I don't want to lose any more friends.'

'I'll be careful, Yvette,' Nicole said. 'I've survived here for over two years without being caught and I know what I'm doing.'

She spoke with more conviction than she felt because the occupation always seemed to be getting worse, but she was determined.

Yvette nodded. 'I hope Paul comes back for you. I don't know when I'll ever see my boyfriend. We send those awful cards to each other now and then, but he seems a long way away these days. We'll be grass widows together, Nicole.'

'Paul is a friend. That's all,' Nicole said.

Yvette smiled, but she said nothing more.

***

Nicole regretted her decision not to accompany Paul. Had she been right to dismiss the chance of fleeing to safety with him? There had been little time to think it through, yet it was too late now. She wondered how he was getting on and pictured his arrival at various points on the long journey to England. He was bound to meet obstacles on the way, but he was capable and resilient.

She was glad that her life allowed little time for reflection. Now that she was the editor of *Valmy*, both Gérard and Berthe looked to her for leadership. Other journalists, frustrated by the day job of keeping in line with the Vichy government and the occupier, supplied material and more students were willing to take *Valmy* onto the streets and into cafés. In the later months of 1942, the growing belief that the Allies would win was leading to more activity against the occupation.

Nicole went back to writing the diary for *Valmy* that she had abandoned after Miriam's arrest. People still liked reading her account of daily life under the occupation as a reflection of their own experience. She aimed to entertain, to cheer her readers and to undermine the occupier. She never stopped fearing another police raid.

Valmy was only one of many underground newspapers and not the most influential, but it played its part in the growing resistance to the occupier. Being increasingly well known made it more vulnerable to discovery and some changes were needed.

'We're part of the Resistance and so I want us to continue what Paul and David and Miriam were doing, even though we've lost them,' Nicole said, meeting Berthe and Gérard in a café early one evening just after Paul's departure.

'We need to sharpen up a bit. Paul was sure that the police are looking harder for us since the July round-up. We need to make some changes to frustrate them. We must never leave anything about *Valmy* in Denise's shop. No piles of the latest issue, no copies of old issues, nothing to identify us in any way. So, no sloppiness. This must be like a military operation,' Nicole said, knowing nothing of such things, but sure of what she was saying.

'Any one of us can still be caught outside with it,' Berthe said.

'We'll have to be extra careful outside as well, but we must protect Denise. She's the one who's there all the time and she'll have to deal with the police if they turn up. We'll meet every week at the same time to agree the next edition, but always in a café. That way, we'll be less likely to arouse suspicion. We'll arrange where to meet as we go along and only use the shop for typing and duplicating once a week. If you need me in between, leave a message with Denise. She's agreed to that,' Nicole said.

'Suits me,' Gérard said and Berthe agreed.

'And we need more people to write for us, so let's think about that. Now, about the next edition…'

Nicole, Gérard and Berthe held regular low-voiced meetings in cafés, never the same one twice and always after Nicole and Berthe had finished work. Gérard was flexible. Without a regular job, he existed on doing things for a variety of people. He was mysterious about his activities outside *Valmy* and Nicole and Berthe knew better than to question him. He moved from one person's flat to another. Nicole always made sure to arrange a next meeting with him as the best way of keeping in touch. Gérard wanted to be hard to find, at least by anyone in authority. Berthe kept her link with *Valmy* a secret known only to Nicole and Gérard, in order not to risk her job.

THREE

DEPARTURE

As an escaped prisoner, now wanted by the Gestapo, Paul dared not use his real name for the permit he needed to travel into the unoccupied zone. Instead, Berthe gave him a blank from the police headquarters, which Nicole used to forge a permit for him. When the train to Toulouse stopped at the border between zones, he held his breath for a moment, remembering the soldier who had disappeared for agonising minutes on his last train journey. He was relieved that this time his papers received no more than a cursory glance.

The train arrived in Toulouse in the late afternoon and Paul left the station to find himself in the warm and sunny September weather of the south. He took a deep breath and felt a release of tension. He had spent less than a year in occupied Paris and now he was in an unoccupied French city. He might have little money, nowhere to live and no job, but he felt safer among the pink brickwork and narrow alleyways, familiar from his brief stay the previous year, than he had during his months in Paris.

Threading his way through the network of streets to the central Place du Capitole, with its grand buildings and arcades, he found the café where Jorge worked – the one person he might know in Toulouse. He had the address of a Jewish organisation that could help him find his feet in Toulouse if Jorge had left the city, but he was relieved to spot a familiar figure balancing a tray with one hand while taking payment with the other.

'Paul! A moment and I'll be with you,' Jorge said with a broad smile, seeing him arrive.

'On the house!' he said, a few moments later, setting a beer down with a flourish. 'I didn't expect to see you again.'

'I had to leave Paris,' Paul said, explaining briefly.

'You can stay here on the floor tonight, maybe longer if you need to. I'm still in the room upstairs.'

'Thanks, I will, if that's all right.' He sipped his beer. 'I'm on my way to London eventually, but a billet here would help and I like Toulouse. I feel like staying here for a while.'

'Many refugees arrived after you left,' Jorge said.

'Yes, from the occupied zone. It looks more crowded now,' Paul said, watching people moving to and from the streets that led from the Place du Capitole.

Jorge's café had no vacancies for staff and Paul began looking for work elsewhere. Early that evening, in the window of a nearby bookshop, he saw a handwritten notice asking for an assistant. He was prepared to take any job that paid him, but he liked the idea of working in a bookshop.

Inside, the shop was narrow but deep and stacked from floor to ceiling with books. Running his eye over the shelves, he recognised names of novelists like Émile Zola and Victor Hugo, but also those of politicians, scientists and philosophers. The books about politics were the most numerous and included some in Italian.

Behind a central counter, talking to a customer, stood a dark, thickset man with a big face, which was rescued from plainness by a genial expression. He seemed to be running the shop alone, at least at that moment. Customers stood or sat around, some leafing through books, others chatting. The atmosphere was relaxed and welcoming.

Paul waited, turning the pages of a book that he had plucked off the shelves, but not concentrating on it. When he saw that the man behind the desk was free, he slipped the book back into its place and went up to him.

'Good afternoon. I'm looking for a job and I see you need an assistant.'

'*Buon giorno.* You must have seen my notice. It's only just gone up. I need someone for three days a week, but how do I know you're any good?' He spoke French with a strong Italian accent.

'I was a journalist in Paris. I love books and you have a fine collection here, especially about politics.'

'Ah, you noticed my special interest! But your accent isn't local. Even a foreigner like me can tell that. What are you doing in Toulouse, young man?'

'I'm Jewish, from Paris, at least recently. I had to leave. It's getting too difficult there. I'm staying with a friend while I sort myself out.'

The bookseller was looking at Paul, summing him up, but then he seemed to come to a decision. He nodded.

'Well, I'll give you a try, from tomorrow morning at eight o'clock sharp, so I can show you round before we open.'

Paul smiled and thanked him. Over the course of the next few days, he learned about the trade from the bookseller, Mario, an Italian anti-fascist in exile. Mario taught Paul about the stock, how to order books, how to use the cash register and to look out for book thieves.

Paul became a regular customer of Jorge's as his café was nearby. It was a good spot from which to watch people and learn what was going on. He stayed with Jorge for no more than a few days and then rented a room from a customer he met, who lived in a large apartment in the city centre.

The bookshop was a meeting place for people who wanted to resist the Nazi presence in France. Paul told Mario that he would like to join the Resistance in Toulouse. Mario advised him to take on a false identity.

'Do you know anyone who can fix the papers for that?' Paul said.

'There's a printer who works with his brother. They produce underground newspapers here and you might have seen one of these.'

Mario handed Paul a leaflet with a headline in bold type urging people to join a demonstration in two days' time against the Nazi occupation and the compliant Vichy government. Paul found the printers' workshop later that day. He had already chosen the name of Jacques Charpentier from a book in the shop. His connection with Mario meant that the printer was willing to help him. Within a few days, Paul had the required false papers.

It might have been easy to find the name Paul Lévy in a list of escaped prisoners, but Jacques Charpentier had never been to prison. He was a local man who had grown up in the town of Villefranche-de-Lauragais near Toulouse. Paul had plucked the name of the town from a map and had spent a day visiting the town in case anyone questioned him about it. Although conscripted in 1939, Jacques Charpentier had survived the Battle of France without injury or capture. Listening to the voices around him, Paul did his best to adopt the strong, local accent for his new identity. He was encouraged when his false papers were checked on one or two occasions by the Toulouse police without any query. His enquiries of Mario about joining the Resistance led him to a man called Gilbert, leader of the first Resistance network to be set up in Toulouse.

'You're not from round here,' was Gilbert's immediate reaction to Paul, even though he had used his new identity to introduce himself.

Paul admitted that he came from Dijon, via Paris, but had assumed a false identity. Gilbert, a Toulousain, understood without needing to know the details. He was used to false identities, but he had to know that Jacques Charpentier could be trusted and questioned him closely about his motives.

'It's not what you might expect,' Gilbert said, having decided that Paul was acceptable. 'You're not in Paris now, you know. You won't be blowing up bridges, collecting information about troop movements or escorting downed

Allied airmen to safety, like the Paris Resistance. Our war is about propaganda.'

'I was doing a kind of propaganda in Paris,' Paul said. He told Gilbert about *Valmy*.

'Good. You can write. That will be a help here.'

Paul attended his first meeting of the Resistance group in a room above Mario's shop. Several young men and women were already there with Gilbert when he arrived after work one afternoon. A few minutes later, a solid young woman entered the room.

'Hello, Agnès. Aha! You are the bringer of gifts,' Gilbert said, with an expansive gesture, as she put a bulging paper bag on the table with a broad smile.

'Help yourselves,' Agnès said.

They all tore into the paper bag, devouring the pastries it contained.

'They're always hungry,' Agnès said to Paul with a laugh, as Gilbert introduced her to Jacques Charpentier.

In the mornings, Agnès worked in a bakery, but her spare time was devoted to the Resistance. She and Paul and the others worked together on preparing leaflets, organising meetings and demonstrations, and she often brought pastries.

Paul was soon writing and distributing flyers and newspapers, in touch with a larger group of trusted people than he would have been in the occupied zone. His job and that of the others in the group was to emphasise how wrong the occupation was, as well as any collaboration with it by local people and by the Vichy government.

At Paul's suggestion, Jorge joined the group. He belonged to a loose network of Spanish refugees in

Toulouse, but he was ready to play a part in the Resistance. His dream was for Spain to be liberated from Franco's rule, so that he could return to his country. Together, he and Paul joined clandestine meetings in Jorge's café as well as Mario's bookshop.

The bookshop also saw the birth of a movement unique in France, stemming from Mario's wish to see a federated Europe. Paul was sympathetic to its aims, but his main goal was to help undermine the Vichy government and the occupation, so that France would be liberated from the Nazis. Thinking ahead about the kind of France that people would want after the liberation could come later, although he enjoyed talking to others in the bookshop. In quieter moments, when minds expanded, people reached for ideals and dreams rather than being absorbed in daily events.

He was not surprised to meet David in the bookshop one day. As a big, southern city outside the occupied zone, Toulouse was continuing to attract Jewish refugees fleeing from the occupation. He did not notice him at first, because David had grown a beard, but when a young man leafing idly through a book looked straight at him, he felt the jolt of recognition.

'David!'

'Paul! You got here in the end.'

'My name is Jacques now,' Paul said in a whisper. 'It's good to see you. When did you get here?'

'I took my mother to stay with relatives and I came on here because I'd heard it was becoming a centre for the Resistance. I've joined the Jewish Army.'

Paul had already joined his resistance group by the time

he heard about the Jewish Army, based in Toulouse, which had been set up in 1941. It aimed to rescue Jews interned by the Nazis and the Vichy government and supported the French Resistance.

Paul told David a little about his life in Toulouse. He did not know all the customers in the shop and did not wish to be overheard, so he arranged to meet David later in Jorge's café where it would be noisy enough for them to talk freely. It was then that he told David about his work for the Resistance. He was glad that his friend had turned up in Toulouse and kept in close contact with him.

***

Relieved as he was to have escaped from Paris, Paul missed Nicole. He had fallen in love with her during his few months in Paris and had been disappointed by her refusal to come with him. They had drawn closer to each other because of the July round-up, but he had held back from telling her of his feelings when she was so troubled by the loss of Miriam and her family. He had not wanted to take advantage of her distress. He had stayed longer in Paris than he would otherwise have done because of her, but the break in at his flat had made up his mind to leave. He was sorry that they were now apart, but it was increasingly clear that Jews were unsafe in occupied France. One day he would return as he had promised and find her.

He sent cards to her signed Jacques, certain that she would guess who had sent them. He wanted her to know he had arrived in Toulouse and was surviving well enough for the present. Despite his false name, he dared not give an address for a reply in case any of the cards fell into the wrong hands and the police came looking for him.

***

As the autumn progressed, Paul became more aware of the growing unpopularity of the Vichy government and the rise in resistance as the public began to take note of its harshness. In September that year, the government had passed a law whereby all men between the ages of eighteen and fifty were liable to labour conscription. Factory workers were rounded up and sent to Germany, which led to strike action.

Paul's resistance group produced leaflets urging young people in Toulouse not to go to Germany, but to evade the draft in any way they could. A labour camp was a prison, with long hours of back-breaking work, little to eat and every chance of being bombed by the Allies. Paul was certain that conditions in the labour camps would be worse now than when he was in prison because the war was biting deeper into people's lives.

In January 1943, a police force, the *milice*, was introduced with the aim of fighting the Resistance and ridding the country of its Jewish population. Paul wrote leaflets from his heart, for distribution where young men gathered, in the stations, cafés and cinemas where they were likely to be rounded up by the *milice* and sent off to labour camps.

At Gilbert's suggestion, the Resistance group held a demonstration against the draft, just after it was announced. A handful of young men and women gathered outside a popular café, just off the Place du Capitole, early one morning, to catch people on the street. The demonstrators were carrying placards and handing out leaflets to customers and people passing by. On a cold, bright morning, Paul longed to be inside the warm café, not outside with his hands and feet frozen. Agnès was standing next to him, pale and miserable-looking.

'I can't do this any longer,' she said after an hour, stamping her feet to keep warm. Her leaflets had nearly all gone, but she barely seemed to be able to hold them in her hands.

'What's the matter?' Paul said, passing a leaflet to a young man entering the café.

'I don't know. My fingers are all numb and I feel peculiar. I must sit down.' Her voice was no more than a whisper.

'Agnès isn't well. I'm taking her inside,' Paul said to Gilbert, who looked surprised, but nodded. Paul shepherded her into the café full of men beginning their day. He found a couple of seats and ordered coffee. He rubbed Agnès' hands, which were indeed frozen.

'I nearly fainted out there. I didn't have any breakfast. It was stupid of me, working in a bakery, but I could only think I had to get here early, so I ran.'

'Are you feeling better now?' Paul asked, as she drank her coffee and chewed on a bread roll that he obtained from a passing waiter.

'Yes. Thanks, Jacques. I was feeling worse and worse, but I didn't want to cause a scene in front of everyone.'

Colour was returning to Agnès' face and her voice was stronger. Leaving the café, they saw their fellow demonstrators had gone. Paul walked her back to the bakery. There had been no sign of the *milice*.

The Resistance group organised another demonstration against the draft, this time outside a cinema in the evening, where a popular film was showing. Paul, Gilbert and a small team leafletted the queue and engaged them in discussion. It all seemed to be going well until the *milice* turned up. Dropping their few remaining leaflets and their placards, the demonstrators ran, scattering in different directions into narrow, dark streets where they would be hard to find.

Agnès made it clear that she liked Paul and wanted more than to work alongside him in the Resistance.

'I already have a girlfriend in Paris,' he told her. It wasn't quite true, but he hoped that it would be one day.

'Yes, Jacques, but not in Toulouse, whereas I am here.'

'Not only do I have a girlfriend in Paris, but I am not staying long in Toulouse. I'm thinking of going to London.'

'Yes, but you're not going today, are you?'

'That's true, but...'

She gave a rich, knowing laugh. 'Are you afraid I shall expect you to marry me? That's not what I'm thinking at all. I want us to have some fun together. Or do you think I'm ugly?'

'Not at all! You're very attractive!' he said, liking her appearance and especially her laugh.

'Then will you come back to my room?'

He did not take much persuading to have what she called fun as long as it was clear there was no future in it. When Agnès assured him that no one where she lived would be curious about him, he accepted her invitation. Being with her did not diminish his feelings for Nicole. It was a pleasure of the moment and a way of forgetting the war, which he knew would soon present further dangers.

FOUR

LONDON

Paul had formed the habit of having lunch every day in Jorge's café. He was sitting on the terrace in the Place du Capitole on Armistice Day in November that year when he saw the arrival of Nazis. He swallowed, stopped eating and his body tensed at the unexpected sight. There was no mistaking the marching columns filling the enormous square, while a band played deafening military music. The feeling of greater safety that he had acquired from living in Toulouse vanished in an instant. Seeing the grey-green uniforms and the hated swastikas on their flags, so familiar from his imprisonment and his time in Paris, reminded him that he was an escaped prisoner and belonged to a hated race.

Jorge came up and stood beside him for a moment. 'Look who's here. The uninvited guest. Now no one is safe.' 'I wish I'd known. I needn't have left Paris,' Paul said.

He had been pleased when the Allies had invaded North Africa earlier in the month. He had begun to believe that they would win the war and that France would be a free country again, even though no one had any idea when that would happen. He had felt safer in Toulouse than in Paris and the idea of London had receded. Now, the enemy had overrun France to forestall an Allied invasion from the south and everything had changed.

He finished his meal quickly, hardly tasting it, and returned to the bookshop, where he spent the afternoon talking to customers about the new arrivals. He feared round-ups of Jews as had happened in Paris, but he quelled an impulse to flee and instead decided to wait and see what happened. It would take them time to get a grip on Toulouse.

***

Gilbert was breathing heavily when he arrived at a hastily convened meeting of the Resistance group after the invasion of Toulouse.

'Things are different now,' he said to those gathered in the room above the bookshop, their most usual meeting place. 'With them in control, we're not doing propaganda anymore. It's the hard stuff now. We need guns and explosives. Without a French army in France, we'll be relying on the wretched British for equipment. Their planes will drop supplies by parachute. At least, that's the plan.'

As a former soldier, for however short a time, Paul knew something about weapons and fighting a real battle, but others in the group, including Agnès, had done little more than write and distribute leaflets and take part in demonstrations. Paul saw a difficult time ahead. Some members of the group were eager to hear what Gilbert was saying, but others seemed nervous.

After the meeting, Gilbert received a wireless message from the regional head of the Resistance in the Toulouse area and led a small team to secure airborne supplies. In a truck lent by a supporter, they drove to a field outside the city after dark. They had torches, but once they separated for the search, it was hard finding each other, let alone the supplies, on a cloudy December night. When it began to rain heavily, Paul did his best to stay with Agnès, remembering the incident outside the café and trying to help her keep warm. The group waited in vain for hours, long past the expected time, but bad weather had prevented the arrival of the plane. Discouraged and wet, they trudged back to the centre of Toulouse in the early hours of the morning.

Another wireless message told Gilbert to try again the following night. Borrowing the truck again, the Resistance group were in place as ordered. There was no rain, but it was still cloudy and although they heard the plane arrive, it was too dark to see where the supplies were dropped. Their torches were not bright enough and they did not want to attract attention. Precious time was wasted searching through fields until, at last, when it was becoming dangerously light, they stumbled over first one and then more heavy bags of equipment.

'Right. We've got the stuff. Now, back to the truck and we're off,' Gilbert said with relief, as he shouldered one of the bags.

They were not sure that they had found everything, but they dared not look further as it was almost dawn and they returned to where they had left the truck. They drove back into Toulouse with their cargo without being caught. The guns and explosives that they had secured kept them well supplied for some months as they became an active Resistance group.

***

In February 1943, all young men eligible for military service were required to go to Germany to work. Paul fell outside the group called up, as Jacques Charpentier had served in the army already, but the new order meant that all young men were more likely to be arrested on the street and questioned.

Paul did not evade the *milice* for long. He was stopped on the street and questioned one day. Fortunately, he was carrying nothing incriminating and aroused no suspicion that he might be Jewish. The police scrutinised his papers, but they let Jacques Charpentier go. That incident made Paul feel certain that it would be unwise to stay in Toulouse. He was likely to be picked up again and could be questioned more closely another time.

He could almost feel a net closing around him. With the call-up on top of the invasion, Toulouse now seemed much less safe. Round-ups could take place as they had in Paris and his false identity might be penetrated. He began to long for an escape and his thoughts turned back to his original plan to go to London. He had saved money for the journey in his few months of working for Mario because he had been almost certain that he would need to leave France. He was sure now that he would feel safer on the move.

Other young men were going to the *maquis* – the rank and file of the secret army that was growing in France and which took its name from the scrub, the uncultivated French countryside. Many were fleeing there to avoid being sent to Germany. Paul had heard that the chief of the Free French Forces in Toulouse and the surrounding department of the Haute Garonne commanded a *maquis* force of a thousand men. Yet he felt that he was too urban at heart for the *maquis*. London, although much further away, had the greater appeal. With his brother in Dijon to give their parents any help they needed, he felt free to go where he wanted.

'Why don't you come to London with me?' he said to David one day after he had decided what to do. 'I'm going to cross the Pyrenees and get rides to Lisbon. I've done it before the other way and so I know the route.'

'No. I don't want to leave Toulouse, even now they're here,' David said without hesitation. 'I don't speak any English and I don't want to risk the journey across Spain. I'm going to stay here with the Jewish Army.'

Paul would be travelling on his own, but he was not deterred. He sent a card from Jacques to Nicole to say that he was leaving Toulouse. He missed her and thought of her a lot, sometimes wondering if he had made a mistake in holding back from her. There was no point in dwelling on it, but had he missed the chance of a lifetime? He had been attracted to her from the start, not simply because of the warmth of her smile and the sparkle in her eyes, but because of her courage and sense of purpose. He had wanted to protect her, but he had been able to do nothing more than comfort her in her distress and he felt now that he had failed her, just as she felt she had failed Miriam.

In March 1943, he counted his savings and said goodbye to Mario in the bookshop, to Gilbert and the Resistance group, including Agnès, to Jorge and to David. Through contacts he had made in the Jewish Army through David, he crossed the Pyrenees with a guide. The journey was hazardous in the cold and ice of late winter, but he had done it before the other way and would not let it defeat him. Descending into Spain, he followed in reverse the route he had taken in late 1941, hitchhiking on the main roads and avoiding any military or official-looking vehicles. He had a narrow escape in Valladolid when he was stopped by the police. He was afraid of being imprisoned, but he spoke enough Spanish to persuade them that he was on his way to Lisbon and would not be staying in Spain and, fortunately, they let him go. He was relieved to cross the border into neutral Portugal without any further incident.

In Lisbon, he secured a place on a British merchant ship travelling in convoy. They were attacked in the Bay of Biscay by a Nazi warship, but the military escort attached to the merchant convoy drove it off and they arrived safely in Southampton.

It was springtime when he arrived in London again, some eighteen months after leaving. He had one or two contacts in the French community there, especially Sylvie, who had been so helpful to him before. He telephoned her from a booth at Waterloo Station on leaving the train. She was fortunately at home and she remembered him straightaway, inviting him to come and stay with her and her husband, Thierry.

After his exacting journey from Toulouse, Paul was grateful for the invitation. He remembered the way there and was soon in Notting Hill. He found Sylvie at home and free to spend an hour talking to him about wartime London and listening to stories about his travels since she had last seen him. Paul told her what little he knew about Stéphane and Philippe, whom he had last seen on the road outside Lisbon and not heard from since.

Sylvie passed him the newspaper lying on the coffee table in the sitting room.

'As you're a journalist, have a look at this. It's a daily newspaper for the French community in London. I know the editor and if you want work in London, he might be able to help.'

The newspaper was simply called *France*. It was written in French and was a single folded sheet more professional-looking than *Valmy*. Paul glanced at articles and pictures about the war, mainly events in France and England of interest to the French in London.

'That would suit me well,' he said, thanking Sylvie. 'I need a job and I could write about life in France now.'

Sylvie telephoned the editor and reported the next day that Paul would be a welcome visitor. At the newspaper's office, Paul's experience of the occupation of France, combined with his professional background, secured him a job. The pay was poor, but when Sylvie and Thierry offered him a room for a low rent, he decided that he could manage.

He spent his spare time wandering the streets of central London, trying to get to know the West End and the City as he had begun to do before. The Blitz was long over, but bombsites remained and London was clearly much more damaged than Paris.

He wrote a letter to Nicole's parents, introducing himself and offering news of her. Nicole's mother replied quickly, inviting him to come to a place called Queensbury in north London and giving him a phone number and a date. Phoning from Sylvie's house, he accepted the invitation.

After a long, noisy journey on a tube train, Paul emerged from the underground at Queensbury on the day in question. He asked for directions and walked along streets made up of rows of little houses, quite unlike anything in Paris. He was carrying a bag of apples bought from a barrow outside the underground station. Much food in England was rationed and he knew that anything would be a welcome addition to the household.

He found the house easily enough and knocked on the door. He had studied English at school and had a working knowledge of the language, with the help of his first trip to London. The door opened and a middle-aged woman greeted him. She was an older version of Nicole and she smiled warmly.

'Hello, Paul. How good of you to come all this way. I am Nicole's mother, Anne. Come and meet the family.'

Paul followed Anne into a small sitting room with a curved window. She introduced him to Jessica, the friendly and vivacious wife of Nicole's brother, Ralph, who was away in the RAF. Their two little daughters stopped a game they were playing to stare at him. Nicole's father, Jeffrey, who was working for the RAF as a translator, arrived shortly afterwards. With everyone delighted to meet a stranger from France, Paul felt almost overwhelmed. Being with them for the evening felt so comfortable and safe, after the privations of his war, that it was scarcely believable. Their lives had not been entirely peaceful as a nearby bomb during the Blitz had shattered the windows of Jessie's house, but no one in the family had been hurt.

'Of course, you want news of Nicole, but it is some months out of date,' Paul said straightaway. He explained that he had not brought a letter in case of being arrested and searched at any point on his long journey.

They sat down together before the meal and Paul told them everything he knew. There was Nicole's journey back from Bordeaux, the death of Marcel, her life with Miriam and the Weiss family and the dreadful round-up, her job and her work for *Valmy*. Her parents had received one or two letters from her, but they were touchingly grateful to meet someone who knew her and had seen her fairly recently. Anne told Paul the story of last seeing Nicole on the quayside in Bordeaux in 1940.

'But you abandoned her in Paris?' Jeffrey asked.

Nicole had warned him that her father could be blunt, but Paul was still taken aback by the accusation.

'No, I wanted her to come with me, but she wouldn't,' he said.

'But why not? That would have been the perfect escape.' Anne was looking perturbed.

Paul struggled to remember Nicole's exact words. 'She misses you, but she doesn't want to give up on being French. She has a job and a home with Yvette and she wants to continue with *Valmy*. She believes the Nazis will lose the war and that you will be able to come back to Paris and, of course, she sends her love.'

He did not want to worry her parents, so did not add that since the round-up of Miriam and her family, Nicole had been taking more risks with work for the Resistance. Jeffrey and Anne had to accept what Paul said, but they wished that their daughter had made a different decision.

'It all goes back to choosing French nationality,' Jeffrey said. 'We wanted her to choose British. We argued and she wouldn't listen to my advice.'

'Was it our fault, bringing her up in a foreign country?' Anne said and Jeffrey disagreed.

Conversation, in a mixture of English and French, moved on to more general questions about life in London and the progress of the war. For the evening meal, Jessica produced what she called a Woolton pie.

'It's a recipe from the Ministry of Food. I've turned our garden into a vegetable patch and I'm growing potatoes, carrots, broad beans, runner beans and onions,' she said, putting it down on the table with a flourish.

Before the war, Paul might have been less enthusiastic about the vegetable pie, although it did not contain swede, but after a year of prison food and then years of being hungry in France, he praised it wholeheartedly. He even accepted the second helping that Jessica urged on him. An apple crumble with substitute cream followed. Jeffrey opened a bottle of wine, which he had been saving for the end of the war.

'Your news of Nicole is certainly worth celebrating, young man,' he said, as if trying to atone for his earlier criticism.

Paul left with an invitation to return, which he welcomed, and he saw the family several times during his stay in London.

***

After a year of working for the newspaper *France*, Paul began to feel restless. He was safe from persecution in London, but he had, by then, said everything he wanted to say about the Nazi occupation of his country and he was looking to the future. In the spring of 1944, he joined the Free French Forces in London. He had begun to hear rumours of a big push that would take place in the summer and he wanted to be part of it.

By then, he had not seen Nicole for eighteen months. He still thought of her often, wishing that she had accompanied him to England and wondered sometimes if he should have stayed in Paris with her. Was he a coward to have fled the Nazi occupation once it began to hunt him down? Should he have stayed in Paris with the woman he wanted, rather than fleeing as he had done? Jeffrey's accusation that he had abandoned her was unfair, but it still rankled.

Was Nicole taking risks that would put her in danger? Cautious Yvette would try to put a brake on her, so would Denise, who was a sensible woman. He could only hope that Nicole was not in some danger, arrested by the Gestapo or the *milice* for her resistance activity. *Valmy* had survived for a long time in the occupation and its luck could run out.

He looked forward to returning to France, to helping to free his country, and he wanted to find Nicole. As the spring of 1944 turned to summer, he began to be impatient to leave London, city of refuge, which had welcomed him and yet was not his home.

FIVE

PURSUIT

Nicole was delighted to hear the news of the Allied landing in North Africa one morning on the wireless and set off for her job at the art school with raised spirits, despite a leaden November sky. An Allied victory was looking more likely, yet the war was by no means over. When the Nazis invaded the unoccupied zone later that month, she could only hope that Paul was by now safely outside France. However, she realised with a sinking heart that he was still in Toulouse when she received one of the cards from Jacques that he had been sending to her. Yet the card offered some reassurance that he was all right.

The production of *Valmy* continued without interruption until one day in December when Nicole arrived at the typewriter shop after work to find it closed. This was unusual. Denise was always there during her opening hours. As she stood uncertainly outside, a man from a neighbouring shop came up to her.

'She had to close. She's been arrested,' he said.

Nicole was aghast. 'When?'

'About an hour ago. She asked me to look out for you. Well, she said a customer was coming. I suppose she meant you.'

'She did. Were they local police?' Nicole said, wondering if the Gestapo had arrested Denise.

'Yes, the *flics*.'

In that case, they had probably come from the nearest police station. Nicole knew where it was. Thanking the neighbour, she set off, determined to ensure Denise's release. If necessary, she would take her place.

'I have come about Denise Dupont, who was brought in for questioning,' she said, boldly, to the policeman on duty when she arrived. He told her to wait. She found a seat and watched comings and goings impatiently for about a quarter of an hour. She spoke to the policeman a second time, more insistently. Ten minutes later, a different policeman came out to speak to her.

'I've come to vouch for Denise Dupont. I was told that she's been arrested,' Nicole said.

He interrupted her, asking who she was. He was a weary-looking middle-aged man and she sensed that he was giving her a chance to be persuasive.

'I'm one of her customers. She has done nothing wrong. Please release her.'

'*Madame*, she is suspected of supporting the Resistance,' the policeman said.

'Oh, that's impossible. Look, it's a typewriter shop. It doesn't make enough money for her to live on, so she's allowing people to use her duplicator. Of course, it's printing leaflets and notices, but only to help other businesses. She's not doing anything wrong at all. I'm one of her customers. Now, why have you arrested her?'

She spoke with assurance, knowing that they had no evidence against Denise. She and the others had left nothing in their room at her shop.

'She's accused of printing the underground rag called *Valmy*.'

Nicole sounded incredulous. 'Underground? Mme Dupont would never do anything like that. She's a respectable, law-abiding woman – a local businesswoman trying to make ends meet in these difficult times.' She smiled at the policeman. He looked as if he understood what she meant.

'Very well, *mam'selle*. If you can vouch for her, I'll let her go, as we need the space. But we have her name and if there's any further trouble, she'll be charged.'

He disappeared through the door behind the reception desk and returned with Denise, who was immensely relieved to see Nicole.

'I told them I'd done nothing wrong. I showed them the duplicator. I said I had to make a living, so I was letting people use it,' she said as they left the station.

'Who do you think reported you to the police?' Nicole asked.

'I have no idea, but it was somebody with a grudge and sharp eyes.'

'Somebody who was right about what we're doing. Denise, you're in danger now. We'll have to find somewhere else,' Nicole said.

'Nonsense! I won't let you. I'm not afraid of them.'

'Well, you should be afraid. What if they come again when we're printing? They'll arrest you along with me. No, we'll have to find somewhere else.'

Nicole was not only protecting Denise, but everyone involved. She, Gérard and Berthe racked their brains and contacted everyone they knew who might be able to help. The Paris Resistance was growing in strength by the end of 1942 and Gérard knew a printing business whose owner, Antoine, was sympathetic and would print *Valmy* free of charge. Antoine's premises were in a small building that housed several businesses off the Rue Daguerre, not far from Denise's shop. He was also prepared to let the *Valmy* group have a certain amount of ink and paper, when it was available. Hearing this, Nicole made the change. *Valmy* missed only one issue.

***

The winter of 1943 was gruelling and Nicole was freezing, although she was grateful for the clothes that she had rescued two years previously. At home, Jacqueline, Yvette and Nicole lived in the kitchen most of the time, where the stove provided some warmth. They took hot-water bottles to bed and were reluctant to get up in the morning.

When the siege of Stalingrad ended with a Soviet victory over the Nazis in February 1943, *Valmy* and other underground papers welcomed the news. The Resistance and the Gaullists were heartened, but a blow fell in that same month with the Vichy government order that all men aged between eighteen and fifty and women aged between twenty-one and thirty-five must go and work in Germany for two years.

'I can't do this,' Yvette said to Nicole when she heard the news. 'I won't work for them when they're responsible for my father's death. I'll see if I can get some sort of exemption, being a nurse. But what about you, Nicole?'

'From what I've heard, women are not being called up. It will only be men,' Nicole said.

'How do you know?'

'I don't know for certain. It's just what I've heard.'

Nicole would not say that she had heard from Berthe that women would probably not be called up. She never mentioned her to anyone except Gérard. It turned out that Berthe was right and Yvette and Nicole were spared being sent to Germany.

She hoped that Paul would leave France. It was no country for Jewish people now and he might not have survived being sent to Germany. When a card from Toulouse told her that Jacques was leaving, she knew that Paul was on his way to Spain and then London. Dangerous as the journey might be, she felt relieved.

The Allied bombing of factories in the suburbs of Paris raised hopes of Allied landings soon, but they only led to the introduction of a blackout in the spring. Even though the evenings were growing lighter, the blackout made Paris seem darker and more alien at night than usual. Nicole, Yvette and Jacqueline lived in a bubble of light in their flat, feeling more imprisoned by the blackout and even worse during increasingly frequent power shortages when they had to resort to candles or oil lamps. Yvette's hospital hours meant that she often had to come home in the dark, feeling her way and fearful of attack.

Antoine had the latest in printing machines. It made life easier that Nicole, Gérard and Berthe no longer had to wrestle with Napoleon or type onto skins and duplicate *Valmy*. They had more time to concentrate on gathering news and writing.

Nicole soon discovered that Antoine was not personable. He was always busy when she took in the copy for typesetting and did not welcome interruption, but he did exactly as he had promised and the only delays with the print run were because of a shortage of supplies. The day after he received the finished copy, stacks of *Valmy* were ready for distribution unless there was a paper crisis. The other advantage was that he was fearless about the danger he was putting himself in by printing an underground news-sheet. The group took him the occasional bottle of wine or pack of cigarettes.

At the art school, Nicole was punctual and attentive, doing her best to turn in work on time and maintain her reputation for a high standard. *Valmy* could sometimes be pressing, but it was important not to skimp on her job. She made a point of getting along with Sandrine. After almost three years, she was well known and well regarded at the art school, but Serge was a continuing pest. She hated doing any work for him, but could not always avoid it. One morning he leaned over her desk, a heavy hand on her shoulder. She wriggled out from his clasp.

'Come on, meet me for a lunchtime drink,' he said as he often did.

Nicole sighed. 'Stop asking me that. I haven't got time. You are interrupting my work.'

She spoke more brusquely than usual and this time he seemed to believe her. His smile vanished and his eyes glittered coldly.

'You don't know what you're missing, frigid cow,' he said, pulling the last page of his lecture notes, which she had just finished, out of her typewriter and walking away.

'You've seen him off. Well done.' Sandrine leaned over from her desk nearby, with a smile.

'I just hope I haven't made an enemy,' Nicole said, with a shrug.

'You might have done. Watch him, though. The word is that he's a *collabo*.'

'I know. I'll look out for myself, don't worry.'

After the incident with Denise and the police and then with the unwelcome news in the spring of 1943 of the Gestapo assuming control in Paris, Nicole was doubly careful about the need for secrecy. She had lived with the fear of discovery for so long that it was almost part of her existence and vigilance was second nature. Yet without Paul's reassuring presence and after Denise's encounter with the police, she felt more vulnerable. The person who had reported Denise might be gathering more evidence or someone else might be trying to destroy *Valmy*.

Nicole kept an eye on the newspapers, skimming through them with *Valmy* in mind when she could. Waiting for Gérard and Berthe in a café late one afternoon, she opened the copy of *La Presse Parisienne* that was available for customers. Her attention was drawn to a short piece condemning *Valmy* for encouraging resistance and undermining the government. It included a picture of the latest edition and encouraged readers to find and report those behind the underground paper. It mentioned Michelle Laforte. She showed it to Gérard and Berthe when they arrived.

'Good. We're making an impact,' Gérard said.

'It makes me nervous,' Nicole said.

'They don't know anything. Someone at *La Presse Parisienne* has seen a copy of *Valmy*, that's all,' Berthe said. 'Otherwise, they would have done an *exposé* or reported us to the police.'

The next issue of *Valmy* came out on time with no reference to the article in *La Presse Parisienne*. Nicole had decided that it was best ignored. She was hoping that no more would be said, even though she appreciated Gérard's view that they were making an impact.

A few weeks later, the three of them were in another café, discussing the next edition of *Valmy*, when Gérard handed Nicole a copy of *La Presse Parisienne* folded to show a photo. 'Have you seen this?'

Nicole glanced at the newspaper, which she had not yet seen that day. Above a clear picture of her was a headline asking who she was and whether she was Michelle Laforte, journalist for the underground newspaper, *Valmy*. Worst of all, she was carrying copies of *Valmy* – the first three letters of the name clearly visible. She also had Kim on a lead.

Carrying a stack of copies of *Valmy* gave her away. One copy could have meant she was simply a reader, but a pile of them suggested she was at least distributing it. The presence of Kim did not help when few people now had dogs in Paris. It was not clear where or when the photo had been taken, but Nicole was in no doubt about it.

'Once, when I was taking copies to a list of cafés that you'd given me, Gérard, someone took a picture of me and I realised too late that I was displaying *Valmy*'s name. This must be the picture. Well, I can't ask *La Presse Parisienne* for their source, but can I hold on to this?' she said, folding the newspaper to hide the picture and slipping it into her bag.

Gérard nodded. He was looking serious. 'You must lie low for a while.'

Nicole did not let Gérard see how perturbed she was, but she spent the rest of the day wondering what to do. That evening, she showed the photo to Yvette.

'Why would anyone take your picture?' Yvette asked.

'I don't know why the man took it in the first place, but it shows someone behind *Valmy* and there's been speculation in the press about that. Why the picture is surfacing all this time later, I can't imagine. It must be two years old.'

'*Valmy*'s better known now. Maybe someone was going through old prints and came across it. Take precautions, Nicole.'

'Gérard said pretty much the same thing. I'm much more careful about *Valmy* these days. We all are.'

'People might be looking out for a young woman with a dog now. It would only take one person to link you with the picture and report you. You must stop taking Kim for walks. *Maman* and I will do it. She's taken to him and I've often caught her giving him a treat.'

Nicole was touched by her friend's concern. 'I love walks with Kim, but you're right. And I'll cut my hair. It's grown anyway as I don't have it cut anymore, but I'm still wearing it in the style of that photo.'

'I can do that now. You know my mother does mine and I do hers, to save money. I can't bear to think of you being caught. I wish you'd give up *Valmy*.'

'All right, go ahead, if you're volunteering to be my hairdresser. I'll disguise myself with an urchin cut, but I won't give up *Valmy*.'

Yvette opened a kitchen drawer, took out a large pair of scissors and set to work, draping a towel over Nicole's shoulders for protection. Nicole sat still, listening to decisive snips and watching her hair fall. Before long, the floor was scattered with thick hanks and Yvette was handing her a mirror.

'You look *chic*! And nothing like the photo,' she said.

'Thanks, Yvette, that's perfect. If you ever give up nursing, you'll know what to do instead.' Nicole was standing up, admiring the result.

'No walks with Kim, just in case.' Yvette's voice was stern.

'All right. At least for a while, until people forget the photo.'

Nicole followed Yvette's advice about Kim. She felt that she was treating him badly and he seemed puzzled. Jacqueline worked in the mornings for a shop that altered and mended clothes, but her afternoons were free and she willingly took over the walking duties. She took Kim to a small park nearby, where dog walkers congregated. She enjoyed talking to people she met about the pleasures and problems of having a dog in the occupation.

***

One evening, Nicole worked late in Denise's shop to finish her weekly diary. Even though *Valmy* was not printed there anymore, it was a convenient place to work as they now had no office and Antoine's print shop was nearby. She had kept a key at Denise's suggestion and she was so absorbed in writing that evening that she forgot the time. She was not in danger of missing the curfew, but it was dark when she left the office and the blackout made it worse. She had not ridden the bicycle that day and she took the metro home.

Leaving the metro at Pont de l'Alma, she felt unnerved by walking alone in the dark even along the Quai Branly – a familiar area. The streets were black, not even lit with the dim blue lamps that had preceded the blackout. Windows were curtained. It was quiet, with few people around. She was nearly at the *passerelle* where she would cross the Seine, when she heard booted feet behind her. The sound of boots or shoes was always louder with so few cars on the road.

A wolf-whistle reached her and she glanced around to see a cluster of Nazi soldiers. They had obviously been drinking. She ignored them and pressed on, but they gained on her, calling more loudly. With no one else around, she was afraid.

She doubled her pace, but they did the same. A hand reached out and grabbed her arm. She turned around and found herself staring into the face of a drunken soldier. She shook off the hand and hurried on, but he grabbed her again. She was saved from a struggle or worse when a loud German voice broke into the scene, roaring at the men. They scattered instantly. With a swift '*Merci*' directed at the boots of the owner of the loud voice, she fled, running across the *passerelle* into her old street and up the steps without a backwards look, resolving never to be out alone in the dark again.

She wrote about her experience with the soldiers in her *Valmy* diary, adding news of a woman beaten by a drunken soldier for refusing his advances and another woman raped when she accepted a lift in a Nazi car. Women were vulnerable under the occupation. The days when the soldiers had seemed correct in their manners were long over. These days, they were either almost too young or too old and seemed less disciplined. They were to be feared.

PART SIX

ONE

REVENGE

The photo in *La Presse Parisienne* made Nicole even more watchful, never knowing when she left home whether she would return that night. She acquired certain habits, pausing at street corners to look behind her. If she entered a café or a restaurant, she would survey the scene before sitting down. She would notice who was leaving a metro carriage with her.

Vichy government supporters continued to denounce to the authorities anyone they suspected of resistance. Life was becoming harder. Harsh reprisals, imprisonment and execution were increasing. Air raids over Paris became more numerous in 1943 and frequent air-raid warnings sounded. Every day, Nicole wondered how much longer the occupation would last and how much more of it she could stand.

Gérard was already there when she arrived in a café one afternoon to discuss the next issue of *Valmy*. 'Someone wants to see you. The British want you to help them,' he said as she sat down.

More groups were not only publicising the wrongful nature of the occupation, but also passing information to the British, helping British airmen brought down by air battles, as Nicole had done, and trying to undermine Nazi troop movements and supply lines.

'I've been expecting this,' Nicole said. She had been aware for some time that the British had agents in Paris. She had even heard, but did not say so, that a group of British agents met in a certain café, against all their rules. They were lonely in Paris and could not resist the desire for company of their own kind.

'They need people who speak both French and English as well as you do,' Gérard said.

Nicole nodded. 'I'll help where I can.'

She met one of the British agents through Gérard after that conversation. She began to act as an occasional interpreter and an escort for them, and she put them in touch with British people in Paris who might be of help. She was firm about how much she would do for them. She needed her job and her loyalty to *Valmy* was important. Her critical view of French government under the occupier did not extend to regrets about her decision to choose French nationality. She loved her country even though it had fallen on hard times and she believed fiercely that the Vichy government would be defeated and that a better France would arise from the occupation.

***

Some new blow was always landing on Nicole. She came home from working on *Valmy* one evening in the spring, not to the usual eager greeting from Kim, the jumping up and the wagging tail, but to an altogether different dog. He was lying down in the kitchen, whimpering in obvious pain. Jacqueline, in a state of some distress, was fluttering around him, not sure what to do.

'I let him off the lead in the park, as I usually do. He ran off and I was chatting to someone for a few minutes. When I looked round, I couldn't see him at first, but then I noticed a man feeding him something. I didn't think much of it at the time. I put him on the lead and we set off for home. He was all right at first, but then he started dragging behind me. He never does that.'

Nicole was horrified. 'You mean he's been poisoned?'

'It looks like it. By the time we got home, he could barely walk and so I carried him. He was in obvious pain. Of course, it could have been an accident, but…'

'But you don't think so. If it was deliberate, why would anyone do such a thing?'

'I don't know. Some crazy person full of hate,' Jacqueline said. 'Or someone who thinks dogs are eating meat that should be kept for people.'

'No one would like what Kim eats,' Nicole said, thinking of the entrails on which she fed her dog.

'No, but they might imagine he's being fed on steak!'

Food was becoming scarcer as the war ground on and there were now three days in the week without meat. Nicole looked at Kim, her companion throughout the occupation, and was afraid that he might die. He was nine years old and had suffered the occasional thorn in his foot and had once been bitten by another dog, but he had not been ill before. She had never seen him look so lifeless. Close to tears, she picked him up and took him to the bed that she had constructed for him from cardboard and old blankets. He lay there, hardly moving. She prepared his dinner, but he refused it.

They heard a key in the door. 'Here's Yvette. A nurse will know what to do,' Jacqueline said.

On Yvette's advice, Nicole wrapped Kim in a towel and, using a spoon, attempted to give him a strong dose from a jar of mustard that Jacqueline had in the cupboard. She stroked his throat to cause him to swallow. A few minutes later, he vomited. He seemed a little better after that, although still listless.

Over the next few days, he was able to take a little food and he became more alert. It was fortunate that Yvette was on nights that week and able to be with Kim in the mornings when Nicole and Jacqueline were out at work. Jacqueline promised not to let Kim off the lead again. It was a pity, because he loved a run in the park, chasing around with other dogs, but there was no choice. He recovered slowly, getting a little better every day, and Nicole was relieved to see his appetite return.

***

One summer morning, Sandrine came and stood by Nicole's desk.

'Serge has been saying that he suspects you of being the woman who writes for that underground paper that people have been talking about,' she said, without preamble.

Nicole, preparing to start work, froze and stared wordlessly at Sandrine.

'I don't want to know whether you are or not. It's up to you what you get up to outside work,' Sandrine said. 'I don't want to get involved. I've got my family to think of. I'm just warning you that he could inform on you. He's that kind of rat. Be careful, Nicole.'

'Thanks for the warning, Sandrine. Maybe I'll think of something to say about him, if he's just trying to get me into trouble.'

Nicole spoke lightly to persuade Sandrine that Serge was being unpleasant for no good reason. She had never taken anyone at the art school into her confidence about *Valmy*, but Serge could have recognised her from the photo in *La Presse Parisienne*. Later that day, she told Gérard and Berthe about Sandrine's warning. She would be extra alert, but she would wait and see what happened.

Valmy was becoming known in Paris and these days there was no shortage of students and other people ready to contribute copy or to distribute it. Gérard had set up a system involving a post-office box for people to send copy to, the number being distributed only by word of mouth. A sympathetic postal worker ensured that Gérard received the post for that box.

When Sandrine came over to her desk one afternoon, not long after the conversation about Serge's suspicions, Nicole felt a flicker of alarm.

'The police were here at lunchtime looking for you, Nicole. You were out, but I saw them talking to Serge. Then they came over and questioned me.'

'What did they want?'

'They had a copy of that news-sheet, *Valmy*. They had your name, from Serge no doubt, and wanted to question you about someone called Michelle something. They asked for your home address.'

'Did you give it to them?'

'I gave them the old address, where you used to live with the Jewish family.'

Nicole breathed a sigh of relief. 'Thank you so much, Sandrine. No one there knows where I am, so the police will have a wasted visit if they go looking for me there. But I can't stay here now. It's too risky. They'll come back here looking for me. I'm sorry, because you're going to have to replace me, but I must go now.'

'Yes, of course. You don't want the police to find you here and the college won't like them nosing around. Don't tell me anything, because when they come back, I don't want to know anything. I'll get a typist from the agency to replace you, but I'm sorry to see you go. You've been so good at your job.'

Sandrine was looking over her shoulder, as if afraid that the police might turn up there and then. Nicole put on her coat, picked up her bag and said goodbye, slipping out of the door, down the steps of the art school and into the street outside without a backwards look. She had been paid in cash as usual the day before and so would only lose the pay for a morning's work. She would not have a reference, but that could not be helped.

Walking fast towards the metro station, she wondered where to go. Yvette was at work and Jacqueline probably out with Kim, who had recovered from the poisoning and was back on his feet again. She would go and see Denise, who was resourceful and would help her. She arrived to find Denise at her counter, but with no customers. She explained what had happened.

'You've had a narrow escape. Let me make some coffee,' Denise said.

Nicole nodded. 'I'm glad to have got away from Serge. He's bad news and I'll never have anything to do with him again. I'm sorry to leave Sandrine, who's been so loyal and helpful, but it won't be hard to find another job. Typists are always in demand.'

Once again, Nicole silently thanked her father for his insistence on her learning such useful skills as shorthand and typing. She gave Denise a cigarette and they both lit up.

'Nicole, are you really thinking of getting another job, just like that?' Denise said.

'Yes, why not? Typing will stand me in good stead until after the occupation. Then I'll find a place at an art school, one without Serge.'

Nicole did not stop to think what it would be like if the Allies lost the war. By the middle of 1943, she, like many people, believed that an Allied victory was only a question of time. She began to feel better despite the setback of losing her job, but she sat up at Denise's next words.

'You can't just get any job. If the police or the Gestapo put out a wanted poster, someone will give you away. You need to work for someone in the know, in the Resistance or sympathetic to it, at least.'

'You're right. How stupid of me,' Nicole said.

'You need time to think it through, that's all. I'll ask around – discreetly, of course.'

That evening, hearing Nicole's news, Yvette was worried. 'You're taking too many risks, Nicole. Losing your job is a chance to do something else. Give up *Valmy* and find something that isn't going to land you in prison.'

'I can't do that, Yvette. It's not just the news-sheet. There are other things, too.'

Nicole had told Yvette about her work for the Resistance beyond the news-sheet, despite having been drilled in the need for secrecy. She needed to be able to talk freely to someone and Yvette was her oldest available friend now.

'I know, but I'm frightened for you. People disappear these days,' Yvette said.

'Don't we know it? Let's not forget Miriam. It's partly because of what happened to her that I'm doing this.'

'I know. I don't stick my neck out. You're brave, Nicole, and I admire you, but you could be arrested. You were nearly caught at the art school and if those police yesterday had found you, they would have locked you up and we wouldn't have known where you are. I don't want to lose another friend. I suppose I want a quiet life.'

At their next meeting, Nicole told Gérard and Berthe about the loss of her job and that she was looking for work.

'Why not go to the café where Paul used to work and ask around? Maybe start by doing odd bits of typing here and there and build up from that. You could say you're a friend of his. We distribute *Valmy* there, so people might help you,' Berthe said.

Nicole thought that a good idea. The following morning, she went to Paul's café to see if she could pick up some work. Paul had liked the people there and so it seemed a good place to start, if she chose the right time of day. The writers and thinkers who frequented the café might not be early-morning people.

Outside the café, in the Place Saint-Germain-des-Prés, tables were full when she arrived, but she found a seat in the spacious interior. The café was grander than those she was used to. She took a newspaper to read with her coffee, but she had barely sat down when she was hailed by a couple of women she had met through Paul – the kind of women she could talk frankly to about the trials of the occupation, always being careful not to say anything that might compromise others, but without fearing informers. She passed a pleasant hour with them.

'I'm looking for work as a secretary or typist,' she said when they asked for her news.

'There's a noticeboard here where you can advertise. Just ask for a card at the counter,' one of the women said. 'Lots of people keep an eye on that noticeboard. They're the right sort of people, of course.' She seemed to understand Nicole's need for discretion.

Nicole was wary of filling in a card and leaving her name and address for anyone to see, but she was pleased when the two women offered to mention her need for work to others of their acquaintance and to vet anyone who responded.

Denise and Berthe were right. Spreading the word informally was the best way to find work without taking too much of a risk now that she was wanted by the police. She felt increasingly vulnerable these days, but she would try to survive on small typing jobs and keep *Valmy* going.

Nicole began to build up a modest business by typing for writers. She went back to Paul's café several times and one of the two women she met on her first visit put her in touch with a writer who gave her some work. He praised her speed and efficiency and gave her more to do, as well as spreading the word about her. This led to other commissions.

'You can use a typewriter in my shop and make sure your charges cover the cost of paper and ribbons,' Denise said when Nicole arrived with news of her first commission.

'That's just what I was hoping you would say, but...' Nicole said.

'No buts.'

'Well, there's a risk. After all, you were arrested.'

'But *Valmy* isn't here anymore, so it's all right. I'll tell you if I'm worried. Now, come along, Nicole. Don't make things more difficult for yourself.'

Nicole accepted that and Denise liked having her in the shop. It livened up the day and even helped sales for customers to see a typewriter in use. Gérard and Berthe were able to see her there if they needed to in between their café meetings. Nicole made enough money to pay her rent and feed herself and Kim, but for anything else she had to use her savings, which dwindled.

Valmy stressed that Paris remained a dangerous place for young men and Nicole liked to say in her diary for *Valmy* that it was dangerous for young women as well, judging by the harassment and rapes that she heard about. The Nazis assumed that young men were engaged in resistance activities and Nicole was glad that Paul had left. She teased Gérard that his underground connections added up to a magical capacity for survival unharmed.

When members of the Resistance burned the files of thousands of French conscripts in the Place de Fontenoy in February 1944, *Valmy* reported that this action made it more difficult to send men to the labour camps in Germany and Poland. In March, the Resistance paper *Combat* called for people to act and for total resistance – a call that *Valmy* echoed. Yet events moved against the people of Paris as well. In April, the underground press reported hundreds of deaths from the Allied bombing raid of the station at La Chapelle. Nicole knew that the Resistance was stronger now, but it would never be able to defeat the occupation alone. She could not feel safe yet.

***

It was never easy, having a dog in Paris during the occupation. It was not his fault, but hers, that they had missed the boat in Bordeaux. He was part of her life, but the difficulties of having a dog under the occupation were not over. One evening in May 1944, Nicole returned home to find a worried Jacqueline.

'You'll never guess what's happened now! The government has requisitioned all dogs that are more than forty-five centimetres at the shoulder.'

Nicole, taking off her coat, asked Jacqueline the reason for this stupidity.

'No one knows for certain, but the rumour is that they want to train them to run under tanks with a dynamite charge strapped to their backs.'

'I'm not a tailor's daughter for nothing. Have you got a tape measure?' Nicole said.

Jacqueline produced one and passed it to her. Nicole drew Kim towards her and measured him. 'Forty centimetres,' she said, with a sigh of relief, a few seconds later.

'Some of the dog owners I meet in the park are afraid and are keeping their dogs indoors for fear of losing them,' Jacqueline said, putting the tape away.

'We'll have to do the same if they decide they want smaller dogs as well,' Nicole said, stroking Kim, who wagged his tail. She hugged him. No government official was going to lay hands on her dog.

Nicole now rarely took the risk of taking Kim for a walk, even with her different hairstyle. She left that to Jacqueline. When no decrees appeared concerning smaller dogs, Nicole and Jacqueline relaxed.

TWO

CAPTURE

An increase in personal messages transmitted by the BBC to the French Resistance led Parisians to expect Allied landings to take place soon. They were desperately needed, because supplies were running out, transport routes were being closed and gas supplies were low; there were power cuts, an increase of round-ups and newspapers were not being printed. *Valmy* appeared only occasionally because of the shortage of paper.

Nicole could not be certain why it took the police a year, if they were going to do it at all, to circulate a poster of the photo that had led her to change her hairstyle and stop taking Kim out. It was headed by the word "*WANTED*" and beneath the photo was the name "Michelle Laforte" and the explanation that she was behind the notorious underground newspaper, *Valmy*. She first saw the poster plastered onto a large advertisement hoarding near

Antoine's printworks one morning in late May 1944. Despite her new hairstyle, she was sure that she would be recognised. Feeling shaken, she hurried on to see Antoine.

'Antoine, I'm wanted by the police. I've just seen a poster...'

'I saw that. Go underground,' he said, scarcely looking up from his work.

Nicole's mind raced. If she were caught, Jacqueline and Yvette could be accused of shielding a wanted person. She should leave their flat now, but where could she go? Gérard could help, but she was not due to see him yet and finding him could be difficult. She would talk to Denise, just as she had done when she left her job at the art school. Within a few minutes, she had reached the typewriter shop.

'Come and live with me. I'll hide you and you can have Marcel's old room, if you don't mind,' Denise said, on hearing Nicole's news.

'That would put you in the same danger as Jacqueline and Yvette, because I'm a wanted person.'

'I don't care. This wretched war is coming to an end. I'm not frightened of them. We'll beat them at their own game.'

Denise's determination showed in her face and Nicole felt reassured. She clearly relished the prospect of defeating the police and her spirit tempted Nicole to accept her invitation. There was one problem.

'Thanks. All right, I'll move in with you. I feel I must do something, but what about Kim?'

'Well, you know I'm not a dog lover...'

'It's all right. Jacqueline has rather taken him over recently and I'll ask her to keep him for me. At least he doesn't cost anything.'

'I should warn you about my neighbour, old Mme Clément. I suspect her of informing on me. Remember the day you rescued me from the police station?' Denise said. 'I'm sure she was behind that. She'll be inquisitive, but I can pass you off as a niece.'

With her short hair and without Kim, Nicole looked different enough from the young woman of the wanted poster not to fear being recognised by Denise's neighbours. There was no knowing for how long it would be, but Nicole arranged that Kim would stay with Jacqueline and Yvette until she could reclaim him. Jacqueline would brave any hostility to Kim and would collect his food from M. Thibaud. Nicole would move into Denise's flat, at least until the hunt died down, visiting Jacqueline, Yvette and Kim when she could.

That evening, she packed her case and said goodbye to Jacqueline and Yvette. They did not try to stop her from leaving, seeing that her mind was made up. Kim was used to her going out without him and he took little notice of her departure. She was sorry to leave everyone, but relieved that she was doing something to defeat the intentions of the poster. At Denise's flat, she unpacked her case in Marcel's old room, among his possessions, which Denise had not touched. It was now three years since his death, but his room reminded her strongly of previous visits.

When it could appear, *Valmy* included Michelle Laforte's diary. Gérard, Berthe and Nicole, with help from Denise, tore down the wanted posters where it was safe to do so.

The approach of summer in 1944 made life seem easier. There was no longer a battle to keep warm and long, light days encouraged the hope that the Allies would invade. When they landed in northern France on Tuesday 6th June that year, Parisians were delighted.

'The occupation is coming to an end!' Nicole said, as she and Denise heard the news on the wireless.

'Be careful. It's not over yet,' Denise said, but her eyes were sparkling.

The news raced through the city as people assumed an Allied victory was not far away. Military traffic increased in Paris as the Wehrmacht forces set out to combat the Allies.

It was a mark of the growing confidence of the Resistance in Paris that the police chief Henriot was assassinated later in June. On Bastille Day, 14th July, Nicole noticed that the French *tricolore* and its colours of red, white and blue were everywhere, in shop windows or worn on clothing. She and Yvette, who had the day off, joined the crowds gathered at the Place Maubert, near the Sorbonne, where demonstrations had often been held before the war. People were waving flags and shouting. *Valmy* reported the demonstration, how the police were present but held back from the crowds. Expectations of liberation grew in Paris as the summer advanced.

On a sunny morning in early August, on her way to see Antoine with a copy of *Valmy* in her bag, ready for printing, Nicole was walking briskly along the Rue Daguerre when a car drew up beside her. She froze as a voice addressed her in German. She did not speak the language, but there was no mistaking the words, '*Halt, Fräulein!*'

Two soldiers jumped out of the car and arrested her. Trying to run would have been a waste of time as they looked muscular and fit, if not young. She had no choice but to allow them to push her into the back of the car where they handcuffed her. It drove on and it was not long before she realised that they were going to the Gestapo headquarters on the Avenue Foch. This was far worse than being captured by the French police. The Gestapo were famous for their cruelty. She feared torture and worse as she sat stiffly in the car between the two soldiers. She was trembling and could scarcely breathe.

The car parked behind the building and the soldiers indicated to Nicole to get out. There was no point in trying to run from a courtyard guarded by other soldiers. She was not athletic enough to leap over the wall, especially in handcuffs, and would have been caught in seconds trying to escape from the entrance.

The soldiers directed her to a small room inside the building where one of them emptied her bag, examining the contents and taking everything away. She had to surrender her watch and a silver ring she was wearing. Her possession of a copy of *Valmy* ready for printing was proof of her association with an underground newspaper, which had existed for four years without anyone connected to it being caught.

She was taken up to the top floor of the building. A guard removed her handcuffs and pushed her into a narrow cell, locking the door behind her. Silence fell and there was nothing to do but examine her Spartan quarters. The only furniture was a bed with a thin, dirty mattress and a single blanket. A bucket stood in the corner. A small window was too high up for her to see anything but sky, but it did, at least, provide some daylight.

She sat down on the bed. They had known who she was when they picked her up, but how had they recognised her? Had Serge seen her on the street one day and followed her out of vindictiveness because his previous effort to inform on her had failed? Had he then gone to the police with information about her movements? Had Mme Clément from Denise's block informed on her? Or was someone else, some unsuspected enemy, behind her arrest? With nothing else to do, she entertained all kinds of ideas, some plausible, others fanciful, but never one she felt was conclusive.

Did someone link Kim to the dog in Michelle Laforte's diary? She had written about Kim in her *Valmy* diary and had not changed his name as she had her own. She remembered her dilemma about whether to include Kim in her diary and her decision to do so. That may have been a terrible mistake.

People would be looking for her. Denise would realise, when she failed to return home, that something was wrong. She knew both Gérard and Berthe and would find a way to alert them, as well as Jacqueline and Yvette. They would be trying to find out where she was, at least. The thought gave her some comfort.

When a grey soup and stale bread were delivered to her door, along with water in a tin cup, she forced herself to eat to keep up her strength. Hunger meant that she spent hours thinking about food and she made a game of remembering and tasting her favourites.

What would happen now? Before her arrest, she had heard rumours that the Nazis had decided to deport the remaining political prisoners in Paris to concentration camps in Germany or Poland. Perhaps that was why no one was interrogating her. They had already put her name on a list of those to be deported. She would be sent to Drancy or a similar camp and then put on a train for the east like Miriam and her family.

Yet she must expect to be interrogated and not to say anything that would give away other members of the *Valmy* group or Antoine. She would give them her name, would admit to her connection with *Valmy*, and to being Michelle Laforte if they asked. Those admissions would not harm anyone else, but they would not be enough. They might torture her. Could she stand that and not give away information that would lead to other arrests? She did not think of herself as an especially brave person.

When it grew dark, she tried to sleep. Her cell was high up in the prison and her first night was hot and uncomfortable. She slept badly, waking several times in the small hours of the morning, trying to understand such noises as she could hear in the building. Doors were slammed and voices raised. A scrabbling sound made her think of rats.

Her cell door was thrown open later in the morning and a guard she had not seen before motioned her to leave. She was taken to what she saw at once was an interrogation room on a lower floor. It was small and smelled of stale cigarette smoke and something unpleasant. The guard who had escorted her disappeared. A bright light shone on her so she could barely see the man behind a desk. She was frightened, but not unprepared. This was what she had expected. The man behind the desk was a Nazi who spoke bad French. She had to stand. She told herself to be angry, not afraid.

'You look German,' he said, smiling.

'I'm French.' They knew that because they had her identity card. She did not smile.

'Your name?'

She gave her name. The copy of *Valmy* that she had been carrying when she was arrested was on his desk. He was a middle-aged man, with a nondescript face and a soft voice. He picked up *Valmy*.

'You work for this newspaper?'

Again, she nodded. There was no point in denying it.

'But you don't use your name. What name do you use?'

'Michelle Laforte.'

He nodded and wanted to know the real names of the other journalists. She would only give the pseudonyms he already knew from the copy of *Valmy* that he was holding. She said that she did not know the real names. She said nothing more, shaking her head. He kept on and on, trying to wear her down. He lost patience suddenly and shouted.

Someone else came into the room, a bigger, hard-faced, younger man. Nicole was terrified, seeing a thug. She shivered. The light seemed brighter. The first man began to question her again, but she was silent. The thug began to slap her and push her around. Still, she would not answer. She tried to force the thug to look at her, to realise he was hitting a woman, much smaller than he was – to shame him, if he could be shamed. She was wasting her time. He would not look at her. He began to punch her and she fainted.

Later, she awoke on the floor of her cell, bruised from the beating and from being thrown unconscious onto the floor. Her head thudded. She dragged herself onto her bed and collapsed.

Waking the next morning, she expected to be interrogated again and that it would be worse this time. At different times in the occupation, she had heard rumours of electric shocks and water torture, but nothing happened that day except for the arrival of a kind of soup with stale bread and water. Her head ached still and she was bored and anxious, certain that she was being made to wait to break down her defences.

One day succeeded another. Every day she expected another interrogation, but her only contact was with her immediate jailors, who did not seem to know anything or were unwilling to speak when they delivered her food twice a day or collected her bucket. She was losing weight. She spent part of each day doing physical exercises to strengthen her muscles and the rest of her time went on thinking and on playing memory games that she devised for herself.

She thought of Paul. If she were free and were to meet him again, how would she feel about him? It was not hard to imagine, to leap over the high wall of prison in her mind to such freedom as Paris could offer. She longed for freedom and for a normal life and she began to wonder if that life would ever include Paul. He seemed close to her in his absence. She remembered that she had liked him immediately. He had been good to work with, concerned for her safety and had comforted her when Miriam had been taken. He had not tried to take advantage of her distress.

She thought of him more and more, drawing from his strength and wishing she had agreed to go to England with him. Being in prison stripped away all the small things in life and emphasised what was most important. Paul, whom she had not seen for nearly two years and who for all she knew had not even survived his perilous journey to England, mattered to her.

Using the fork that she was given every day with her midday meal, Nicole scratched a line on the wall from the beginning of her imprisonment, so she could count the days. She reached seventeen. August was well advanced now and she had no idea what was going on, but she was feeling weak from lack of food and inactivity and she was still frightened. Why didn't they interrogate her again? Were they still softening her up after all this time?

When her cell door was unlocked on the nineteenth morning, at an unusual time, the bulk of a silent guard filled the doorway. He motioned to her to come with him. With no possessions, all she had to do was climb off the bed where she had been sitting and follow him. Bedraggled, hungry and feeling distinctly unwashed, Nicole obeyed.

Her mind raced as she walked behind the guard. The corridor was narrow and there was nothing else to do but follow him. This was going to be the interrogation she was dreading, with torture. Or was she going on a train journey to a labour camp, or a camp where she would be killed? Was that what had happened to Miriam and was it her turn now? She remembered the leaflet Miriam had shown her two years previously, about people being gassed. There had been similar suggestions since then. Or was she simply going to be shot in some courtyard in the centre of the building where no sound would penetrate beyond the outside walls? The guard said nothing to her. She did not try to speak to him, to discover her fate sooner than necessary. Every moment was suddenly precious. Her feet dragged as she followed him.

They descended the stairs, flight after flight. This did not seem like the way to a torture room, more like the way out. So that was it; a firing squad, or a journey to a death camp.

THREE

LIBERATION

At the foot of the staircase, they entered a room. Standing behind a desk, a Nazi soldier was ticking off names. He checked Nicole's name, passed over her handbag and told her to go. She took it feeling confused. Go where? He motioned towards a door with a jerk of his thumb and Nicole found herself in a foyer where people were waiting.

'Nicole!'

She turned towards the sound and caught sight of a familiar face. 'Denise!'

'Nicole, you're coming home with me. You're released!' Denise had jumped up and was hugging her.

Nicole did not grasp what was happening at first. She stood still and stared at Denise.

'Let's get out of here. Can you walk?' Denise said.

She nodded and found she could speak. 'Yes, I can. I'm

not used to it. I've been sitting most of the time, but I did some exercises in my cell, to keep fit.'

They left the station and began to walk slowly down the street. It was sunny and Nicole, blinded by the unaccustomed brightness and feeling unsteady, held onto Denise with one hand and a nearby wall with the other.

'Some prisoners are being released,' Denise said once they were outside. 'As soon as I heard that, I came to get you, in the hope that you were one of them. And here you are!'

'How did you know where I was?'

'Berthe found out. I knew something had happened when you didn't come home that night. You would never stay out without letting me know. Luckily, Berthe came to the shop with a message for you, something to go into *Valmy*, and I told her you were missing. She found out at work where you were and then she heard about the truce and we agreed that I would come and get you if you were released!'

Nicole pressed on, one foot in front of the other, knowing now that she was free. She wanted desperately to put as much space between the Nazi headquarters and herself as possible, yet she was feeling weak, like someone learning to walk again after an illness.

'What are they doing?' she said as they came to a group of young people tearing up cobblestones and dragging a bench and other moveable items into the road.

'It's a barricade! Yesterday Colonel Tanguy asked the city to rise and barricades are going up everywhere. So are French flags. Now, come on, Nicole, let's go,' Denise said, propelling her towards the metro.

Nicole was conscious of little more than Denise's firm hand guiding her as she stumbled along. They could not take the metro, which had stopped running because staff were on strike. Instead, they squeezed onto a crowded bus, which went only part of the way. Nicole was exhausted by the time they reached the flat and collapsed into a chair in the sitting room.

'I thought that I would be shot or deported,' she said to Denise, who was passing her coffee, bread and jam.

'Either or both of those things could have happened if you'd been caught earlier, but they're in retreat at last,' Denise said.

'You mean I've been lucky. It doesn't feel like luck to be banged up in a prison for all this time, but you could be right. So, there was a truce. That's why I wasn't interrogated again. They had other things on their minds!' Nicole gave a weak laugh.

Later, when she had washed off the dirt of prison, Nicole examined her bag and found her watch and ring. She put them on. Her identity card was there as well and her purse with a few coins and notes. Nothing had been stolen. She felt so tired then that she fell asleep on her bed, feeling relaxed for the first time since being imprisoned. That evening, she told Denise more about her ordeal and listened to her friend's news of Paris.

'Railway workers went on strike and then the police. It's frightening, but, at the same time, it's marvellous. They're starting to leave Paris, looting as they go. They've sent their women back already. Guns are being fired around the city and, this morning, I heard firecrackers in the streets. The occupation is nearly over, but the Allies haven't arrived yet and I don't know what's going to happen. To be honest, I'm a bit scared of street battles,' Denise said.

For the second time that day, Nicole felt a wave of relief, even though she could see Denise was worried. The comfortable chair on which she was sitting seemed to embrace her as she sank further into it. There might be a battle, but the moment of release was approaching after over four long years. She smiled at Denise and accepted a small glass of liqueur in celebration of her release.

***

Exhausted and famished, Nicole needed time to recover from her ordeal, but thanks to Gérard, Berthe and Antoine, *Valmy* was one of the underground newspapers published openly in Paris for the first time on 21st August. *Valmy* had made a lot of Michelle Laforte's disappearance and Gérard and Berthe made headlines of Nicole's return. Even Antoine smiled to see her.

'Thank you so much for what you did to help Denise find me,' Nicole said as soon as she saw the familiar skinny figure and dishevelled hair of Berthe. She gave her a grateful hug.

The truce did not last long. Led by Colonel Henri Tanguy, the leader of the Paris Resistance, people fought street by street from behind their barricades for several days to reclaim their city, using such weapons as they had and tearing down Nazi signs and flags.

The Nazis fought hard against the Parisians and the sound of gunshot was heard frequently over the few days after Nicole's release. People were worried that the Nazi general in charge of Paris would carry out Hitler's orders to lay waste to the city, but, to everyone's relief, he refrained.

No one knew how far the Allies were from Paris or if the Nazis would send reinforcements for their troops. General Leclerc at the head of the Second Armoured Division advanced on Paris, arriving on the evening of 24th August. The city was liberated the next day, after heavy fighting broke out between the Nazis and Leclerc's men. The bells of Notre-Dame rang out after four years of silence, followed by other church bells. The sound of the "Marseillaise" was heard in the streets as the occupier surrendered.

Yvette was on duty in hospital, but Jacqueline, Denise and Nicole joined the welcoming crowd on the Champs-Élysées for de Gaulle's victory parade – Nicole refusing to listen to advice that she was too weak to join in. By then she had moved back with Jacqueline and Yvette, which had the added advantage of reclaiming Kim. He was joyful at her return.

She had missed the entrance of the Nazis to Paris after she had left for Bordeaux over four years previously, but she could guess at how different an occasion it must have been. The Champs-Élysées was now lined with an enthusiastic crowd, waving flags and roaring their welcome to the French and Allied troops. She had to carry Kim much of the time, to protect him from being trampled underfoot. She scanned the faces of the assembled soldiers, hoping that Paul had come to France with the Allies and was even on his way to Paris or had already arrived. There was no sign of him.

In the evening, Nicole, Yvette and Jacqueline, with Kim, came out to join the throng on the streets of Paris.

They made their way to Denise's shop, where Gérard and Berthe joined them.

It seemed as if the whole city was on the streets, talking, singing and dancing, some carrying bottles saved for years for this moment. The "Marseillaise" was sung again and again. Celebrations carried on for hours, late into the night, accompanied by a ceaseless roaring of voices and ringing of church bells.

Denise and Jacqueline gave up after a while and went home, but Nicole, Yvette, Gérard and Berthe, with Kim, walked through Paris for hours. The streets were full of excited groups of people and the noise of jubilation never abated. In the small hours, after they had run into friends and acquaintances, celebrations were continuing with as much fervour as if they would never end. But for the absence of many loved ones, Nicole had never felt so happy and relaxed. Everyone had woken from a nightmare that had lasted for over four years, since the day that the Nazis had invaded France.

Coming home with Yvette and Kim at dawn, Nicole went straight to bed and slept until midday. Waking, she thought about Miriam, as she had done several times in the last few days. If only the Weiss family could have taken part in the liberation of Paris and reclaimed their home and their lives, but it was impossible. Even if they were alive, the war was continuing and whatever dreadful camp they had been sent to would not be liberated yet.

The following days were joyous, but the joy of liberation did not last long, as Paris began to struggle out from under the yoke of occupation. It was a shock to learn that over a thousand Parisians had been killed in the fighting of those few days in August. Divisions created by the war, food and fuel shortages, and unemployment were rife. Even after the Nazis had ceased creaming off food and industry, life for most people was hard.

Most shops were empty or shut, but Jeffrey's shop was open when Nicole went past one day. She was pleased for her father's sake to see the business was still going and waved through the window at Pascal, but she did not go in. She did not want to see Patrick McGrath.

'I didn't want to know what might have happened to him now that people are taking revenge on collaborators,' she said to Yvette later.

'It's worse outside Paris, but I hear they're going to hold the trials of collaborators in Paris,' Yvette said. 'Perhaps you should report Serge to the authorities!'

Nicole shook her head. She was not interested in taking revenge on Serge and in any case had no evidence of what he might have done against her. She was shocked at the revenge on collaborators and saw a distressing scene one afternoon when she was delivering some typing to an author who lived on a narrow street in a part of Paris she did not know well. A woman was submitting to the shaving of her head, while men and women were shouting angrily at her and a child was crying. Nicole retreated quickly, finding another way to her destination.

'I don't agree with all the punishment of women that is going on, but I was too afraid to intervene,' she said to Yvette and Jacqueline that evening.

'Too right. They might have shaved your head. People are so angry these days. It's almost worse than the occupation,' Jacqueline said.

Yet justice was not always done. *Valmy* made clear its disgust that the police chief who had co-ordinated the round-ups of Jewish people was merely reprimanded and resumed his career.

***

Nicole slept badly after her imprisonment. She had nightmares about being in prison. It was comforting to let Kim sleep at the end of her bed. If she woke from a nightmare, he would snuggle up against her.

It was only gradually that life began to seem more normal. Old habits lingered. Nicole still checked to see who was in any café she was entering, who might be following her on the street, who left the metro when she did. Yet life was moving on. Yvette was full of excitement about a new man. The one from Rennes had stopped writing to her at least a year previously and she had since met a doctor at the hospital where she worked.

Nicole met Gérard and Berthe in a café one evening to discuss *Valmy*.

'I have heard that one or two of the Resistance newspapers, like *Libération*, are planning to become Paris dailies, but we're not in that league, especially without Miriam, David and Paul. What do you think?' she asked.

'I agree. I want to finish my course at the Sorbonne if I can get back in there,' Gérard said. He had been studying physics before the war.

'And I already have a job. What are your plans, Nicole?' Berthe said.

'I want to go back to art college,' Nicole said.

'Close *Valmy* down,' Gérard said. 'A liberated city doesn't need underground newspapers and the other papers, from what you say, will fill any gap.'

'We should have a final issue to finish things off properly,' Berthe said.

'We could say something about the sort of Paris we want to see,' Nicole said. 'There is a ferment of ideas bubbling up and we could pour oil on divisions.'

'You'll be lucky, Nicole. People are settling old scores and you won't hold them back, but I'm with you for a final blast,' Gérard said.

They settled on that. A final issue of *Valmy* included a last diary entry from Michelle Laforte. She told the story of her imprisonment and release and made a plea for an end to the shaving of heads and other revenge acts. The wanted posters about Nicole had all but disappeared by then. She tore down a last one to keep as a record.

Nicole continued typing for writers. The war was not over yet, but she was beginning to think about her future. Her twenty-sixth birthday had followed the liberation. She celebrated with Jacqueline, Yvette, Denise, Berthe, Gérard and Antoine over a glass in Denise's shop. Despite having edited an underground newspaper, she did not want to go into journalism, nor was she drawn to politics. It was enough that the occupier should leave the country and that France should be free again.

She needed to find her own life and she wanted to continue with her art studies, although she lacked the money for the fees. It was impossible to go home when her parents were still in England. Nor could she yet discover what had happened to the Weiss family, although she was determined to do that. It would be possible after the war and she still hoped that one day they would return.

Even after her imprisonment, she missed Paul, but she had no idea where he was and had no way of contacting him. He had not been in touch with anyone she knew. If he had come to Paris for the liberation, he could have found Denise in her shop and made contact through her. She often thought of him and longed to see him, but he had parents and a brother in Dijon to think about. She only hoped that he was with his family and had not been injured or killed.

David returned to Paris from Toulouse after the liberation. He appeared one day at Denise's shop and found Nicole typing. He confirmed that Paul had left Toulouse in February 1943, for England, but he knew nothing more. He asked about Miriam, but Nicole could only say that there had been no news.

***

Nicole's wish to return to her art course depended on not having to see Serge again. Apart from anything else, she thought it most likely that he was responsible for her imprisonment. She wondered about applying elsewhere, but first she would see what was happening at her old art school. She cycled there one day and was pleased to find Sandrine at her desk.

'Oh, look who's turned up out of the blue. Hello, Nicole!'

'You're looking well, Sandrine.'

'Well, things are slowly getting back to normal. And your old bugbear has gone.'

'Serge? That's what I came to ask you. I'd like to come back here as a student, but not if he's around.'

'He's not. I heard that he's even left Paris, but don't ask me where he's gone. He didn't say so, of course, but I reckon he's scared of reprisals against collaborators.'

'That's good news. Then I can come back. I don't care where he is as long as he's gone,' Nicole said.

That evening, she talked to Yvette about her visit to the art school. 'I'm so pleased to think that I can go back there as a student. If I earn enough to pay the fees, I could enrol for the autumn next year.'

'And I'm so pleased you're going to lead a normal life,' Yvette said, with a smile of relief.

The art school had replaced Nicole after she had left her job and there was no vacancy for a typist, but she was free now to work without fearing arrest and she found a job in a notary's office nearby, which paid well.

***

Months of war followed as the Nazis were chased out of France and their domination of Europe collapsed. Some of the privations of the occupation, like rationing, continued and Parisians, like people elsewhere in Europe, lived on a diet of vegetables. In early 1945, Nicole, like other women, was still wearing wooden shoes without stockings. January and February that year were as cold as most of the winters of the war, with little coal for heating. Nicole continued to live with Yvette and Jacqueline. There was still no sign of Paul.

In April that year, French municipal elections allowed women to vote for the first time. Nicole, Yvette, Jacqueline,

Denise and Berthe all voted. It was also possible in April to see films of the concentration camps in Paris cinemas. Nicole went with Yvette to see one film as the first step in discovering what had happened to the Weiss family. They emerged shaken and in a sombre mood as they began to understand the nature and extent of the Holocaust.

After the war ended in May, people began returning from the Nazi concentration camps. Nicole knew by then that few people had survived, but she was clinging to a thread of hope that Miriam and Louis, young and determined, might still be alive, even if Sonia and Daniel had not survived.

'I'm going to the Gare de l'Est tomorrow at lunchtime. A train is coming in from the camps and Miriam might be on it. I know it's only a small chance, but will you come with me?' she said to Yvette one evening.

'I'm working until late afternoon. I could probably change my shift, but I don't want to go with you,' Yvette said, her face strained.

Nicole understood. They had both been horrified by the film about concentration camps and Yvette had avoided talking about it since then.

At the Gare de l'Est, like other Parisians watching the survivors leave the train, Nicole found herself in tears at the sight of the wretched, thin, exhausted passengers, some of them unable to walk, who arrived. Would she even recognise Miriam and her family? She scanned faces with a growing sense of hopelessness as people passed her and she finally gave up.

Making more enquiries led her to the Hotel Lutetia in the Varenne district of Paris. It had been the Nazi headquarters and was now displaying lists of those who had been deported, with a record of the outcome. Again, she was disappointed not to find any mention of the Weiss family. She visited Jewish organisations that were trying to help people who had survived the camps and the occupation. Her hope that the family might be among the survivors dwindled as she searched lists of dead and missing people, but she would not give up until she knew for certain.

Eventually she found what she was looking for. It made it easier that she had never forgotten the date of 17th July 1942. From Drancy, the family had been sent to Auschwitz in Poland. It appeared from the recorded date of their deaths in late July that they had all been gassed on arrival or shortly afterwards. Seeing this entry on a list made Nicole weep. She emerged from her discovery into the Paris spring sunshine scarcely able to believe that the world around her was so ordinary and that people were carrying on with their lives.

Early that evening, in the café where the three girls had often met in the years after leaving school, Nicole met Yvette as she finished work. They sat on a crowded terrace under lime trees and breathed in the scent of their flowers. As Nicole finished telling Yvette of her discovery, they were silent for a moment, neglecting their coffee, oblivious to the hubbub around them and the people passing by.

'Thank you for checking, Nicole. I thought of doing that, but I kept putting it off,' Yvette said at last, with tears in her eyes.

'I understand why. It was horrible, but I had to find out what happened to them.'

'I don't know what to say. At least they didn't spend months suffering.'

'Do you remember Miriam's plan for the three of us to meet every year on May 19th, on that bench in the Luxembourg Gardens?' Nicole asked.

Yvette stirred her coffee. 'I remembered the date for some years. The last time was just before Miriam and her family were taken.'

'Well, it's nearly May 19th. Let's go then and, if we're both living in Paris, we can meet there every year to remember Miriam,' Nicole said.

'Good idea. Of course, we'll remember her at other times as well, but that will be her special day.'

On the chosen date, Nicole and Yvette visited the Luxembourg Gardens after work. Walking past the iron railings, they saw welcome changes. There was no sign of the vegetables that people had grown during the war or of the enormous flags of swastikas that the Nazis had draped over the palace. A few summer flowers were out. The rows of trees and the central pond were unchanged. They made their way to the spot where they had met Miriam every summer since they were schoolgirls. They sat quietly together, remembering the lively spirit, generosity and hopes of their friend.

FOUR

HOME

'*Maman*, is that you?'

'Yes, darling. Oh, how lovely to hear your voice! Are you well? I've heard such terrible things about Paris.'

'I'm fine. Thinner and badly dressed, but I'm surviving!'

Nicole was in a public call box in Paris, shouting over a crackly line. The war was over and it was now possible to phone London. There was no time to go into what her mother had heard about Paris, which was probably about reprisals against collaborators. What mattered was being able to talk to her for the first time in five years. The postal service between France and Britain had been restored and they had exchanged letters, but this was the first phone call and there was something she wanted to know. She shouted her question, but her mother didn't hear it the first time. It wasn't just the crackly line that was making conversation difficult. More traffic was appearing in Paris and noise on the street outside the call box didn't help.

She shouted again, more slowly this time. 'When are you coming back to Paris?'

'In September. Your father hasn't been demobbed yet and we need to arrange about the flat and so forth.'

Nicole had not doubted that her parents would return after the war. Paris had been their home for over twenty-five years and was where Jeffrey had his business. Little might remain of it, but he was not one to give up on things easily.

There was still no sign of Paul. Nicole had begun to wonder if he was all right or whether something awful had happened to him as it had to Marcel. Or did he no longer want to see her? Denise's elder son, Jean, came home unscathed and slipped back into running the family business. In the summer of 1945, closing the typewriter shop, Denise and Jean, with Nicole, visited Marcel's grave in Normandy, staying overnight in the small town nearby. He lay in a section of a First World War cemetery reserved for soldiers who had died in the Battle of France. His name, the years of his life, 1917–1940, and the name of his regiment were engraved on a simple tombstone. They left some white flowers there. Denise crossed herself and said a prayer for her son, but she did not cry, saying she had done all that already. Nicole felt the sadness of the loss of her future with Marcel and she and Denise consoled each other by telling stories about him.

Denise had been collecting copies of *Valmy* since the early days and wanted to find a way of publishing Nicole's occupation diary after the war. Nicole assured her that no one would want to read it. With the war over, Paris would want to move on.

***

Three months and several phone calls after first talking to her mother, Nicole and Kim met Anne and Jeffrey at the Gare du Nord on their return to Paris from London. Nicole was leaving Jacqueline and Yvette's flat and returning to her family home, at last. She carried the small suitcase with which she had left Paris in 1940. What wouldn't fit in was tucked into a large shopping bag slung over her shoulder.

Standing at the end of the platform, she waited as the train carrying her parents pulled in. Doors were thrown open and people poured onto the platform. Nicole scanned the passengers moving towards her for some time before she saw her parents emerge from the crowd. They had not seen her yet. She felt a pang at first. They looked older, weary perhaps from the journey when they were no longer young. She had not seen her father since the journey to Rick and Georgie's flat, and she would never forget her last sight of her mother on the deck of the boat leaving Bordeaux. Five years was a long time.

Now her parents caught sight of her. She was touched by the delight on their faces. Then they were by her side, saying her name as they hugged and kissed her in turn, while Kim, who clearly had a long memory, was beside himself with excitement.

'You've still got that dog – cause of all the trouble,' Jeffrey said, releasing his daughter, but he was smiling.

Anne, overwhelmed, searched for a handkerchief. Tears

might not have been far away, except that Jeffrey bustled everyone towards the taxi rank. Looking out of the taxi windows, Jeffrey and Anne contrasted Paris with London. Paris was shabby, with blackened stone facades, cracked stucco and peeling paintwork, but the centre was almost intact, whereas London was pockmarked by bombsites and, in some places, devastated. Nicole explained that the Nazi occupation had spared the centre of Paris after the early days of the invasion and that little Allied bombing had occurred over the centre, although the outer industrial areas had been hit.

Entering their old block, they pressed the bell for the concierge to obtain the keys to their flat. M. Lebrun emerged and greeted them. Nicole had not seen him since she had persuaded him to unlock the family flat so that she could rescue her clothes five years before. He looked older and more careworn, but he managed a smile.

'You did well to be away,' he said to Jeffrey and Anne, then added to Nicole, 'I see you haven't got rid of that dog yet.'

He handed keys over to Jeffrey and the family climbed the stairs to the first floor, where Jeffrey unlocked to the door to their flat. He had made sure to write to M. Lebrun about their return as soon as he could.

Once inside the flat, empty since the departure of the Nazis the previous year, they went quickly from room to room, looking for any changes. Anne caressed favourite pieces of furniture.

'We're home,' she said. 'Remember that day we left in such a hurry? It's taken us more than five years to come back, but we're here at last!'

'Don't be too sentimental, because it's not going to be the same as it was,' Jeffrey said.

'So much has happened that the day we left belongs to another life,' Nicole said.

She could tell that her father was worrying about their immediate future. It was hard for her parents, now in their mid-sixties, to have to pick up the threads of their old lives.

How different her life had been from their lives during those five years. The girl – so cosseted, so full of hope – was gone and in her place was a woman who had given her youth to a war she would never forget, which had brought hunger, fear and loss. It had brought friendship as well and she hoped for more than that.

She followed Kim into the kitchen where he looked up at her with an expectant whine. She searched the cupboards and, finding his bowl, gave him some water. Seeing him in his old home at last, remembering the puppy who had come to live there before the war, she noticed for the first time that the fur around his mouth was going white. He was getting old.

'Well, they didn't steal Kim's bowl,' she said with a laugh, returning to where her parents were examining the living room. 'I don't know what I would have done without Kim,' she said, prompted by her observation in the kitchen. 'He was such good company all the way through the occupation – the one constant in my life.'

Her parents nodded and her father refrained from teasing her about Kim.

'Did they steal anything?' she said next. All the big items of furniture that she remembered were there, including the piano where she had practised for so many hours.

'My Marie Antoinette dressing table is here. Of course, I took all my jewels to England with me, but… oh dear… there are things missing!' Looking at blank spaces where she had been expecting to see pictures or ornaments, Anne's voice was a mixture of relief and distress.

Nicole's gaze fell on an Art Nouveau vase that had always been a favourite of Anne's and, next to it, a Bristol blue glass vase that Jeffrey, who had grown up in Bristol, had often told her had come with him when he and Anne first moved to Paris. These familiar objects, like others she could now see, had accompanied her all through her childhood. She was comforted by recognising them.

'A lot of French art has been shipped to Germany. They could have taken everything and we're lucky that they didn't. Of course, they may not have thought we have much worth stealing,' Jeffrey said, with an uneasy grin.

'It's nothing when you think of what happened to people,' Nicole said.

She had yet to tell her parents face to face about the Weiss family, but there would be time enough for that. Miriam was never far from her mind. Nor, on a lesser scale, had she told them about her own time in prison.

For the moment, she was enjoying the luxury of a family reunion. How could she ever have found her mother intrusive? Yet it could easily happen again now that she was moving in with her parents.

'We'll have the flat cleaned thoroughly.' Anne spoke with a slight shudder, but she did not seem to smell smoke and Nicole decided not to mention the smoking she had seen on her first visit to the flat under the occupation. She did explain that, on a later visit, she had persuaded

Monsieur Lebrun to unlock the flat so she could obtain her winter clothes and that she had run into one of the Nazis living there.

'Nicole, you should never have done that. Anything could have happened to you!' Anne said, but Jeffrey looked at her admiringly.

'I'm glad they've been gone for some time. And the one you met sounds like an officer. I prefer to think they were officers rather than men,' he said.

In her bedroom, Nicole was reminded of the last time she had been there, frantically seizing her winter clothes and being terrified by the sudden appearance of the Nazi in the doorway. She recoiled from the thought as she moved her clothing to fill the spaces available. She was the occupier now. She unpacked her few things and explored the wardrobe and drawers. What she had left behind had been pushed to one side as if to allow for someone else's clothing, but at least her things were still there.

She took her autograph book out of her suitcase and opened it. Something fell to the floor. She picked it up, recognising the rose she had taken from the Standard Club garden in June 1940, just before leaving Paris with her mother. Long dead and faded, it still held some colour. It was the rose she had taken as a souvenir of her life in Paris before the war, when she had thought she was leaving, not knowing how differently everything would turn out. She looked at Marcel's signature, read with difficulty words by Miriam about friendship and moved on to a little poem Yvette had written.

Later, over a scratch evening meal, Nicole asked her parents about their lives in London. Jeffrey had spent the war interpreting and translating from French to English and vice versa. Anne had helped Jessie with the grandchildren and written a stream of letters to Ralph and Christopher. Her parents had received some of the letters that Nicole had sent from the unoccupied zone in the early years of the war before the invasion of almost the whole country.

Nicole described her life during the occupation. There was her time in Bordeaux and her journey back to Paris. Then had come the hospitality of the Weiss family when she had turned up on their doorstep, the long period in which they had gradually lost their freedom, their deportation and Nicole's subsequent discovery of their fate. There was the strength of Denise to talk about, as well as the friendship of Jacqueline and Yvette. There was *Valmy* and its group and the art school job and Sandrine, even the hated Serge. She skated over her spell in prison, but Anne, although pale with shock on hearing about it, refrained from saying it would never have happened if Nicole had caught the boat.

'I was so sorry about Marcel. But what about Paul? Such a nice young man. You know he came to see us several times. We kept our French going with him!' Anne said.

'He came to see you? Oh, of course, I gave him your address,' Nicole said. 'I haven't seen or heard of him for ages and I don't have an address for him. But when did you last see him?'

'Well over a year ago now. It was May last year, I think,' Anne said.

'That's right. He'd joined up with the French forces in London and was expecting to go to France with them,' Jeffrey said.

'I've been hoping to hear from him. Something's gone wrong,' Nicole said, her heart sinking.

She thrust the thought aside, not wanting to spoil her parents' homecoming with her problems. Kim was, by then, dozing by her chair, but alert enough to the sound of his name to wag his tail as Nicole told her parents about what good company he had been throughout the occupation and how M. Thibaud had kept him fed. She also told them about the hostility of hungry people to dogs.

'Things have calmed down now,' Nicole said, after describing the joyous liberation. 'People are concentrating on putting their lives back together. There's more food around now that it's not being siphoned off to Germany, but it's still rationed. I only get a hundred grams of butter for a whole month! And many shops are shut or empty. Collaborators are being harshly treated. And people often don't understand or accept what happened in the death camps and the few survivors are sometimes ignored or dismissed. And there are other displaced people, like returning prisoners of war.'

She went on to explain that Paris had been changed by the war, despite the centre having escaped bombing. The fabric of the city was dreary and depressing after several years of war and being a fluent French speaker gave Nicole easy access to despondency and bitterness discernible beneath a superficial gaiety. Little was said openly about France's part in the war, the rift between those who had collaborated and those who had not, and the treatment of Jewish people and others thought undesirable by the authorities, but these matters were noticeable even if only by silence surrounding them.

Jeffrey was eager to know what Nicole could tell him about his tailoring business. Under Patrick McGrath, whom Nicole had not seen since her visit to the shop in 1940, it had survived. Jeffrey had heard from him recently.

'It survived because he became a collaborator and made Nazi uniforms,' Nicole said flatly.

'Perhaps he had no choice if he wanted to keep things afloat,' Jeffrey said, clearly hating the thought that his shop had been drawn into supporting the Nazis. Jeffrey was planning to revive the business. Christopher would soon be joining them in Paris with the English wife he had met during the war.

'Enough orders are coming in to stop us from starving and I'm looking forward to Ralph and Jessie's return,' Jeffrey said, explaining that they, too, would be coming to live in Paris with their daughters in a few months' time and that Ralph would also be helping Jeffrey.

Nicole laughed. 'Do you remember how pleased Christopher was to go off to war and escape tailoring?'

'Well, he's changed his tune because he'll be working with me as well. The trouble is that bespoke suiting isn't going to be top of many lists. It won't be easy to get the business back on its feet again.'

There was no mention of the English branch of the tailoring business that Ralph had managed before the war. It would be enough to revive the business in Paris. Nicole was glad that her father did not expect her to become a tailor. For the last year, she had been working as a secretary and her plan was still to study art again.

Jeffrey and Anne knew that some of their English friends and business contacts, who, like them, had fled to Britain during the war, would not return. Rick and Georgie had decided to stay in England after five years away from France. Jeffrey and Anne had written to French friends once it was possible, but many people had moved away or just moved on. Social life would revolve largely around family for the present, with old friends and contacts thin on the ground.

The pre-war social life of the Standard Club at Meudon, where the family had spent so many happy Sundays, had not disappeared altogether, but it had changed. The club had opened again after the war, but many of the members had not returned and new people were coming in.

'Nicole, you're not looking as chic as you used to and is that an ink stain on your skirt?' Anne said, as the long conversation wound down.

'Oh, Napoleon!' Nicole said, laughing. 'That was what we called our first printing machine. I swear it used to squirt ink at me. I've got hardly any clothes now. It's just as well there are some here, because most of what I've been wearing is threadbare.'

'And what have you done to your lovely hair...'

'Yvette cuts it for me.' Nicole explained about that first cut to disguise her appearance.

Jeffrey whipped out a tape measure from a drawer where it had lain for years and took measurements for a new suit that he would run up for Nicole, using material from pre-war stock that he had been assured remained in the shop.

'It's just as well that I missed the boat in Bordeaux,' Nicole said at one point.

'Why? It was one of the worst moments of my life, looking at you on the quayside getting further and further away and not knowing what terrible things might happen to you,' Anne said.

'It was dreadful at the time, but if I'd caught the boat and gone to England with you, I might have married an Englishman and lived there for the rest of my life. I know we've missed out on five years, but in future we'll all be in Paris together! And because I became a French citizen, I never had the fear of being interned during the occupation.'

'I didn't think of that when I was advising you to become British. I was only thinking of getting you to England and safety. All I can say is that you seem to have become more French in the last few years,' Jeffrey said.

'Whereas we must have become more English,' Anne said. 'I do hope I can remember what little French I knew!'

'I suppose that's true, but you're still my parents and I'm so glad you've come back at last.' Nicole was smiling.

'And we're delighted to be back here with you, whatever the problems,' Anne said. Jeffrey echoed her.

'It takes me back, being here. I had such a lovely childhood and I was happy before the war,' Nicole said.

She looked around the room that was both familiar and unfamiliar. Over four years of occupation had been hard, but, since the liberation of Paris, she had been trying to be positive about the future. She could believe in happiness for herself, but it was still out of reach.

FIVE

REUNION

As the following morning was a Sunday, Nicole and her parents were able to linger over breakfast, still reviewing the five-year absence brought about by war. Jeffrey was in no doubt about the change in Nicole.

'You're not my little girl anymore.'

Nicole laughed. 'You wouldn't want me to be! You were always trying to make me tougher and more independent.'

'It's the war that's done that, not your parents. But I'm proud of what you've done to make a life for yourself here and what you did for the Resistance. That newspaper must have played its part and you obviously did quite a bit otherwise, more than you've told us.'

Anne, agreeing with Jeffrey, slipped out of the room for a moment and returned with a folder of cuttings from newspapers they had read in England. Flicking through the folder, Nicole noticed copies of a newspaper called *France*.

'It's the paper that your friend Paul worked for. I collected issues with articles about Paris. Have a look and see how it compares with your underground newspaper,' Anne said.

'It's more professional-looking than *Valmy*,' Nicole said.

Her attention was caught by an article about a journalist who had fled Paris in 1942 and escaped to England. It was dated April 1943. Her heart leaped at the name of the journalist – Paul Lévy.

She had never seen his real name in print before, being used to his pseudonym of Richard Simon, which he would not have needed in London. 'Here is an article by Paul and there are more articles by him,' she said, looking up from her search through the folder.

The nightmares that Nicole had experienced after her spell in prison were less frequent now that a year had passed. That night, she dreamed about Paul. He was simply there with David, Gérard and Berthe, as if he had never gone away. She awoke, relieved to have had a pleasant dream about the past for once.

The next day, Nicole put the clippings from *France*, which Anne had given to her, into the scrapbook with her diary pieces and articles for *Valmy*.

'I don't think Paul has forgotten you,' Anne said. 'My impression was that he was rather attracted to you, at least admiring!'

Nicole's answering smile faded quickly. 'We're just friends, but he said that he would find me after the war. He knows Denise's shop well and could write to me there. I'm sure he's not in Paris because there's been no hint of him here. He could be in Dijon, where he comes from, but he could still have written. But perhaps a letter's gone astray.'

'Well, yes, of course. Being Jewish, he must have been worried about his family. Surely he would have gone to Dijon as soon as possible?'

'But why would he have stayed for so long? He said he'd come back here.'

'I don't know. There could be all sorts of reasons… Why not make more enquiries?'

'I'm encouraged that he saw you several times in London. It shows he didn't forget me straightaway. I'll go and see Miriam's boyfriend, David. He managed to get his old newspaper job back and he might be able to give me names of newspaper people to contact in Dijon,' Nicole said.

'I'm not sure I approve of all this chasing after a young man, but I'm curious now to know what has happened to him,' Anne said.

'Not as curious as I am!'

***

Jeffrey and Anne were settling back into life in Paris. Patrick McGrath had paid the rent on the shop and the salaries of two people working there, so things were in good order for their return, but, as Jeffrey feared, it was not easy to revive the business after the war. Former customers had either largely disappeared or could not afford a new suit. Jeffrey decided that he must offer more than bespoke tailoring. Using old bales of material, he and his employees began to make off the peg menswear for sale.

Nicole noticed that her parents were struggling and did her best to help by taking an interest in them, bringing home gifts of food and paying a good rent. Five years of separation had changed her relationship with them. These days, they treated her as an adult and they respected her for the way she had coped with staying in France during the war. She even felt that they were looking to her for a lead on living in liberated Paris.

Jeffrey asked Nicole to come to the shop for a fitting of the new suit that he was making for her. Patrick McGrath had gone back to Ireland with Jeffrey's return to Paris and Nicole was spared having to see him again. She tried the suit on one day and Jeffrey made a few adjustments.

'This is just what I need for the office, Papa. I feel so smart and you haven't lost your touch after all those years in the RAF!' Nicole said, twirling around in front of a long mirror.

'Good. I'll finish it tomorrow and then it's yours.'

'Now, how much do I owe you?'

Jeffrey hesitated. 'I'd like to make you a present of it, but...'

'Oh no. You must treat it as an order from a customer. After all, I'm a working woman!'

'All right, my dear. Thank you,' Jeffrey said, naming a modest sum.

When Jeffrey went on to lament his lack of customers, Nicole remembered what Miriam had said years before on hearing that Patrick McGrath was making Nazi uniforms.

'Why don't you make women's clothes?' she said to her father. 'After all, you've already started with my suit.'

'I've only made women's clothes for your mother and

you,' Jeffrey said. 'But it's not a bad idea. It wouldn't be *haute couture,* of course.'

'No, of course not, just ordinary suits and skirts, tailored clothes for women. Most women I know are desperate for new clothes. They've worn everything to rags during the occupation. They don't have much money, so prices couldn't be high. I can advertise among people I know at work and my friends. I could make you a special business card with a picture on it. I'm sure Antoine would print it for me.'

'You would make a good business manager, my girl,' Jeffrey said, with a smile.

***

David had heard nothing from Paul, but he knew the name of a regional paper that might have once been edited by Paul's father. He had consulted a directory and given Nicole an address. She had written to the editor, asking if anyone at the newspaper knew of Paul Lévy. She had posted it and waited, but there had been no reply. She had to think again. She knew that the Free French Forces had become part of the French army after the liberation of France and she went to the army headquarters to enquire about Paul.

'He was demobbed in May 1945, madame,' an official told her when she had explained her quest and he had consulted the army records.

'Oh, that's a relief. Can you give me an address?' Nicole said.

'Yes, if you tell me your relationship to him.'

'He's a friend.'

'Then I can't help you. We can only give an address to a relative,' the man said.

Seeing Nicole's disappointment, he agreed to post a letter on her behalf and she took one to him, with Paul's name and a stamp on the envelope, the next day.

A week later, a letter arrived for Nicole from Dijon. She recognised the handwriting on the envelope straightaway and tore it open.

Dear Nicole

I am so pleased to hear from you! I'll keep this brief because I'm coming to Paris next week – can you meet me at 6pm on Tuesday, at the café near Denise's shop where we used to go? If it's no longer there, wait outside the shop for me. All the best, Paul.

He sounded like the Paul she had known and she was pleased to be seeing him so soon. Tuesday was in three days. There was no time to write back and no phone number on the letter, so she would simply turn up at the café. She had no other plans, but nothing would have stood in the way of seeing Paul again.

Yet, when Tuesday came, she felt a kind of anxiety that lasted all day. What would it be like to see him? She could be disappointed or upset. He might be changed by his experiences, whatever they had been. Seeing him again might be so different from remembering him.

She did not even know for certain why he wanted to see her. It was three years since he had left Paris, during the war. Things were different now. The war had been over for four months and it was over a year since the liberation of Paris, when she had expected him to return. He might have met someone else and was simply wanting to catch up with her as an old friend who could give him news of *Valmy* people.

She left Kim behind. He was less patient with waiting around these days and Anne liked looking after him. Leaving the metro, she passed Denise's typewriter shop, scene of many memories, not stopping even though lights were on. She went directly to the café.

Inside, she spotted Paul straightaway. Seeing her at the same time, he sprang to his feet, enveloping her in a long hug. As he released her, smiling, all her uncertainty about him vanished and she was simply delighted.

'I was so pleased to hear from you. When I came back to France for the liberation, I wrote to you several times at Denise's shop,' he said at once. 'When I was demobbed in May, I came to Paris to the shop, but it was closed. I spent all day looking for people we had known, but Gérard seems to have vanished and I didn't know how to contact Berthe. I asked David, but he didn't have your address. I went back home disappointed and kept writing. Then your letter arrived.'

'I was there most of the time, but I never heard from you. Denise can't have received your letters. It must have been the post. Paris was chaotic after the liberation and even now things are not back to normal.'

'I began to think you'd forgotten me or didn't want to see me again.'

'No, Paul.' Nicole shook her head. 'I missed you and I've been hoping to hear from you. I didn't have an address for you, but the army kindly sent a letter for me. I think we've been looking for each other,' she said, brushing away a feeling that threatened to overwhelm her.

Paul was looking better fed and better dressed than she remembered, with neatly clipped hair, but he seemed otherwise unchanged. She had wondered how she would look to him after three years and was wearing her new suit for the occasion.

'You look different. It's your new hairstyle,' he said, appraising her, but not noticing the suit.

'My urchin cut. Yvette does it for me.'

'And where is Kim? He was always with you.'

'Oh, he's all right. He's at home with my mother and getting on a bit.'

'Your parents are back in Paris then. You know I met them several times in London. They were kind to a French stranger!'

'Oh yes, I've heard all about it and that inspired me to start looking for you again. I'd lost hope of finding you.'

Over a drink, Nicole gave Paul an edited version of her story, not saying how much she had thought about him when she was in prison. She still didn't know if he had met someone else, but she felt no need to rush things and they had so much to say to each other. Being with him was mixture of excitement and comfort. Paul told her about his resistance work in Toulouse and his journey to England.

'I worked for a French newspaper called *France*,' he said.

'I know.' Nicole told him about finding his name in the newspapers that her parents had shown her. 'You fell on your feet then. I'm not surprised, coming from Paris.'

'Yes, I'm sure that helped. Everyone wanted to know what it was like under the occupation. I kept going on that for quite a while. Then I wanted to be more active, so I joined the French forces in London and in June last year I came over with the Normandy landings. I've been in Dijon, looking after my parents, ever since I was demobbed in May.'

Paul's parents had survived the war, but his only brother had been arrested one night in Dijon in 1943 and sent somewhere that no one knew for certain. Nothing had been heard from him since then. His father had lost his job during the occupation and found it difficult to work after that. His parents had gone into hiding and had suffered from malnutrition. They were taking time to recover from the war. After much searching, Paul had discovered that his brother had died in a death camp at a place called Dachau, near Munich in Germany. Paul had been living and working in Dijon to help his parents get back onto their feet since his return to France.

Nicole commiserated with him and told him about Miriam and her family. Paul listened in silence, saddened by the news, although not surprised, especially after what had happened to his brother.

He explained that he had had an interview for a job as a journalist on his old newspaper, *La Presse Parisienne*, that day.

'Oh, that's why you're smartly dressed!' Nicole said. 'Did you get the job?'

'Yes, I'm coming back to Paris next week and I've even secured my old flat.'

'Which you always said was too small to live in!'

'Yes, but there's only me. I'll squeeze in somehow. It

was only when things began to seem a bit better with my parents that I could think of coming back,' he said.

'I understand now. I had started to believe I wouldn't see you again,' Nicole said.

'Never! Now, I haven't eaten all day and I'm starving. Will you join me in at the bistro nearby, the one we used to go to?' he said.

She took his arm as they walked the few steps to the bistro. Inside, it was much the same as Nicole remembered, with net curtains, but lampshades were now covering bare bulbs. Intent as they were on each other, they ordered the dish of the day without checking what it was. Even after the food arrived, they ate distractedly while talking, until Nicole noticed something.

'It's rabbit. That's what you promised me the first time we had a meal together. It's taken you years to fulfil your promise!'

He laughed. 'Remember the swede we had that time? In England, I had to eat all kind of horrible vegetables like swede and parsnip!'

They went on to talk about Nicole's life after Paul had left Paris. 'Gérard and Berthe and I continued to produce *Valmy*. I carried on being a courier when Gérard asked me to deliver something. But before the liberation, I lost my job at the art college, probably because I made an enemy there – a man who was pestering me,' Nicole said.

'I remember. You told me about him once. Wasn't he called Serge? I wanted to go and beat him up.'

Nicole laughed. 'You have a good memory. Well, I kept going with freelance typing jobs. Then a wanted poster went up with a picture of me.'

'Hang on. How did Serge cause you to lose your job?'

'He could have worked out my connection with *Valmy*. The first time I helped with distributing it, I was stupidly carrying copies displaying the name and someone took a picture of me. I was worried about it at the time, but then I forgot about it. Much later, after you left, that picture appeared in *La Presse Parisienne*. I have no idea why it took so long, but Serge may have seen the picture, recognised me and gone to the police. Fortunately, I wasn't there when the police came to the art school looking for me, but when I heard about their visit, I left the job immediately.'

'So the picture in the wanted poster was the one the photographer took. As *Valmy* became better known, he might have realised that his photo could be used against you, then perhaps Serge saw it and contacted the police. They made the wanted poster, but what happened then?'

Nicole told Paul about her imprisonment and release. He listened in silence, looking concerned.

'I don't suppose I shall ever know for certain what Serge did,' she said as she finished.

'Do you need to know?'

'No. I've got better things to do. And it's over now.'

Nicole told Paul about her job in the notary's office and her plan to return to the art school in the Rue du Dragon where she had been a student before the war.

'So you're going back to your old life, like me?' he said.

'On the surface, perhaps. The life before the war has gone and much of it will never come back. Sometimes it seems so difficult, not just the struggle to survive, but to hope for better times. When I think of the French police who took Miriam and her family away, I wonder if we can ever heal our divisions. But I try to be positive.'

'Having lost my brother, I know exactly what you mean.'

Nicole looked sad. 'I remember Miriam saying that she had never felt as Jewish as she did when Jews were being persecuted.'

'We'll talk more about this, I know, but now I want to see you home and I need to get back to Dijon tonight,' he said.

They looked around them. It was not late, but the bistro closed early and was emptying. The waiter had brought the bill without being asked. Paul paid it and they left.

Outside, it was dark and gloomy. Few people were about on the quiet street. Nicole wanted to tell him how much he meant to her, but she hesitated. Three years was a long time and she felt uncertain about taking the initiative. Had he not missed her?

He turned towards her. 'Dearest Nicole, I am sorry for everything you went through after I left. I've missed you so much and I'm so pleased to see you again.'

She told him then how she had missed him after he left Paris and how she had survived the ordeal of her imprisonment by thinking about him. There was enough streetlight for her to see the impact of her words. He drew her away from the light and, taking her face in both hands, he kissed her, slowly at first and then with passion. Nicole closed her eyes as she clung to him. They drew apart and hugged before they let go of each other. She was almost breathless with joy.

'I wish we could go back to my flat now, but I haven't taken it yet,' Paul said.

'There's no rush,' Nicole said.

There was time now. Before they were free, time together had been snatched, but in future it would be plentiful. On the metro, he wrote down her phone number. They reached her stop at Iéna and walked down the steps to her flat.

'My mother is watching from the window,' Nicole said, as they neared her building. 'She'll be worrying about where I am. Would you like to come up and say hello to my parents?'

He shook his head. 'It will have to be another time.'

'Oh, of course. You must go.'

'Not for long, my dearest Nicole. I'll ring you next week and we'll make up for lost years,' he said, embracing her.

She watched as he walked away, remembering the last time she had said goodbye to him and had looked at his receding figure, not knowing if she would ever see him again. He had turned round then and waved. He did the same now and she waved back before going indoors.

AFTERWORD

It had been a long lunch and the restaurant was empty of other customers by the time they finished their meal and coffee. Nicole had talked almost the entire time, while Nicolette had listened, questioning here and there, but not saying much. Nicole had not needed any persuasion once she had started talking and her words had flowed.

'Thank you for telling me, *Maman*,' Nicolette said as Nicole finally finished her story. 'So, but for the war, you would probably have married Marcel. And I hope it wasn't too painful to talk about Miriam.'

'I always thought it would be, but it's a relief now, after so many years. And with your father gone, I feel I need to talk about things more. He knew it all, you see, so we didn't need to say much about the occupation,' Nicole said. 'Yvette and I have met every year on May 19th since then to think about Miriam and her family, so I have talked to her. Now, I'm going back home for a rest and you had better get back to your family. Of course, I miss your father all the time, but we had many years together for me to think about.'

'All right,' Nicolette said. She had a lot to think about as well after hearing about her mother's war for the first time. 'Will you be all right?'

'Don't worry about me. I'm a tough old bird and I'll be fine. But come again soon and you can read my diary and the newspaper clippings if you want to.'

'I will,' Nicolette said, as they stood up to go.

On the bus going home, Nicolette reflected on her mother's story. How brave she had been in such a frightening time. She had recovered from missing the boat in Bordeaux, she had taken part in the Resistance, she had suffered the loss of Miriam and her family, and she had even been arrested and imprisoned. She herself had never had to face any such challenge. The Paris student uprising in 1968, which she had eagerly embraced, bore no comparison to the Nazi occupation. And how much more open and friendly her mother had seemed talking about it all, as if she had been released in some way. Nicolette's heart no longer sank at the thought of seeing her mother and she looked forward to meeting her again soon.

ACKNOWLEDGEMENTS

My mother, Andrée, who gave me her name, grew up in Paris before the Second World War in a British family as the youngest of three children. She and her parents escaped from France in June 1940, leaving their dog behind, and flew to England. There, my mother joined the WAAF and then met and married my father. She never returned to live in France, but my brothers and sister and I grew up hearing about her childhood in Paris and exchanging visits with our grandmother there.

After my mother's death, I found a book of wartime newspaper clippings among her possessions. Searching through it, hoping she had written something about herself, I was disappointed, but I wondered what could have happened if a young woman of British origin had stayed in France during the Nazi occupation. Nicole is from a similar background to my mother, but her story is quite different.

I found the following books and articles helpful in writing Nicole's War:

1. *Divided Loyalties* by Janet Teissier du Cros, Hamish Hamilton, 1963.
2. *Fighters in the Shadows* by Robert Gildea, Faber and Faber, 2015.
3. *Fleeing Hitler* by Hanna Diamond, Oxford University Press, 2007.
4. *Les Parisiennes* by Anne Sebba, Weidenfeld & Nicolson, 2016.
5. *Love and War in the Pyrenees* by Rosemary Bailey, Phoenix, 2009.
6. *Mon Paris, ma mémoire* by Edgar Morin, Fayard, 2013.
7. *Occupation* by Ian Ousby, Pimlico, 1999.
8. 'Paris Under the Occupation' by Jean-Paul Sartre, in *Sartre Studies International*, Vol. 14, No. 2 (1998), published by Berghahn Books.
9. *The Unfree French* by Richard Vinen, Penguin, 2007.
10. *When Paris Went Dark* by Ronald Rosbottom, John Murray, 2014.

In addition, I visited the Musée de la Libération at Denfert-Rochereau in Paris. Their guide to the collections is available in English and in French.

Although I have drawn on my mother's background, all the characters in this novel are fictional. There was a Resistance newspaper called *Valmy*, but I have done no more than use the name. Passages quoted from *Valmy* in the novel are fictional. There was also a newspaper called *France*, published in England for the French community here.

I am especially grateful to my husband, Alan Rushton, for a close reading of drafts and for many helpful discussions over the years of research and writing and visits to France. I should also like to thank Ruth Cohen, Linda Edmondson, Morven Leese and Patricia Wyatt for their scrutiny of drafts, and their thoughtful comments and suggestions. I also benefited from many discussions with family members. Finally, I wish to thank Book Guild staff for their considerable skills in editing, marketing and production, as well as their friendliness and efficiency.

Andrée Rushton